A Carmel McAlistair Mystery

ST. JUDE
UNDONE

LIZ GRAHAM

OneEar Press

Happy Reading!

2022

St. Jude Undone

Copyright © 2022 by Liz Graham

This book is a work of fiction. Names, characters, businesses, organizations, places, events and incidents either are the product of the author's imagination or are used fictitiously. Any resemblance to actual persons, living or dead, events, or locales is entirely coincidental.

ISBN: 978-1-990667-01-5

First Edition: March 2022

B rigid Ryan was ignoring her, she could tell by the way the woman flicked her long red hair as she left the bungalow across the way, by the careful stiffness in her back, and by the casualness of each step made by her black boots along the gravelled road of St. Jude Without. She was pretending to be entranced by the fog that lay thick over the mountains and sea, yet there was nothing visible at all within this heavy blanket of moisture, nothing except for the sight of Carmel McAlistair herself sitting in her living room window.

And the tourists of course, but everyone was trying their best to ignore *them*.

The church bells tolled across the stretch of sea to St. Jude Without, slipping through the thick mist shrouding the trees and the houses and the boulders on the sides of the roads, the echoes magnified in this watery world as they washed down the granite cliffs looming over the village on this dreary Sunday afternoon in the middle of June. These slow doleful notes might be sounding the death knoll of St. Jude Without, the village as she knew it, as it had stood for hundreds of years since the pirate claimed the land from the last of the First Nations. This tiny community was dying a tortured and unpretty death, and Carmel knew it was all her fault.

At least, she was being blamed for its demise. She'd just returned from a whirlwind tour of the Atlantic Provinces to promote her book, but unfortunately, her flight to best-sellerdom had launched St. Jude Without's fame too, and that wasn't sitting well with her neighbors. This small village had flown under the radar of mainstream society since being founded by the Captain Jeremiah Ryan sometime in the eighteen hundreds. His descendants kept up the family tradition of skullduggery, smuggling and other anti-social behaviors, and they didn't appreciate being exposed to the outside world.

Over the past year since she'd moved to this hidden harbor just north of Portugal Cove, her life had been plagued with crime and murders and mysteries. And if the dead bodies weren't enough, there were also legends of ghosts, fairies, witch craft and pirate treasure in the small cove.

St. Jude Without was a writers' dream, and so she'd written about it all, just whimsical short stories to while away the long late winter nights. Truth can be stranger than fiction, yet she was the first to admit she'd embellished quite a lot.

Overnight, the village was a tourist attraction, with everyone and their dogs flocking to see for themselves this tiny cove peopled with the ne'er-do-wells and bikers and witches and fairies and ghosts of her stories. The result was horrible. From her perch in the old red armchair at her living room window she watched as the after-lunch crowd of cars and minivans negotiated the narrow gravelled road that was North Point Road Extension, one Ford Capri now stuck in the steep mud lane leading to Phonse Ryan's house and the wharf, churning its wheels uselessly as if it was the deepest winter snow. Vee Ryan now had a legitimate cause to hate her.

So the undoing of St. Jude Without? Yeah, Carmel McAlistair was directly responsible for that.

She brushed her messy brown curls out of her face and frowned at the water dripping down the window pane. 'I have to get out of this place,' she said aloud. Out of this house and the confines of the village if just for the afternoon, and the only way out was the single road leading to Portugal Cove. With her zebra stripe rubber boots on and the hood of her bright yellow raincoat securely fixed, Carmel splashed her way down the road, ignoring the tourists and the looky-loos. Brigid had disappeared by this time and none of the other inhabitants of St. Jude Without were showing their faces.

The only positive outcome of all the murders of the previous year, well, besides the fame and promise of royalties (and she was an optimist at heart), the great thing that had come out of all this, was Inspector Darrow of the Royal Newfoundland Constabulary. Or, as she said to herself when absolutely no one else was around, her New Boyfriend.

Their relationship had developed slowly and sweetly over the past year. Not a traditionally handsome man, John Darrow was tall enough (but not too tall), had dark Celtic hair and eyes, and the sexiest Scottish accent. Carmel and Darrow had in common the kind of mind that likes to figure out puzzles, and a physical attraction which was working well, very well indeed.

• • • •

'A two-week course in Community Policing? In Toronto, at this time of year? You can't be serious.' Inspector Darrow lowered himself to the chair in front of Chief Yvonne Hender's desk, watching his plans for the summer drain down the open sewer that was often the lot of the policeman's life.

'Herb Laney is just back from rehab,' she said curtly. 'I'm keeping him under close observation, although God knows he could do with more education on how to treat the public. The hotel and flights are already paid for from the education budget, and we need to send an Inspector. You're the only one who's got a clean desk, no major investigations ongoing.'

'I do my work, so I'm the one that gets punished?' He was only half joking.

'Accreditation is coming up in the fall, and I can't risk failing that. We need to prove we're staying on top of Best Practice, and that means offering educational opportunities.'

'What exactly is this course going to teach me that I don't already know? Will you be sending me out on the beat next?' The frustration in his voice couldn't be hidden, and as always when emotional, the Scottish accent was coming through strong. 'Christ's sake, we have cops on horses trotting up and down Long's Hill, squad cars trolling through residential neighborhoods, isn't that evidence enough of our community policing policies?'

'Calm yourself,' she snapped. Her short bobbed hair gleamed silver in the fluorescent lights. She caught herself and gave a small half-smile of apology. 'Look on the bright side, at least you'll have your educational component over with for the fiscal year.'

He stared across the table at his boss, keeping his glare just this side of subordinate. This was mid-June. His children would be heading for their mother's right after school finished on the twentieth. 'The kids are leaving next weekend. I won't see them for a whole month.'

Yvonne sighed and almost rolled her eyes, acknowledging his point. 'Yeah, okay, you can skip the last week of the class. It's just soup-kitchen detail, really. Hanging out with the homeless, seeing them as human beings, that sort of thing. I'll excuse you from that.'

He nodded.

'Another reason I want you to attend is that they're going to be unrolling the new Policy Directive on Community Policing during the first week. I want to send someone who can regurgitate it into plain English for the rest of the force.'

A new Policy Directive. Darrow had been around long enough to know what that would entail. Entire forces all over the country would spend valuable time and resources changing all the ways of doing things that had just been hammered out from the last new Policy Directive. The things that were working, for the most part, in as much as things worked. And if this new Policy Directive was focused towards police interactions with the public... Darrow groaned.

'What direction will we be taking now?'

A glint of humor showed in Chief Inspector Hender's eye. 'A kinder, more community involved police force. Basically, crime is a result of bad parenting, and the state is the parent. We need to show understanding, love and...' She glanced at the paper on her desk. 'Ah, and goodwill to the criminal classes.'

'In other words, kill the crooks with kindness?'

'You nailed it.'

'That'll be a tough sell here.' Darrow leaned back in his chair and shook his head at the ludicrousness of it all. He'd been in the business long enough to know when he had to accept his lot. 'Can you see Laney and his sidekicks on George Street on a Friday night, sitting down with the drunks and bonding?' He stood up to go.

'Darrow,' Yvonne said with a note warning in her voice. 'Thanks for this. And you're excused for duty this weekend. Turn your phone off. Enjoy the kids.'

• • • •

The TV weathermen called it RDF – rain, drizzle and fog. It was common enough weather throughout the year there at the very edge of the Atlantic Ocean, where life was surrounded by water on all sides. Meteorologists claimed the frequent fog and rainclouds onshore were directly caused by the collision of the freezing Labrador Current with the balmy Gulf Stream flowing up from Mexico. It kept the winters moderate in temperature, usually, and a pair of rubber boots could do you all year round if you lived in town where they cleared the sidewalks of snow. Add a thick pair of hand-knit socks and you were all set for winter.

But the thick RDF of June – now, this was special weather, much anticipated by those who lived around the bays and made their living from the ocean. The old folks called it the Capelin Weather, when millions of those tiny fish tossed themselves upon the beaches, the bounty of the sea coming to the land for a change instead of the fishers having to go and haul it out of the ocean. Perhaps it was the dreariness of the endless rain and fog which magically summoned those tiny fish to suicide, throwing themselves on mass out of the ocean and onto the beaches all around the island. When the capelin were rolling onto the shores, folk would go down with their buckets and nets and grab as many as they could. A day out for the family, a boil-up and picnic on the beach in the damp. Carmel shivered at the thought.

The heaviness of this weather matched Carmel's present mood, yet it hadn't affected everyone in the cove thus, for as she passed along the top of Snellen's Field she heard a single voice rise in song from the wetness. It was a male voice, deep and resonant and hoarse, and she recognized the tune though the words were slurred. The singer was ranting and roaring like a true Newfoundlander, and she could barely make out the tall hefty figure as he stood at the end of the field looking over the ocean, for all the world like a captain surveying his domain. The song ended on a hiccup, followed by the sound of glass smashing on rocks.

'Screw you, Bell Island!' he shouted across the shrouded stretch of water that lay between him and the unseen island across the way. 'We – will – win!'

He laughed and began another song, a verse which should have been sung smoothly and lightly, but coming from this man, sounded spooky and threatening. 'We're in the money!'

The man doffed an imaginary top-hat and as he turned around, Carmel hurried back on her way to the next cove over. She had no desire to find out what beef Nate O'Reilly had with the small island across the water, or why he was rip-roaring drunk at three o'clock in the afternoon. Some things were better left unknown.

She reached the end of North Point Road in Portugal Cove and turned down towards the wharf of that fine town. The ferry's mournful cry sounded again, muffled through the fog and distance, and the place was deserted with not a living soul in sight, not even a seagull. She walked along the breakwater to stare at the wake of the ferry still churning in the gloomy afternoon.

Huge boulders surrounded her on this man-made breakwater, a finger pier of charcoal and gray rock with deep shadows in between. All color had been swallowed up by the endless fog. Leaning against a pole at the end, the one which held the light to show mariners the way to safety, her foot scuffed against something soft in this otherwise hard landscape.

Even before she looked down, the smell broke through her thoughts, the metallic, coppery odor of blood overlying the salt in the air. She could pray all she wanted that it would be a dead dog or a seal, but the unmistakeable waft of human death told her different. That, and the sharp tang of whiskey.

There, finally, was color in the world, but it was deep red against the gray tarmac, the bright black and white stripes of her boots awash with carmine. She looked past her feet at the body of a giant lying between the boulders.

'Oh, God, not again.'

And then the wind rose and with it came the rain finally, breaking through the fog for real this time, heavy drops filling the air and lashing the boulders and washing the man's blood away into the sea.

2

Her heart sank again when she saw who had been called out into the wet cold afternoon. Darrow had told her Inspector Herb Laney was just back from his stint in rehab. She could tell by the scowl on his face that he was in an even more rotten mood than usual.

'They never even gave me the night off to reconnect with the guys in the Police Bar, no, it was back to business straight away,' she heard him complain to his sidekick as they got out of his vehicle. 'Fricking Hender is one hard-assed bitch.'

His expression didn't improve when he saw Carmel standing in the lea of the ferry terminal, the flashing blue and red lights of the squad cars running over her in an unending pattern.

'So of course you called it in,' he said directly, ignoring any niceties. He sneezed in her direction, not bothering to cover his nose, then wiped his face with his sleeve.

She flinched and nodded, silent, already tense with anticipation for the interview. Laney was the officer who had taken over from Darrow just this past spring when her boss had been killed in the Archives. Being no fan of the Scottish Inspector Darrow and his 'uppity ways', Laney had been all set to pin the crime on her as the most convenient suspect and in doing so discredit Darrow at the same time. Killing two birds with one stone, so to speak, something which appealed to Inspector Laney's sense of justice and lack of work ethic.

The two officers crowded too closely to her under the overhang of the terminal, but even this didn't offer shelter from the rain as the wind threw it every which way but down.

'Friend of yours, I suppose?' Laney flicked his head toward the activity at the end of the breakwater. The Scene of Crime officers were trying to affix a canvas tent over the body in the gusts of wind but were having a hard time securing it with no purchase in the rocks. Carmel's bloody footprints had long since washed away.

'No... I don't know,' she said. 'I didn't look.'

'Touch the body?'

'My foot hit him, I wasn't looking down, I was watching the water.'

'But you know it's a man? Strange, that.'

'I assumed...,' she looked toward the tent. 'He's a really big man... person. The body is huge.'

Laney appeared to be paying little attention to her words, trying to light a cigarette in the wind and rain. Frustrated, he threw the soggy mess of tobacco into the nearest puddle.

Although just late-afternoon and close on to the longest day of the year, the breakwater felt dark as night outside the bright lights of the terminal.

'Any ID on the body?' Laney turned his back on Carmel to ask the officer approaching.

'Easy enough to recognize him,' the young man said. 'It's Lars Andersen, from Bell Island.'

'What? Christ, no. What happened to him?'

'Looks like his skull was bashed in on the left temple.'

'With what?'

'A rock?' All present looked around at the breakwater on which they stood, edged by boulders on two sides. The structure had been created by heaving large rocks and other heavy debris into the water, then the middle was filled in and paved over. There was no shortage of potential culprits for the damage done to poor Lars' head.

'Christ,' Laney said again.

'He was probably drunk and slipped in the dampness, though God knows what he was doing at the end of the breakwater.'

'Taking a piss while he was waiting for the ferry, I'd say. Unless...' Laney turned to squint at Carmel through the rain. 'Unless it was murder.'

She stood before him, drenched, her curls flattened and dripping. Was he eying her suspiciously? This was ridiculous, and she said so.

'I'm five foot six. Do you really think I could have... *would* have bashed that giant on his head?'

Laney looked pointedly up the coast towards where St. Jude Without lay hidden in the fog. 'Not you necessarily, but you have some pretty shady friends who make no secret of the fact they don't like Bell Island. Looks like it could be their crude kind of handiwork.'

'Want me to round up the usual suspects, sir?' This was said with a great deal of enthusiasm.

'Wait on it,' Laney said, and he cleared his throat and spit out the side of his mouth. 'See what forensics says first.'

'Can I go?' Carmel spoke up against the wind to remind them she was still there.

He slowly turned to look her. She could tell by the wrath in his eyes that he held her solely responsible for his presence here on the rain lashed pier, dragged away from whatever comforts the life of Inspector Laney might hold on a June evening.

'No,' he said, already turning back to his sergeant. 'Give your statement to the constable here first. And don't even think about leaving town, I'm watching you.'

The statement was given in the relative dryness of the squad car, but after that Carmel was left on her own to make her way back home. She climbed up the short hill to North Point Road, fuming to herself all the way. Laney was such an ass. Carmel was hardly a candidate for smashing in the head of a six foot six giant. Lars Andersen was well known, recognizable if only for his height and size, for he was as broad as he was tall with the largest gut Carmel had ever seen on a man. All the Andersen clan were oversize, something to do with the genes of the Nordic ancestor who had come to work in the Bell Island mines back in the 'thirties.

Stomping her way along the gravelled road around the turn of the mountain with her head bent against the elements, she kept her eyes on her zebra-print boots splashing in the rapidly filling potholes of mud, unmindful of passing vehicles that sprayed the legs of her jeans. What odds, she was soaked through to her skin anyway. And the discomfort, the cold and wet were almost enough to keep her so angry at Laney that she didn't have room to allow for the shock which inevitably is felt when one stumbles over the lifeless body of a fellow human being.

And the tears coursed down her face unnoticed, as salty as the sea-whipped spray of the wind and rain on this misplaced spring day.

3

S he passed the stump of the old pine tree which, legend said, was the site of Captain Jeremiah Ryan's lynching two hundred years ago. The branches of the lilac bushes rubbed together, the new leaves susurrating in a rogue gust of wind, heavy with buds just waiting for a bit of sun to help the blooming. Carmel hurried into her home, eager to light the fireplace to take the damp out of her bones even though it was scandalous to think of turning on the heat so late in the spring. She needed to get dry and warm to rid herself of the chill, and as she sat before the fire, drowsily soaking in the heat, her mind naturally replayed the events of the afternoon.

How long had Lars Andersen lain on the rocks at the end of the breakwater? The blood pooling at her feet had been liquid, fresh from what she could see, and had washed away easily in the torrent of rain without leaving an outline. It hadn't had time to clot and dry on the wet rock. The ferry had just left the port when she got there, and there had been no one in sight on the breakwater.

Had it been as the sergeant had suggested, the man was on a Sunday afternoon, end of the weekend drunken binge at the local pub in Portugal Cove and paused to take a leak into the ocean before getting on the ferry to go back home? Wouldn't his friends have noticed his absence on the ferry and sounded an alarm?

No, probably not. The new ferry was large enough that any companions might assume he was elsewhere.

As the darkness of the wet evening deepened, Carmel was beginning to feel the need of company, to shake off the horror of that afternoon's grisly discovery. Her tenant Ian, the Irish musician, had finally moved out, and after all she had put up with him and his non-payment of rent, Carmel hadn't had the heart to get someone else in. Not really worth the bother, and she found she didn't much like being a landlord.

Yet Ian had been lively, and it did get lonely here without another person around. Over in Portugal Cove, she heard the ferry's mournful cry to announce the last trip out to Bell Island, the boat almost invisible except for a faint twinkling of light through the thick cover of moisture, like a ghost ship sailing through the mists of Avalon. She turned away from the gloom of the fog-shrouded June evening.

Lost in thought as she gazed toward the flames, it took her a while to become aware of another presence in the room. She hadn't been expecting company. The slightest movement above the easy chair opposite her broke into her consciousness, and the sound of an impatient huff of air caused he to lift her eyes.

In the dim light of the burning logs, Carmel found herself staring at the outline of a pirate hat with the ostrich feather bobbing above it. She had imagined she'd seen this sight before out of the corner of her eye, and always scolded herself for an overactive imagination. She blinked, then blinked again, but the hat was still there.

And more, now she could even make out a watery body shape below it, comfortably ensconced in the dusty red armchair.

'Can you see me now, girl?' A deep rumbling voice, heavy on the Irish accent. 'Took ye long enough.'

Yes, she could see him, that is, if she wasn't dreaming. How did you know if you were dreaming or not? And why would she conjure up a pirate ghost making himself at home in her living room and speaking to her?

She shook her head. This wasn't real, it was just the stress of the long day, and perhaps she'd become ill with a fever. Yes, that might be it. She felt her forehead with the back of her hand, but it remained chilled.

The firelight glinted off the beady eyes peering at her from under the brim of the large feathered hat. The apparition was taking on strength even as she watched, and now she could hardly make out the chenille design on the armchair.

Was it a trick of the light? She squinted as if that would clear her vision.

'Captain Jeremiah Ryan, as you are no doubt aware,' it said. Or he said. Whatever it was.

Dear God. The founder of the cove who had passed on centuries ago. The very one she featured in the scary ghost story of St. Jude Without. Had she written him into reality, like some grown-up version of Simon in the land of chalk drawings?

'You're a skinny thing, indeed, not much meat on your bones.'

She almost murmured a thank you, although his voice hadn't sounded complimentary. She was proud of the fact she could fit back into her jeans without too much of a muffin top.

But back to the fact that a ghost was sitting in her living room, conversing with her.

'You're Cap'n Jem,' she stated.

'And me just after telling you my name. Not the brightest spark in the fire, are you?'

'You're a ghost.'

'We're all ghosts, one way or another,' he said. 'Just depends on the level of physicality we manifest, I've discovered.'

'But you died. Centuries ago. Outside on the pine tree.' She pointed to the window, as if that was proof.

'Details.' The old pirate shook his head, manifesting more solidly with every moment. She could make out the worn braid on his coat sleeve now, and there was also a smell rising from him, an earthy, musty odor with a sulphurous undertone. A bit like the cellar below the house, truth be told, which she had only ever dared to visit a couple of times. But how could a ghost give off a smell?

'Ye've done the place up then,' he said, looking all around him at the shoddy furniture, thread-bare carpet and shelves still full of the previous owner's books.

'Not so much, no...' She looked around. This was too weird for words. Brigid and Phonse had spoken of this ghost quite casually. However, she'd put that down to the general strangeness of the pair of cousins, of the cove itself. They also believed in the fairies in the graveyard for God's sake, all of which had given her the ideas for her stories.

Carmel turned her attention back to Cap'n Jem, or his spirit or whatever he was, and studied him. His form was quite distinct by now, yet there was still a sort of wateriness about him that hinted of not being quite of this earth. She searched around inside herself, to test what she was feeling. Apart from incredulity of course.

Shock, yes, which was perhaps a leftover sensation still in her body from finding Lars' body that afternoon, yet it did lend to the air of unreality the evening was quickly taking on. It didn't leave a lot of room for her to be feeling anything else, at least not until she could process it all.

What she *wasn't* feeling, was fear. This phantom wasn't scary, she realized. Unorthodox, yes, and a little smelly, and while he didn't seem to be a particularly likable spirit, she didn't feel threatened by him in the least bit.

'Why are you here?' She found herself wondering aloud. 'I mean, now. Why show yourself now?'

A gleam showed in his shadowy eyes. 'I'm showing myself because I know you are the one.' He gave an eerie chortle that morphed into a racking cough as if he had spent the past two hundred years in the smoky environs of hell.

"Twas me that brought you to the cove, as you know,' he added with an air of self-satisfaction.

'Brigid said something along those lines but...'

'I told young Frank to give you the house, as you play a part in my redemption plan.' He sat back to watch the effect of this honor which had been bestowed on her.

'Young' Frank Ryan was Jeremiah's descendant who used to own this house. She'd never met him, only corresponded through email because after his beloved wife had passed away, Frank had hot-footed it down south to the friendly climate of Florida, eager to be shot of the Newfoundland weather which played havoc with his elderly bones. He had no plans to return, and had been very happy to sell the house to her.

But redemption plan? Captain Jeremiah Ryan had been a pirate, and by all accounts one of the bloodiest in the island's history, plying his trade in the shipping lines between Bermuda and Europe. Many pirates (or privateers as they called themselves) had been given carte blanche by the monarchs of England and France to attack ships belonging to other nations, thus saving said monarchs the expense of outfitting a royal navy to grab all the goodies being sent back to the other monarchs of Europe. A win-win situation for all involved, and everyone tended to act quite civilly.

But no, not him, according to the legends. He was not and never had been a gentleman pirate. His work had been fueled by pure spite and greed, attacking the wealthiest ships of any nation he came across and rarely taking prisoners alive. Cap'n Jem was not redeemable.

'Y'see,' he began, settling himself into the chair as if for a nice fireside chat. His voice still had the strong Irish lilt from his early years. 'You mentioned the old pine tree outside, where I met my untimely death at the hands of the Catholic priest and his mob of townies.'

'The Clerkwell son who became a priest,' Carmel said, remembering the research she had done earlier in the spring.

He spat a ghostly wad of phlegm into the fire, which sputtered in response. 'That bastard. Don't say his name in this house.'

'He led a mob against you and you were hanged.'

'And my body suffered the indignity of being tarred and feathered, then tossed into the back of a cart and trundled up to Gibbet Hill to dangle exposed to the elements for all to jeer at. The most unjust end for an honest man who only wanted to live in peace with his family in his own village of St. Jude Without.' This was a sad memory for the ghost, she could tell, although it was a different interpretation from the version in the historical documents.

'Hmm,' Carmel replied. 'That's one side of the story, I'm sure. But... how am I supposed to help you redeem yourself?'

Perhaps he would tell her where his pirate treasure was buried, the treasure that just this past spring Phonse and Nate had been looking for, the gold which would help Nate catapult into politics. It never had been found. Everyone assumed it had been blown up in friendly fire from the Brits during World War II, but perhaps it was still lying intact somewhere. Maybe Jem wanted her to find the stash and give it back to the original owners as an act of atonement to allow his spirit to rest. Carmel felt a trickle of excitement at the idea.

A pair of frameless spectacles had appeared out of nowhere and he placed them on his nose as if to give himself an air of gentle learnedness. He looked over them at Carmel.

'Your writing of stories has caught my eye,' he said. 'And I want you to tell my story.'

'I did already,' she pointed out. 'In the story about how you snatched the Clerkwell bride and killed every other person on the ship and then married her with yourself acting as the minister.'

He brushed aside this version of the events of his life. 'No, we're going to tell the true story. The truth of what really happened.' Then he beamed at her and turned on his charm. 'I have chosen you to write my autobiography.'

'I could do that, I suppose,' she said slowly. Would that make her a ghost writer for a ghost, a true ghost writer? The evening was taking on an even more unreal air. 'But how would that redeem you?'

He removed the glasses with a scowl and shook them at her. 'Because you'll tell the truth of what happened. You'll publish the story and hold it out for the world to see.'

Carmel had to take time to digest this. Captain Jem harrumphed with impatience.

'Do you not see? You can hawk each broadside down on Water Street in the city! People will be clamoring for the next installment, every week. And perhaps then you can gather them together into a book, and sell it in London and New York. People love books, I hear.'

'The publishing industry has changed a bit since your time, you know,' she told him, then a thought hit her. The spirit seemed to know some things, like what had been happening in her life, but he wasn't so much in tune with the rest of the world's developments. 'How did you know about my stories, anyway?'

'I inhabit this house, don't I then? My world is limited, so anything at all takes my interest,' he said. An evil leer lit his spectral features. 'It has been quite more titillating since you've moved in, I must say.'

She couldn't help the blush which spread up her neck. Gawd, had this ghost been watching everything she did? Even when she and Darrow... She really didn't like the idea of having an audience to her most private moments. She pushed that thought aside.

'You want me to write your story,' she said, still trying to come to grips with this concept. 'Now, say I do this for you – then what? What do I get out of it?'

'Fame, fortune... You'll get of it what you make of it,' he said. 'Like anything in the physical world. Look at me, I started as a wharf-rat on the streets of Dublin, joined with the merchants (God rot their souls in hell). I took my chances where I could, then the world was mine. But I'm not wanting to get ahead of meself. I'll unravel the tale as it comes.'

'But when it's finished - you'll go away? To heaven or something?' Although she doubted that, for the air was definitely taking on a strong hint of sulphur or bad drainage or something, as his manifestation strengthened. Definitely a whiff of hell as imagined by Dante.

His eyes slid away from hers. 'Mayhap.'

'That's not a definite answer.'

He gave an ethereal shrug, and his feather danced above the hat. 'And if you don't do it I'll stay here anyway,' he pointed out.

'Right,' she acknowledged, as she slowly nodded her head. She was caught between a rock and a hard place – she could refuse to do as he asked and be stuck with a stinky ghost watching her every move. On the other hand, she could write his stupid biography – or ghost-written autobiography - maybe make some money off it, and perhaps get rid of him. However, she was going to use her position of power to lay down some ground rules, first of which – he was to respect her privacy. Carmel looked up. 'Okay, I'll do it.'

She drew her breath to continue but the ring tone of her phone cut her off.

Cap'n Jem looked askance at the phone buzzing on the coffee table. 'That's grand then. I'll be in touch when I'm ready,' he said hurriedly. And then he disappeared, suddenly, with just a whiff of sulphur lingering in the air to prove he'd been there in the first place.

4

She stared at the chair where the ghost had been sitting, then grabbed the ringing phone and went to the kitchen. She felt in desperate need of a cup of tea.

There was a significant pause on the phone after she told Darrow the news of Lars' death. She couldn't bring herself to tell him of Jeremiah's visit.

'You really need to move out of that place. It's not a safe environment.' Darrow's voice was lined with worry. Like all the local cops, he was aware of the lawlessness woven into the fabric of life in St. Jude Without. 'And now another dead body. You know there's affordable housing in the center of the city. In nicer neighborhoods.'

'But Lars died in Portugal Cove, not here,' she argued, once more ignoring his attempts to persuade her to leave her adopted home. She poured the almost boiled water into the mug holding the tea bag. 'And it's not like it was murder, for there was nobody else around.'

With the exception of Nate O'Reilly singing his victory song just half a kilometer away from the ferry terminal. No need to bring that up for it would only add more fuel to Darrow's arguments on the benefits of her exiting the cove. Nate had merely been drunk and being his weird self. Although, come to think of it, Lars was a Bell Islander, and Nate had specifically ranted against that island's inhabitants. But she really didn't want to go there in her thoughts.

'Does Herb Laney feel it's a suspicious death?'

'Yes, but...'

'The ferry had just left, you said. Someone could have smashed his head in and hopped on the boat.'

'Stop it! Not every unexpected death is a murder.' She fervently hoped this was the case, anyway. 'Besides, if Lars was purposefully killed, which I can't believe for a moment, then the murderer belongs across the water and not to St. Jude Without.'

20

She squished the bag against the sides of the mug with more force than necessary and continued. 'Therefore it doesn't reflect on my community, so stop trying to convince me to move.'

Darrow laughed. 'Alright, I'll drop it for now,' he said. 'But I called with news of my own.'

He told her of the unexpected change of plans, of being sent up to the mainland for the mandatory course, and they were both quiet for a moment.

'Well, that sucks for us.' She swallowed her disappointment. They'd had a big date night planned to celebrate the launch of her stories. Carmel had even spent yesterday afternoon at the mall and sprung for a new summer dress with matching sandals for the occasion, she'd been so looking forward to it.

'We'll do it the week after, when I come back,' he suggested.

It would have to do. Disappointing, yes, but on the other hand...

This meant she didn't have to tell him about her spectral room-mate, didn't have to get into details about the ghostly presence in her house at least not just yet, which was a relief because, well, because she didn't want the love of her life to think she was certifiably crazy. By the time he'd returned in a week, surely the situation would have sorted itself out and there would be no need to bring it up for him to worry about her.

'Yes, we'll have a splendid night out when you get back,' she said, with a determinedly cheery note in her voice. 'We'll celebrate my launch then.'

'Ah, well then,' he said, sounding just a tad relieved. 'Brilliant. But we'll keep in touch, of course. I'll phone you in the evenings.'

'Hey, I want to hear all about it,' she said, still forcing the lightness into her voice. 'Community policing. Sounds like fun.'

'It'll be a blast, I'm sure,' he said wryly.

• • • •

Carmel put the phone down on the oak table next to her untouched mug of tea. So much to wrap her mind around, never mind the disappointment in her personal life. The materialization of Captain Jeremiah Ryan was surely the strangest thing yet in the string of odd happenings since her move to St. Jude Without, if you didn't count the dead bodies she kept finding around the cove. A spirit living in her house, if ghosts could be said to live, that is – perhaps 'dwell' was a more accurate term, and technically it was his house, anyway, as he had built it two centuries ago.

It was an unhappy turn of events for Carmel. Her mind raced towards the future. Now that she knew about the ghost, how did this impact her life?

The first and foremost issue that sprang to mind was privacy, and she didn't just mean being careful about closing the bathroom door. Besides, ghosts could go through walls.

No, the knowledge of Cap'n Jem's presence might put a damper on any future development of her relationship with Darrow. She was pretty certain there would be no explaining the ghost to him. He was an Inspector with the Royal Newfoundland Constabulary and while maybe he'd seen some weird stuff in his career, she somehow doubted he would be this open-minded. Even if he was a believer in the supernatural, he'd probably just add this to his arsenal of reasons why Carmel should quit the cove.

Outside the kitchen window the granite cliffs of the looming mountain above suddenly bloomed in a reflected rush of golden pink. The fog and rain had retreated in time for a glorious sunset, one that was made all the more vivid by the moisture still lingering in the air, yet the very brightness served to highlight the shadows cast on the village below.

The village. Her neighbors. While the crowd from St. Jude Without would have no issues accepting that their forefather Captain Jeremiah Ryan had finally shown himself to her, how would they feel about her writing yet another book about the cove? The sweat was forming in her armpits at the thought. They were all of them already pissed at her for exposing their home to the outside world, and now this? How would the True Confessions of a ghost work out for them, even if the spirit was their own great-great ancestor?

It was time to confront Jeremiah's descendants, and tell them what was in the works.

• • • •

She grimaced as she looked out the front window at the now empty narrow road hugging the mountain. If even Brigid her friend was ignoring her, it was doubtful that anyone else in this small tight-knit community would break from the herd and welcome her presence.

But stumbling over the body that afternoon, along with finding out that she was sharing her home with a ghost – and not just any spirit, but the founding father of the community who wanted her to publish his biography, which would only bring more fame and unwelcome attention to the community – well, it was all getting to her.

It was time to clear the air between her neighbors and herself, for none of them had any right to judge her for her success. She flicked her fingers through her hair and applied the battle armor of lipstick and mascara and set off to the community gathering spot.

The bar. It had started life as a Catholic church, built by the very priest who'd led the rabble against Captain Jem. The wooden structure was decrepit on its stone foundation yet the church tower still held the rosette stained glass window which glowed at night, beckoning in the flock when the bar was open.

A slight gust of wind caught the heavy church door behind her, slamming it shut at the same moment the music system paused in its endless cycle of 'seventies and 'eighties rock. All eyes turned as one to Carmel at the entrance, then glazed and slid away, pretending she wasn't there.

She'd known this was not going to be easy.

She searched the crowd for a friendly face, but only caught the menacing glance of Clyde Farrell's large black dog who growled at her to keep her distance. At the bar which occupied the former nave of the church, she could see familiar faces in the glow of the colored Christmas lights permanently strung all around. Sid, the owner of the bar, his dark eyes hooded and not meeting hers as he studied the counter he was furiously wiping. Brigid, the red-haired artist and possibly her friend but perhaps no longer as she too deliberately turned her back. The biker gang in their corner next to the smoking entrance, all with their black leather jackets marked on the back with the skull and crossbones, muttering amongst themselves. Phonse, that gorgeous fisherman who only this past winter had been asking her to marry him. Even he refused to acknowledge her presence.

Carmel knew this crowd and their ways, and she understood that the only way to get them talking to her again would be to explain her side of the story. Unfortunately, they were all Irish descendants and the whole process had to be emotional, involving a lot of shouting, drinking, crying and more drinking. She gritted her teeth. So be it.

She marched up to the bar and firmly placed a five dollar bill on it, daring Sid to refuse her service. If he didn't take her money, then all was lost. On the other hand, if he gave her a beer, then everyone else would come around eventually for Sid unofficially called the shots in this cove. Before he inherited the church from his father, he'd held a job with the Coast Guard for many years. A job with a salary and benefits and a pension, one that required a clean police record. The residents of St. Jude Without were still in awe of that accomplishment by one of their own.

Time was suspended as the whole bar waited for Sid's decision, the five dollar bill laying crumpled and worn on the polished stone surface. Carmel held herself in, unable to plead her case or beg or even breathe in this moment of time which would decide her fate.

'Carmel,' Sid said. He nodded, once, and placed an open bottle on the bar as the bill disappeared. He stood back and crossed his arms, framed by the multi-coloured LED lights around his head for all the world like a Roman emperor at the circus with the power of life and death in his hands. Carmel had gotten the thumbs up.

A collective sigh of relief ran invisibly throughout the hall. For all their faults and lawless habits, the crowd in St. Jude Without didn't really like bloodshed or hard feelings.

Phonse was the first to speak out, his long blond curls shaking, the mature silver threads glinting slightly as his blue eyes looked sorrowfully at Carmel. He stepped forward. She could smell the sweat off his white t-shirt and the beer on his breath, and his muscled torso bent towards her.

'Why'd you do it?' It was a plaintive whine. God, that man could be so sexy until he opened his mouth. He stared down at her accusingly.

Brigid, his cousin and confidante was next. She tossed her long hennaed hair and stood next to Phonse, her Doc Martens planted solidly on the ground as she pointed her finger. 'You betrayed us,' she declared.

'Shame, shame.' Ian, the Irish musician by her side, shook his unruly black curls.

'Hang on a minute,' Carmel began.

'What in frig's name were you thinking?' Bill, the mouthpiece for the bikers, interrupted her. When his deep rough voice bellowed at max volume, he could cut through the thickest fog bank. He stood with his hands on his hips demanding an answer from her. 'Two hundred years we've been here, two hundred quiet peaceful years and nobody knew about the cove. Now this!' He lifted his arms to indicate the road out beyond the windows of the old church and presumably the stream of looky-loos who had been haunting the cove during daylight hours.

'But...'

'How could you do it?' This was Brigid again, shaking her red head and looking mad enough to spit. 'Judas! You betrayed us for money!'

'For money.' Ian echoed her.

Carmel was unable to get a word in for her own defense as the rest of the bar's habitués took up the complaints, each adding their own say in how Carmel's unthinkably selfish actions had impacted their lives. Even the other bikers in the corner were rumbling discontentedly amongst themselves, casting dirty glances her way. She had exposed their quiet corner of paradise to the world and it would never be the same again. Before Carmel could interject and point out that actually, she hadn't yet gotten paid for her efforts despite the popularity of her collection of short stories, Phonse was towering at her elbow again.

'You had to open your mouth, huh? Couldn't leave well enough alone,' he added. The buzz in the bar increased louder and louder, all the anger in the small community aimed at Carmel.

Only Sid remained silent as he watched Carmel's lambasting by the village, one hand thoughtfully stroking his long handlebar moustache.

She could only stand in the midst of all this resentment unleashed, quaking so much she couldn't trust her hand to bring the bottle of beer to her mouth. She had been braced for flak, but not for this heavy stream of vitriol. Shock was quickly followed by hurt as if a knife had been thrust into her belly.

These people had been, until the past week, her friends, or at least her adopted family. It was Brigid who had insisted Captain

Jem's ghost had brought her to the village and thus ensured her acceptance in St. Jude Without. Phonse had been bugging her to marry him just this past winter and even Clyde Farrell the farmer had grudgingly allowed her to buy his over-priced free-range eggs.

The old Carmel might have stood there and grovelled before the tribe, begged for forgiveness no matter how unfair the charges, just to stop the waves of disgruntled disapproval aimed at her. But over the past year of living here, something of the cove must have rubbed off on her. Perhaps it was their absolute confidence in their right to live in society according to their own rules, for the cove's prolonged insularity had led to them not even considering that they were society's misfits and not the other way round, and the way they knew they had the right to live to suit their own desires of lifestyle.

Perhaps this confidence was even the legacy of Captain Jeremiah himself. Whatever it was, this confidence had now become an unexpected part of Carmel's makeup, and she finally snapped. The pain quickly turned to anger as the unfairness of their accusations began to piss her off royally and she slammed the untouched bottle of beer down on the bar, unmindful of the splashes of liquid over her hand.

'How dare you turn on me like this?' Her eyes blazed around at the assembly. 'Because of a few foolish stories? Because I'm successful? It's not like they're even believable – fairies and ghosts and witches? Come off it!'

She glared round, catching the surprised eyes of each and every one of them. 'Can you not be happy for my success? You have an award-winning author living in your midst! So there's a bit of interest from the outside, yes it's irritating and they get on my nerves, too.'

She had everybody's full attention now.

5

'I can't believe you crowd!' Carmel shouted over the Rolling Stones. 'Listen to yourselves! It's as if you all live in a bubble. Wake up and join the twenty-first century, for God's sake. It's not like this is the first time people have heard of St. Jude Without – remember last summer and the TV crews when the Premier's brother got himself murdered just down the road there?'

She faced Phonse full on. 'And your stupid 'Mummer's Affray' where you all dress up in your mothers' clothing and beat the hell out of each other on Snellen's Field, when Reverend Wilson got killed last Christmas? That was pretty sensational and drew a lot of attention, remember?'

And then to Ian, her former boarder and now live-in lover of Brigid. 'You didn't help matters much, getting loaded and going on the supper-time news with your stunned-arse theories of a serial killer, did you?'

And then it was Phonse's turn again. She had a lot of resentment to unload towards him, and it was feeling rather good. 'And don't get me started with your mother blabbing on about the fairies and Melba being a witch and all! She was just looking for her fifteen minutes of fame, that reporter Smythe didn't even have to pay her. She was all over him like ants at a picnic, just to get on TV.'

No, the folks in St. Jude Without had no right to make her the scapegoat of their troubles. They were all half-crazy, along with being inbred, the lot of them. As if anyone believed the stupid stories of ghosts and pirate treasures. Opening up the village to the outside was not a bad thing, come to think of it.

A stunned silence met her outburst.

'That's not a very nice thing to say about my mom,' Phonse said in a small, hurt voice, his face crumpling in upon itself. Carmel had hit his most vulnerable spot, for he was close to his mother, the horrid Vee Ryan who hated Carmel with a passion. A quiet murmur of agreement came from over by the pool table, as his various cousins and nephews and uncles paused in their game to take in the drama being played out at the bar.

'That's a low blow,' one of them nodded in agreement.

'Besides, that was just the local news,' said Bill the head biker in his deep gruff voice as he stood up and shook his finger at her. His bushy black eyebrows were drawn together in a frown. 'I heard them talking about you on the CBC FM news this morning, and that's nation-wide.'

This much was true. Carmel had a bunch of interviews last week while on her tour in the wake of the successful launch of the short story collection. Her publishers were pushing for all the free publicity they could get in order to maximise sales and she couldn't argue with that. The fame of St. Jude Without was only going to grow. Slightly deflated now, she gave a sniff, and waited for the next barrage of artillery.

But nothing came. She had fought back against the tide of public opinion and made her point, and her neighbors respected that. The atmosphere in the small old church eased as everyone relaxed, glad to get the air cleared and Carmel breathed a sigh of relief too. This had been a minor storm and she had sailed through it. Perhaps the community could survive this breach. Her stories would probably just turn out to be a seven-day wonder, anyway, and once the initial furor had died down, the books would lie undisturbed in book stores all over the country until they were packed up and remaindered, sent back to the publisher. St. Jude Without would be able to go back to its easy rhythms of daily life unmolested by the outside world again.

Except now she had to tell them she'd agreed to write the biography of the ghost. Even if no one believed the story's source, it would be sure to cause another round of sensationalism. She drew a deep breath to begin the public confession, but hesitated too long and lost her chance when the space in which she would have spoken was filled by the banging open of the smoker's entrance door. All attention was diverted away from Carmel.

It slammed shut again just as noisily, as Dr. Ignatius O'Reilly sauntered into the bar with his briefcase in hand, his eyes reddened and a funk of skunk weed all around him, and a smile reflecting his exhilarant mood. He was a large man in every sense – a strong build that was just starting to run to the early middle-aged spread common to those who spent their energies drinking beer and not getting on with a real life. Nate had left the cove in his younger years for an education, returning this past winter with a doctorate in History from a mainland university. Unable to understand why the local college didn't snap him up and bestow a well-deserved tenured position on this brilliant local-lad-made-good, he usually carried a chip on his shoulder comparable in size to the boulders which littered the road to St. Jude Without. It was a heavy weight to carry, along with his mass of greasy hair which reached down his back. But all his grudges appeared to have been temporarily forgotten tonight, and his smile only increased when he spotted Carmel in the center of the crowd which parted to let him through.

'Carmel McAlistair – just the person I wanted to see! Break out the shots Sid, we got something to celebrate.' His fists banged a tattoo on the bar as he grinned delightedly all around him.

Carmel had never seen him like this, so happy and excited. It was more like mania, to be honest. She watched him closely, her mind flicking back to earlier that afternoon when he'd been singing at the edge of Snellen's Field in the fog. She'd thought him drunk at the time, for she'd heard the smashing of a bottle on the rocks. Right after she'd found Lars' body. A cold feeling crept up her spine. Could he have…?

But what reason would Nate have to harm the gentle giant of Bell Island? Their paths didn't cross in the normal run of things, for the inhabitants of the cove and the island were sworn enemies for reasons that had long been lost in the mists of time. Carmel had always figured that they just liked holding onto grudges, that clutching those grievances closely had become a form of comfort, and the narrative they told themselves to explain their own inadequate expectations from life.

Unless Nate in his mania was ramping up the grudge.

He threw back the tiny glass of amber liquid and slammed it back on the stone bar. Knowing all eyes were on him, he made a show of checking his old-fashioned wrist-watch.

'Give us the clicker-box, Sid,' he said. 'Our lives are about to change.' He looked up and met Carmel's eye, and gave an exaggerated wink.

Sid slid the TV remote to him, whereupon Nate checked his watch again, gave three short nods as if counting down, and aimed the box at the TV on the wall.

'One Million Dollars!' it boomed. And all heads in the bar swivelled towards the corner where the TV sat.

'Yes, one million dollars is up for grabs to the most tourist friendly community in our fair province.' The blonde reporter's hair blew across her brittle smile as she faced the camera. She turned the microphone to a portly man standing next to her. 'Minister White, why don't you tell us about this exciting bit of good news?'

'Well,' the man cleared his throat and smiled into the camera. 'As you know, with the recent legalization of marijuana, the province's coffers have suffered an unexpected windfall in taxes. While sales of cigarettes and alcohol have remained the same, more legal marijuana has been sold in the first quarter in this province than the whole of the other Atlantic provinces combined!' He beamed with pride at this dubious honor.

'So, to boost our tourism industry and the province's morale, we've announced a contest,' he continued. 'And to keep it fair and to prevent any accusations of favoritism, the winners will be decided through FaceBook likes.' His rosy round cheeks shone with pride.

'FaceBook,' the reporter repeated in a less excited tone.

He nodded vigorously, beaming into the camera the whole time. 'We want to involve everybody, including the younger folks, so we thought this... er, platform, was the best way to reach the most people.'

'But young people don't...' She cut her eyes off screen then zipped her mouth and gave a slight shake of her head. 'Okay, FaceBook. But was there no thought to using this windfall for a more serious purpose, like perhaps paying down the deficit? Or subsidizing the ever increasing power rates?'

He shifted uncomfortably, his face still stretched in a large smile. 'No,' he said through his forced grin. 'No, this is a good news story, a bit of fun to lighten everyone's hearts. It's only a million, that wouldn't go too far in either of those arenas.'

'So this money, going to the community with the most FaceBook likes.' Her tone was now totally flat. 'What is it to be used for?'

'Erm... Infrastructure,' he replied, his eyes now shifting off to the side. 'Infrastructure that will encourage more tourism, of course. This is where our future lies,' he continued earnestly. 'Just think - the most tourist friendly town, village or outport will be given an extra million dollars in unplanned infrastructure money, to be spent on whatever the community feels is needed most!'

'What is the timeframe of this... contest?'

'Just one week,' Minister White beamed. 'Next Sunday, we'll count the likes on this news show. It's a great fun kick-off to summer, don't you think?'

She stared at him for a beat more, then turned to the camera. 'Thank you Minister White,' she said in her driest tone. 'This announcement is sure to stir up much excitement around the province.' And the screen cut to commercials before her eye roll was caught on camera.

Almost everyone in the bar was still looking toward the TV in stunned silence. Only Sid shook his head. He took the remote from the bar and turned down the sound.

'What's the place coming to at all?' he muttered.

'Yeah, this is probably the most ridiculous thing they've brought out yet,' Carmel agreed. 'A million dollars for FaceBook likes?'

'A million dollars,' Phonse echoed.

'We could do a lot with a million dollars,' one sage soul remarked.

'Paving the road would be a good start,' Brigid spoke out, looking at the mud on her boots.

'And there'd probably be enough to pave our lane too. Mom can't even get up over it now it's all churned up with muck from the tourists.' This was Phonse.

'How about a big sign with 'St. Jude Without' on it? We can maybe even get Brigid to draw on a pirate.'

'And a new dock for my boat.' Phonse again.

'I'd like to invest in a new pool table.' This from one of the pool players of course, the guy with the bald head and pudgy belly.

'And a fancy juke box with flashing lights.'

'And a ginormous party!' This suggestion was met with loud whoops and cheers.

'With a million dollars, we could do all of that and more.' Sid spoke out over the hollers, ever the voice of reason. 'But think about it, folks. Really, give it a good discussion. Do we actually want this? We don't like people in the cove, right? Didn't we just go through this?'

'But it's a million dollars!'

Sid for once was soundly ignored, the lure of the money overriding his voice.

'We can think bigger than all of that,' Nate thrust himself forward as he laid his bottle on the bar and nodded to Sid for another. 'And besides, before we spend it, we have to win it. And in order to win it, we need a plan. A plan to get people interested in St. Jude Without. Any ideas?'

This had them all stumped. Life in this village had not prepared them for things like planning ahead. They could dream about what to do with the windfall, but how to go about getting it was another matter. The group exchanged uncertain glances amongst themselves, then shuffled their feet, unwilling to open their mouths. They knew if they waited long enough Nate would just organize the whole thing anyway.

'Ah, Bell Island will probably win,' Phonse said, a frown marring his lovely countenance. 'They win everything, especially if it comes down to FaceBook likes. They have people all over the world.'

'I don't know about that,' Nate spoke slowly in his deep commanding voice, the gleam in his eye showing he had an idea. His eyes slid towards Carmel, and the entire room followed suit. 'I think we already have a head start.'

6

Nate believed that he could leverage Carmel's stories to help the cove win the contest. There were many reasons why this whole thing was not a good idea, but Carmel didn't know where to begin with her objections. As she searched for words to express this, the crowd in the bar were buzzing with their newfound lofty ambitions.

She looked to Sid, beseeching him to stem the tide of madness that threatened to wash over St. Jude Without.

He merely shook his head in reply and shrugged his shoulders as if absolving himself of any responsibility and turned the sound of the TV back up to drown out the noise of the crowd. He turned his back and began wiping down all the bottles on the bar.

The screen showed a glorious sunset of orange and purple clouds, the sun finally breaking out through the clouds at the end of the day in a flashy light show as if to make up for coming late to the party. Carmel's heart sank into her stomach. She recognized the scene, and if she chose to look out the window of the bar, she would see the exact same sunset, for the news crew was just down the road in the next town over. Exactly where she had been earlier the same day, back when the fog had shrouded everything.

'Breaking news!' The brittle blonde was back on the screen, her hair flying loosely in the breeze and her face framed by red and blue lights flashing in the dusk of the background. 'I'm here on the breakwater of Portugal Cove where a body was found earlier this evening.' The camera panned away to show an oversize body bag being loaded into the back of an ambulance.

The bar fell silent. Everyone was familiar with the breakwater down the road, though few inhabitants of the village ever had reason to go there. The ferry was the single entry point to Bell Island, and because of the grudge, none of the Ryans would ever visit that small proud country whose cliffs sheered straight out of the ocean.

'Inspector Laney of the RNC is on hand to give an update on the situation.'

The single light source held by the camera operator was harsh on Laney's face, exposing the bags under his eyes and his fleshy jowls. He blinked twice, and after clearing his throat, made as if to spit out his phlegm but he caught himself in time.

He cleared his throat again. 'Well, yeah, we were called out to the pier here as a body was found in suspicious circumstances.' He harrumphed again.

'May we ask what happened, and who it is?' Blondey was agog.

'I'm not at liberty to say the name of the victim, but I can tell you he was a well-respected citizen of Bell Island,' Laney told her, then he turned square to the camera, his eyes squinting in distaste. 'This murder hits home particularly hard for me, as many people will know.'

'Murder?' she squeaked.

He nodded solemnly. 'Yes, murder,' he replied, his eyes never leaving the camera.

She visibly pulled herself together. 'And why do you say you are personally involved?'

'Because Bell Island is my home land,' he said. He thumped his chest for emphasis and his untidy brows drew together. 'My parents are from Bell Island, and I have a lot of family living there still. I just want to say, we know who is responsible for this, and we will be watching every single one of you. We will find the evidence for this cold-blooded deed and will hunt you down, even if I have to throw every last one of youse in jail. I am taking this personally.'

Blondey took a step back. 'So you believe this was planned by a group?' Her face screwed up in puzzlement at this honesty. Police representatives never gave such heartfelt statements, at least not on record, and never if it was televised and broadcast for the whole province to watch.

As if directed, the camera panned away to include the outline of Bell Island in the background with the sun setting behind it. Laney looked off to his left, up to the space between two headlands where the cove of St. Jude Without huddled, hidden behind the rocks. 'There is no doubt in my mind, and I know the motive.'

• • • •

'Shit. What's that all about?' Phonse laid his empty beer bottle carefully on the bar. He was visibly shaken.

'Lars Andersen,' Carmel said in a low voice. 'I found his body on the breakwater this afternoon. I was going to tell you, but you all got so caught up in the contest.'

His head swivelled from the TV to her. 'What do you have to do with the death of Lars Andersen?' This erupted from his mouth loud enough to grab everyone else's attention.

'What happened?' Everyone was crowding around her now. 'How did someone kill Lars, of all people?'

'I found him lying amongst the rocks on the breakwater, I thought he must have fallen and hit his head on one of the boulders.' She shuddered as she remembered the squishy softness of his lifeless body under her rubber boot and the heavy sweet smell of alcohol assailing her nose.

'I think perhaps he was drunk and slipped on the rocks,' she added. 'I don't think it was murder.'

Phonse screwed up his face in disbelief. 'You're kidding me, right? Lars Andersen, drinking? He doesn't touch alcohol, none of his crowd do. He works for Gen, she keeps them all under a tight leash.'

There was a murmur of agreement all round which grew into excited speculation.

Gen Parsons was the proclaimed mayor of Bell Island across the water - for the past forty years every time the election came up, she won by virtue of being the only candidate. Outsiders commented on her popularity and how well-loved she was, but Carmel figured the real truth was that no one would dare run against her. As the matriarch of Bell Island, she called the shots and everybody there listened and obeyed, for the alternative was too horrible to think of. Rumor had it that Gen had exiled folk from the island for the simple crime of questioning her decisions on the island's public radio. She was sort of like the mafia, but without the Italianness.

If Lars worked for Gen, then he didn't drink, and so maybe the cause of his death was not a simple case of drunken accident after all. But in that case...

This meant that maybe, just maybe, Inspector Laney was right for a change. Carmel's mind was now spinning with everything that had happened today. Perhaps someone had it out for Gen and was getting at her through her henchmen. Perhaps it was a rival for her position – but who would have the guts to challenge her? Surely the woman was in her late eighties by now, why not just wait for natural attrition, she had to die soon, after all.

Nate had been silent throughout this whole exchange, but then he spoke out. His ruddy cheeks had paled.

'He was drunk,' he said, his voice uncharacteristically quiet.

'Not a chance,' Phonse insisted, and all the pool players agreed.

'He was loaded. I saw him drunk,' Nate asserted again, louder. 'This afternoon by the harbor in Portugal Cove.' He stared all around as if challenging anyone to contradict him.

Carmel found herself holding her breath. Nate admitted to seeing the man before he died. Surely if he was responsible for Lars' death he would have kept mum about it.

'We were sharing a bottle of Johnny Walker,' he said slowly. 'Down there on the rocks of the breakwater.'

'Jesus, Nate,' Phonse swore softly.

'I know,' Nate relied, then gave a disbelieving laugh. 'Consorting with the enemy, right?'

'What the frig, man?'

Nate shrugged. 'He had a bottle and was offering. Never going to say no to a free drink, now, am I? Guess he didn't want to drink alone, and he couldn't trust any of the Bell Island crowd to know about it for fear they'd tell Gen.'

'Was he okay when you left him?' This came from Brigid. She was worrying her bottom lip with her teeth.

'Yeah, he was fine.' Nate said. 'A little tipsy, but so was I. It would take a lot of booze to bring down a man his size. At least, he didn't seem that drunk, but half the forty-ouncer was gone by the time I met up with him.'

'What did you talk about?'

'This and that,' Nate replied. He was quiet for a moment, as if harking back to the conversation on the boulders, in the lea of the breakwater shrouded by a solid blanket of mist. 'He was at a turning point in his life, he told me. He wanted to move away from the island, in fact he wanted to move up to the mainland, but Gen wasn't letting him go.'

An awed silence filled the bar. No one, and that meant no one, had ever left Gen's employ.

'Did anyone see you?' Brigid asked in a low voice. She didn't need to add that if Laney was looking to pin Lars' death on the cove, he only needed to have one witness to the unlikely friendship between Lars and Nate.

He shook his head. 'I dunno? The fog was really thick, and we were hunkered down on the other side of the boulders on the breakwater, right on the water. He said he didn't want anyone from the island spying on him. You know, drinking booze. Didn't want that getting back to Gen.'

'What happened to the bottle?' Carmel asked tersely.

'He gave it to me, he had to get on the ferry and go home. Couldn't take it with him.'

She nodded to herself. That explained the smashed glass, then.

'Funny,' continued Nate. 'He was the one told me about the contest. Gen knew about it way before it was announced, you know she's in tight with the Premier, and she's been gearing up her crowd to get into action. He gave me some ideas. When I left him, the ferry was just heading into the harbor.'

'Are you going to tell the cops about this?' Carmel asked, just a little hesitant.

'No!' Nate was rightly scandalized at the thought, his reddened eyes wild like a cornered moose. 'You saw Laney there on TV, giving our cove the hairy eyeball. That's all he needs, now, isn't it? He'd have me strung up in no time flat.'

What he said was true, but this still begged the question in Carmel's mind, one that she hated to ask but which crept up anyway. Nate had been appearing more unstable of late, which might just be the result of his overindulgence in alcohol and drugs. On the other hand, perhaps he was suffering mental issues and self-medicating, with the result that his judgement was impaired. Which came first – the chicken or the egg?

Could Nate possibly have been responsible for Lars' untimely demise? He admitted to probably being the last person to see the giant alive, at least to his inner circle if not to the police. Nate liked to think largely, and made no secret of his aspirations for a bigger life. In his present state of mind, could the news of the contest have been the lure which pushed him over the bounds of normal behavior? In a momentary lapse of judgement, had he hatched a plan to discredit Bell Island? Could he possibly have been devious enough to stage the death of Lars just to embarrass Gen and make her lose the ridiculous contest?

Hunched over his beer, Nate tossed back another shot and met her gaze. She shivered at the calculation she saw in those narrowed eyes.

7

Carmel wrenched her eyes away from Nate's and searched all around the bar. Was she the only one with suspicions? The contest with the million dollar prize was now all but forgotten in the buzz surrounding the unexplained death on the breakwater, for everyone in the room was aware of the consequences of Laney's blatant insinuations about the cause of Lars' death and his finger pointing at St. Jude Without, and their voices were full of complaint at this unfair treatment. If Laney had decided to turn his sights to the cove, they were really in for a hard time. That crooked cop would hound them relentlessly and twist everything he heard till he had a suspect neatly wrapped up. She herself had firsthand experience of his methods earlier in the spring, and the police lock-up was not a place she wanted to revisit.

Only Sid was quiet, standing motionless behind the thin stone counter top, the hand with the soft rag no longer polishing its smooth surface. His face was lit by its glow from the lighting underneath and his shadowed eyes carefully watched the room.

'Sid,' Carmel said urgently in a low voice. He was the voice of reason in St. Jude Without, and if anyone could calm the fears in her mind right at that moment it was him. 'What's going on here?'

He slid his eyes over to where Carmel sat at the bar and nodded as if he understood what lay behind her question, and opened his mouth as if to reply to her, but Nate interrupted with a large bellow from the center of the old church.

The man had rallied himself and shaken off all hints of the dark clouds which had lurked over the room with the news of Lars' untimely demise. He was back to keeping his eye on the prize and was hell bent on taking everyone with him, certain that they would all follow willingly.

'Enough of Lars Andersen, that's Bell Island's problem!' Nate roared as he took out his brief case out and thumped it onto a small round table. 'We have a contest to win!'

He stood with his hands on his hips and a self-satisfied grin on his face. 'Give us another beer, bar-keep, I'm going to get this ball rolling.' He rubbed his hands together in anticipation, then began to pontificate as if he was at the head of a classroom.

Ignatius O'Reilly had always known he was destined to be the Alpha in any group. Blessed with a large physical presence, he had even larger aspirations and like any good leader, he always had the best interests of his followers in mind. At the same time he was fully aware that in order to benefit his people, he needed to get himself in the forefront of all action. Ascendance was key, and it was evident (to Carmel and probably Sid) that he had seized on the contest as the means to give him a fast ride to the glory he felt was his due. Everyone in the cove was aware of his plans to be Premier of the province one day, by hook or by crook. And if crook was the easier way, so be it.

From the opened briefcase he withdrew his laptop. 'Sid, would you turn the TV down for a moment? We're going to have a brainstorming session here,' he informed the group at large. 'This is going to require a concerted effort from everyone.'

There was some uncomfortable shifting and mumbling at the threat of work, but no one dared slip out the back door. They all knew they were in for it, for there was no escaping in St. Jude Without.

'First, let's give a toast to the lady who has started the ball rolling for us.' Nate lifted his new bottle up to cheer Carmel where she stood by the bar.

'Me?' Was she hearing correctly? She had nothing to do with all this foolishness of a contest based on FaceBook likes.

'Oh, yeah, you Carmel,' he said genially after emptying his beer down his throat. He signalled for yet another, then sat the table and beckoned all to gather round. 'The contest is all about being the most tourist friendly place, right? And in order to be recognized as being a tourist attraction, well, you gotta have visitors.'

He looked carefully around to make sure he had everyone's attention. He was a master at running a crowd. 'And we've already got the people coming in to see the St. Jude Without that she writes about, correct?' He waited till he had nods from everyone, even the bikers in the corner. 'Her stories are bringing them in for us. They want to see it all. I say we give it to 'em!'

'But,' he cautioned with his finger in the air. 'In order to keep them here, we have to give them a fuller experience. They need to have so much fun here, they'll tell their friends and relatives, and most importantly – we'll get those FaceBook likes!' This was accompanied by half-hearted cheers from the floor. The crowd in this cove liked a leader especially if it meant they never had to do the thinking.

Carmel and Sid were the only ones who didn't cheer him on. She sat on the stool silently fuming at him. Nate O'Reilly had certainly changed his tune overnight. Just yesterday, he'd been the force behind everybody bitching at her for those silly scribblings which had only been meant to idle away the winter nights. She'd been ready to apologize to her friends when her writing had caught the popular imagination, for she'd certainly never meant to expose the village to outside scrutiny. Now here he was acting like it was all his idea.

'First off. Carmel – we need you to write more,' Nate said, turning around and pointing his fresh bottle at her. 'Churn those stories out and get them seen.'

She rolled her eyes. He obviously had no understanding of the publishing world. 'It takes ages to write a book, let alone get it published,' she objected. 'Sorry, but that's not going to happen in the time frame of this contest. You only have a week to get this rolling.'

'Then let's not bother with a publisher,' he said. 'Put it up on a blog. We'll get Ian to make a website for the cove, and you'll be the blogger.'

She opened her mouth to object further but he had already moved on.

He faced to the crowd. 'Those stories are giving us a great starting point and we want to expand on the ideas. Who here has read them?'

Silence greeted him. A little hurt, Carmel shot an accusing stare at Brigid, who merely shrugged one shoulder and let her eyes casually wander back to Nate.

'Hmm. Figured as much,' he said, then leaned back in his chair. 'But I got you covered. I know exactly how to use the themes in Carmel's work.'

That was more like it. The crowd on the floor let out a collective sigh.

'First though, is there anything outside of the stories which you think is important to draw people in?'

Phonse spoke out first, hesitantly. 'Could we like, have a bouncy castle?' he said, hope coloring his voice. He looked around to see how the effect of his suggestion. The nods and murmurs encouraged him.

'One of those great big red and yellow ones! For the kids, I mean. We could put it down on Snellen's Field. Just like at the Regatta.' His blue eyes glowed at the thought. There'd never been a bouncy castle in St. Jude Without, and at forty-five years old, he'd only ever been inside one once, back in his teenage years when a bunch of the guys from the cove had attended the annual St. John's event. They'd been swiftly kicked out, but that had only whetted his appetite for bouncing.

Bill the head biker was the next to be caught up in the excitement. 'A hot dog stand, we got to have that. People got to eat, right? And what's better than hot-dogs?' The three other bikers nodded their beards with enthusiasm. He rubbed his hard man-pregnancy belly with glee at thought of it. 'Hot dogs and beer.'

Sid stood at the bar, shaking his head while one hand toyed with his long moustache and a frown deepened on his face. He raised his voice over the excited noise. 'Hang on just a minute, all of you. Bill, hot dogs are good, but in order to sell hot dogs, we need people here. In the cove. Think of what you're saying, man!'

Carmel had never seen him so perturbed before. No, not even when he'd thought his girlfriend Sharran might be next in line to be murdered last Christmas, back when religious leaders in the next town over were being strangled. The bartender had kept his cool all that while, merely observing from his hooded eyes as he stood at the altar of his bar.

Those same eyes stared down the head biker across the crowd, and Bill soon saw sense and sat back in his chair.

'Well, maybe not such a good idea after all,' he mumbled, and his three companions nodded their heads in reluctant agreement. They returned to their beers, much subdued.

But this interaction went largely unnoticed by the others in the old church who carried on with their plans, dreams of new juke boxes and parties and paved roads dancing in their heads, ignoring the fact that everything in this world has a price and that these dreams could only come about at the expense of losing the cove as they knew it.

Sid gave one last appeal to the common sense which had flown out the window of his bar, then he came out from behind his sanctuary and drew Nate aside. Carmel moved slightly down the bar towards them, the better to overhear.

'Nate,' he whispered furiously, his brown eyes piercing from beneath their shadows. 'Nate, what the hell are you doing? You seriously want to open this can of worms?'

But Nate by this time was drunk on success and his lofty plans and the fun of being a leader. He brushed Sid off.

'Welcome to the twenty-first century, Sid b'y,' he roared in his best fighting Newfoundlander voice. The two men were much of the same height, but where Sid was tall and narrow, Nate was burly and liked to take up a lot of space, and especially liked being the centre of attention. He flung his arms out as if to embrace the cove itself. 'This is our chance to do something with the place! We have an opportunity to build an empire. You're either with us, or against us.'

The other man stood by, slowly shaking his head, refusing to join his game.

Nate sighed and lowered his voice, placing his arm around Sid's shoulder, who visibly flinched at the contact, or perhaps it was the smell from Nate's long greasy hair.

'Look my son, the old ways are gone. Over with. You have to have vision, see where the world is going. Where the cove is going. Pot is legal now, right? Am I right?'

Sid was silent, the frown on his face speaking for him.

'Booze from the French Islands, well, that's not so cheap anymore is it? France is going bankrupt with all that socialism they got over there, and they've started to realize that St. Pierre and Miquelon are weighing them down financially now the fishing isn't so good.'

The two tiny islands off Newfoundland's southern coast had, since time immemorial, belonged to France, the last remnants of the colonial wars. The heavily subsidized French alcohol had always been a money maker for those brave enough to smuggle it into the province.

'You gotta move with the times, Sid,' Nate continued in his deep gravelly voice. 'Your operation is too small to play against the big guys now.'

Sid continued to shake his head, slowly and almost reluctantly. 'I don't understand why you want to open up St. Jude Without to outsiders. And all this stuff you're talking about – there's rules, you know? You think Bill can get a vendor's license for hot dogs, let alone adhere to laws for serving food and the cleanliness that requires? And if there's things for kids – Jesus, we won't be able to move for political correctness. I don't trust this crowd to not cut corners.'

'You of all people are worried about rules, Sid? You're the last person to let a few laws get in your way.' Nate finished off his bottle of beer with a belch. 'I got plans, and this here, what we're doing with the cove? This is just the beginning. You know the only way to make money in this province is through politics, right?' Nate's voice was now a whisper, the volume turned down as low as it could go, but Carmel could still overhear if she edged herself even closer along the bar. 'You know I'm aiming to make it big – go right to the top, that's my five year plan. Stick with me, Sid, and I'll see you get in as Minister of... what? Transportation, with your background in the Coast Guard? Think of the sidelines you can rake in from that. Never mind all this small stuff.'

'Keep your ambitions out of this cove, Nate O'Reilly!' His furious voice rose as loud as Nate's was quiet.

Nate gave a final clap to Sid's slight shoulder before he moved back to the excited crowd. 'You stick with me, b'y, and I'll see you're all right,' he called over his shoulder.

As Sid turned to return to his habitual spot behind the bar, Carmel caught his glance for the briefest second and almost gasped aloud to see the pain within those normally dark and unreadable eyes. He paused before her and pointed an accusing finger.

'You started this, Carmel,' he said. 'You better stop him before this goes too far.'

He turned his back on her, unplugged the cheery Christmas lights around the bar and went over to confer with the four bikers in the corner.

'Enough of this!' She didn't realize she'd spoken aloud till the words were out of her mouth. The contest was not her problem. Lars' death was not a murder case. The feud between St. Jude Without and its neighbor Bell Island had nothing to do with her. Inspector Laney, Nate O'Reilly, Phonse – the whole packing lot of them – were nut cases.

She drank down her beer and laid the empty bottle on the darkened bar, deciding she'd had enough company for the night. She was on her way back out the front door and none of her friends even noticed her slipping away.

She closed her bedroom door firmly that night, wishing she could as easily shut out the thoughts racing in her head. It had been the strangest day ever. Not just the shock of the finding Lars' lifeless body literally under her foot, but also that horrible suspicion which had arisen in her mind that it was possible Nate was responsible.

'No,' she said as she turned off the light. 'Think of something else.'

Like the ghost. There was a spirit in her house, although she was happy to note, no whiff of hell lurked around now. As she tried to relax and allow sleep to come, she idly wondered what her resident ghost could do – what exactly were his powers? Was he stuck to the house, and the spot where he'd died, or could he roam through the world at will?

And perhaps Captain Jeremiah Ryan was in touch with other ghosts. Could he speak with her dead mother? If so she had a lot of questions she wanted answers to from that lady, questions she hadn't had the time to ask before her presumed death in the wilds of Africa all those years ago. Like, the identity of Carmel's biological father, and if he was still living. It had never really bothered her before, but now she settled in her own life, even if children and babies were not going to happen at the age of 43, still, she had a right to know what her genetic inheritance was.

And maybe the pirate would have answers to more pressing questions, being on the other side and all. Like how to deal with the influx of tourists over-running the small village and how to return St. Jude Without back to the stagnant backwater it should be and how to stop Nate's crazy plans for this contest. Perhaps he could materialize and scare all the outsiders away – she could suggest it to him. No violence though, no more bloodshed.

She had almost lulled herself to sleep with these pleasant thoughts when she came back with a start. What with Nate's dramatics and his big plans, she hadn't told the crew about the ghost's materialization.

Thank God. Imagine what Nate would do with that juicy bit of news. An actual ghost living in the cove. She shuddered and turned over. Maybe it wasn't such a good idea to spread the news of Captain Jeremiah's manifestation.

8

Sid left St. Jude Without that night, quietly, taking the bikers with him with nary a rumble thrust of the mufflers to announce their departure. The bar was no longer open for business, the tables were cleaned and the beer and bottles all put away. However, the cove being a place where doors were rarely locked, Nate just as quietly moved in and claimed the old church as his headquarters. Such was the excitement generated by Nate and his big plans that people hardly noticed the bikers were gone. Perhaps only Carmel missed Sid's solid presence and felt the difference in the cove the next day.

By departing the cove, the owner of the bar was letting it be known that he didn't like the new direction that St. Jude Without was taking under Nate's captaincy.

Nate had lost no time in getting his new project on the go. The very next morning, a large banner was strung across the outside of the church, hand-painted in garish colors.

'SJW Come Home Year,' Carmel read the words aloud as she paused her car outside the church. That was fast work. The plans for the cove were expanding in leaps and bounds with Nate at the unstable helm.

The capelin weather had fully lifted by now, showing the miraculous promise of spring to this sun-starved land. The temperature was still pretty low of course, being right by the water during what was now officially iceberg season, and these huge mountains of broken off glaciers could be spotted sailing down the Labrador Current past St. John's harbor. There'd been more than ever in recent years, what with global warming and everything. She planned to take a swing by Signal Hill later on her lunch-break – from that great height the ocean spread down below in a panorama of icebergs, boats and if she was lucky, a whale or two.

Nate was standing on the road, admiring his work. As now befitting a man with his ambitions, he wore a suit jacket over his habitual ratty t-shirt and jeans, topped off with a dusty fedora perched jauntily over his long hair. A large stogie occupied his mouth.

Carmel unrolled her car window. 'Really? A Come Home Year?' she said to him, doubt evident in her voice. From this vantage point of the road overlooking the small community, she cast her eyes over the few houses. She had a lot of questions, and didn't know where to start. 'There's like, a hundred people living in St. Jude Without, Nate. How is this going to help? And... and... where'd you get that hat?'

He removed the cigar from his mouth with one hand while touching the hat proudly with the other. 'Compliments of Clyde. He's not using it,' he said. 'I've moved in with him, to keep an eye on the old guy. Also, I need to be close to the action if we're going to win this war.'

Clyde Farrell lived alone in his farm down the road, with only his dog, chickens, cows and a goat to keep him company. Carmel had witnessed him brandishing his shotgun at tourists who attempted to cross his land - he'd even set that large black dog on Carmel last summer.

'He let you on his property?'

'Clyde's my uncle,' Nate replied. Of course, everybody in this cove was related somehow.

'Alright, but... the Come Home Year idea?' she reminded him. 'I thought nobody ever left this place. Who is there to come home?'

Nate strolled over and leaned on her car's roof. She waved away the smoke from the cigar with no success.

'You kidding me, Carmel? St. Jude Without has been Catholic for over two hundred years. Lots and lots of babies in that time. There are St. Judeans and their offspring all over the world.'

'How are you going to find them?'

'Ian's working on that. Using social media and sites like Ancestry.ca, he's figured a way to reach as many as possible.'

'It's awfully short notice, isn't it? Usually these kinds of celebrations are planned a couple of years in advance, so people can make plans...'

'You think so?' Nate drew back and pointed the stogie at Carmel. 'Let me tell you something. St. Judeans have been dying for an excuse to come back to the mother-cove. Just you wait and see. We'll fill this place to the rafters and over-flowing. We will win the government lottery.'

He turned away from her car and faced St. Jude Without and Bell Island off in the distance, his fist in the air. 'We will win the contest!'

• • • •

St. Jude Without and its denizens were messing with her head, she decided as she put the car in gear and turned on the radio, just in time to hit the half hour news. The announcer sounded excited by the prospect of the province-wide FaceBook competition, exclaiming he was really looking forward to the race over the next week. Carmel suspected it would fill up a lot of air time.

The furor caused by the death of Lars had already faded into the background.

'Bell Island is going to win this one. It's a no brainer,' she argued to herself as she drove along the snaking mountainside into Portugal Cove. She glanced across the bay to where that island's cliffs rose straight out of the water. Atop the heights, Bell Island looked to be a beautiful pastoral setting on this June morning, all rolling green fields and woods, dotted about with little cottages. It was a gorgeous sight.

Once upon a time, Bell Island had almost solely supported the colony's economy, if you believed the people of that place, and it had once sported a population of thousands. The coal mines stretched deep under the ocean, kilometers of seams being harvested, with ships coming from all over the world to load up. Now though, the coal mines were spent and mostly reclaimed by the sea, and a large portion of its population was scattered around the globe, having migrated to look for other work.

Yet the coalminers' experience lived on in the enterprise of the museum and guided tours through parts of the old mine. Carmel shivered. Even though she had once made a living as an intrepid travel writer, she felt no desire to explore the underground of that island. Not with her claustrophobia. God knew what lurked down there.

'Maybe we can encourage our visitors to go over there,' she said to herself as she took the turn down to the ferry. 'We could help Bell Island win the contest, and clear out the lanes of St. Jude Without.'

She paused the car at the bottom of the short hill, her eyes inevitably drawn to the breakwater, and on impulse drove over to the site. Yellow police tape flapped in the never-ending breeze, but that was the only sign of Lars' death on the Portugal Cove breakwater. The tarmac glistened bright in the sun, and the boulders themselves had taken on an almost friendly shade of pale gray. The breakwater was empty of people at this hour of the day between ferries. Further along the water's edge, over by the fisherman's wharf, a couple of men worked on their boats to get them ready for when the ice finally disappeared from the waters and it would be safe to go back out on the ocean. The sun was shining again and the buds were breaking out on the trees despite the chill breeze from the sea.

Lars Andersen. Carmel rested her elbows on the steering wheel and stared out to the island that had been his home. Was his death accidental, the natural outcome of clambering the boulders of the breakwater while loaded drunk, or was it intentional, a political move to discredit Gen?

And was a million dollars enough money to cause a war between towns, with Lars Andersen being a casualty of that war? It was inconceivable, yet her mind harked back to Nate's narrowed warning look the previous night.

It was unthinkable.

Carmel was just about to pull away from her parking spot near the wharf when a car stopped behind her, carelessly blocking her exit. Through the rear view mirror, she saw the distinctive markings of an RNC squad car.

'Asshole,' she muttered. There was no way she would be able to squeeze past it, so she turned the engine off and prepared to get out to ask them to move over a little, but the occupants had already gotten out of their car and were strolling toward the breakwater.

'Don't see why I have to get out of the god damn car just to have a friggin' smoke.' It was Laney's voice. She took her hand off the door handle and hunkered down in the driver's seat. The last thing she wanted was a run-in with him. She heard the flick of his lighter.

The two men paused on the breakwater, looking over the water to Bell Island, Laney puffing like a chimney.

'I'll get those bastards,' Laney continued. 'Lars was a buddy of mine, you know?'

His sidekick said something she didn't catch.

'Oh, I know it was someone from that cove.' He spit onto the rocks below. 'Every single damn one of them was together the afternoon Lars died. If that's not suspicious in itself, I don't know what is.'

'You think they're covering for each other?'

'Not a doubt in my mind.'

'The rain washed everything away, no evidence left at all,' the other officer continued glumly.

Laney laughed. 'Like that's ever stopped us before?' He flicked the lit cigarette butt over the boulders into the sea, then took out another from the packet. 'I'm sure we can stretch something to fit if we look hard enough. Besides, even if they're not guilty of this, they're damn well sure guilty of something.'

Carmel heard the flick of his lighter again, and the deep inhale which followed.

'There's always that.'

'I say we stick it on the blond guy, what's his face Ryan,' Laney continued. 'Never did like him. He stole a girl from me once.'

He had to be talking about Phonse.

'Bastard,' his subordinate commented. 'Was he actually there that evening?'

'Oh yeah,' said Laney. 'Or at least, he was down at the fish and chip takeout van last week, remember that day it was pissing down rain? We got him on the camera. Dave's working on fixing up the CC footage now. It'll work.'

Carmel's eyes widened as she realized what she was hearing. Laney was planning to frame Phonse by doctoring the footage of the camera by the ferry terminal. Was such a thing even possible?

'Too bad there's no cameras trained on the actual breakwater,' the other cop said. 'That would wrap up the whole thing.'

'You kidding me?' Laney's voice rose loud. 'We'd probably find out then that Lars did slip and get himself killed. No, I intend to use this to get back at that woman-stealing bastard.'

'That's alright then,' his companion said, after a pause. 'When we have that, no one'll even question if he denies being there. The jury will just think the others are lying for him.'

'Oh, yeah,' Laney said. 'Been waiting twenty-five years for this moment. How sweet it is. I'd like to get it all clued up before this weekend.'

He flicked the second butt into the water, aiming for a passing gull but he missed by several feet.

'For sure. Shame if we missed out on the rugby tournament because of this.'

'Damn right. We're gonna pulverize the fire fighters. They got it coming to them, after last year, those jeezly cheaters,' Laney replied.

Carmel ducked back down again as they turned to walk back to their car, not lifting her head again until she heard the doors open and slam shut. Peering between her front seats, she watched as the police car pulled out of the lot and headed back to the city.

She started her own vehicle to reluctantly follow them, making sure they got a good head start, and their words echoed in her mind. Laney was in charge of investigating Lars' death as murder, and was manufacturing evidence to pin it on Phonse, and he wanted to clue it up before the weekend. This was crazy.

And Darrow was out of town all this week. Carmel briefly considered warning Sergeant Evelyn, Darrow's work partner, about Laney's plans, before shaking her head. Evelyn Wright had no time for Carmel or for the crowd in the cove. With Darrow out of the picture, she'd probably prefer to keep her head down and turn a blind eye to Laney and his plans, unwilling to rock the boat.

Carmel had promised herself and Darrow she would have nothing to do with the death on the breakwater, but this was a game changer. Old grudges died hard in this neck of the woods - Inspector Laney, the ex-Bell Islander, was trying to frame Phonse as a murderer because of a twenty-five year old love triangle.

The whole thing was ridiculous, she shook her head to clear her thoughts. There was no way it could have been Phonse. If anyone had been a murderer that day, it would have been Nate. He admitted to being on the breakwater with Lars, and said he'd been drinking with him. Yet why would he admit to being in the large man's company if he had killed him? Nate was not her favorite person by a long shot, and he did appear to be pretty unstable these days, but surely he wasn't a killer.

Right?

'Yet everyone except Nate swears it couldn't have been a drunken accident,' she said aloud, drumming her fingers on the steering wheel as she drove unseeing past Winsor Lake. 'Because Gen laid down the law about alcohol. So what really happened to Lars? Is Nate lying about the whole thing?'

And what did Sid know about what had really happened? She had no way to contact him to ask, for he had disappeared from the cove. It was too early in the day to phone Darrow for he was in transit now, not that she wanted to discuss the happenings in the cove with him. He would only sigh and advise her to move away out of there and not get mixed up with it all.

Carmel quickly drove off into the relative sanity of the busy city.

9

Work was a haven of sanity for her, there was no doubt. Some people might be hard put to spend all day inside on this first gorgeous day of summer-like weather, filing and re-filing folders of dusty historical documents, and they might long for the chance to escape out into the sunshine and balmy breezes along the old downtown streets of St. John's. But Carmel was happy enough to be there doing what she did. Everything was filed according to system, and once you became acquainted with that system, everything was at your fingertips. She loved the order the archives represented.

She was even happy to go down to the basement archives when it was called for, and this was huge for her. Never mind her lifelong fear of small dark places instilled in her by a nasty nun in the orphanage where she'd been dumped by her jet-setting mother before that lady's untimely disappearance, presumed dead. And never mind the fact that she'd found her boss of the time murdered down in those same stacks just months ago, and been accused of her murder by Inspector Laney of the Royal Newfoundland Constabulary.

Never mind all that. With time, a bit of therapy and her own Inspector Darrow of the RNC by her side, she was dealing with the demons of her past, and she was happy to be here in the sameness of her job where although she was surrounded by old things, there were no ghosts or FaceBook competitions. And as the icing on the cake, she didn't even have to deal with the tourists who swarmed the front desk looking for their Newfoundland roots.

That was Tina's job. The very efficient, large-spectacled, gum chewing Tina who, while she resented her job, liked well enough the pay cheque and the union benefits and couldn't imagine life without them. For Tina, work was a life sentence that she accepted, having neither the desire to upgrade her skills nor the courage to try something different. Besides, there was a perceived prestige that came with working in The Rooms, the province's main Archive/ Gallery / Museum space. It beat working at Honda Country, even if there weren't as many cute guys here. Tina was still holding out for one of the university types to come in and sweep her off her feet. Now that would be a real catch.

'Leave that stack of folders out,' Tina said in the small archival office behind the front desk. 'All the Bell Island stuff. No sense putting it away, because with their 'Come Home Year', there'll be another dozen looking for those family trees before the day's out.'

She snapped her gum and looked up at the clock on the wall. 'Coffee time, close enough. You coming? Someone brought doughnuts, we gotta hurry to get the best pick.'

'K,' Carmel nodded. She was under no illusions why she was singled out to join Tina at coffee, it was the same every morning she worked, which as her job was only part-time, it only happened two or three times a week. She straightened the pile of folders on the desk and followed Tina down to the staff lounge.

'So what's new in your neck of the woods?' Tina asked casually while hovering her hand over the box of treats as she mentally debated between a syrupy fritter or the allure of the colorful sprinkles on a jam doughnut.

Carmel knew Tina was really broaching the subject of Dr. Ignatius O'Reilly. Nate of the stringy greasy long hair, beer belly and attitude, who could actually be quite charming and flirtatious when he cleaned himself up and was looking to get something from someone.

Tina's question really meant – how was Nate, what was he doing, was he seeing anybody, did he mention Tina at all, how could she angle for an invitation up to the cove as he didn't come in to the Archives anymore?

'Oh things are happening in the cove,' Carmel replied. 'They're having their own Come Home Year.'

'Yeah, I saw it on FaceBook,' Tina enthused. 'It must be so exciting, eh? Dr. O'Reilly's got that all organized so quickly.'

'Ye-es,' Carmel replied, being as non-committed as she could be.

'And I hear there's all sorts of things happening there,' Tina continued as they took a table and brushed off the crumbs of the previous occupants. 'Maybe I should drop up for a beer sometime.'

'You could,' Carmel said. 'But the bar's closed down right now. For an indefinite period of time.'

'Oh,' said Tina, her mouth turning down at the corners. She took a large bite of her doughnut. Sprinkles had won out, and they mixed with a drop of jam on her lip.

A spark of devilry made Carmel open her mouth. She would probably regret it later, but it would be fun to watch, and if Tina saw Nate in his present state, her crush would surely dissipate and she would quickly be turned off him. Really, she told herself, she was doing Tina a favor for her own good.

'Nate set up his headquarters in the back of the church, though,' she said in as casual a tone as she could muster. 'And it seems like he's really run off his feet. He could probably use a hand at getting everything organized.'

Tina's eyes opened wide behind the large glasses and she leaned in toward Carmel. 'Oh,' she said. 'Oh my. I could offer to help. I have lots of free time on my hands in the evenings. Maybe even take some vacation this week.'

'Wow,' Carmel said, a little taken back at her display of enthusiasm. 'I don't know if you should waste your valuable leave time on this, but why not come up sometime and check it out?'

One look at the mess Nate had become would be enough to send Tina screaming in the other direction, Carmel was pretty sure, and would cure the woman of any designs she might have on him. For all of the woman's shallowness and silly ways, Carmel was quite fond of

Tina, and she mentally patted herself on the back for her good deed for the week.

'I will!' Tina replied, then put her finger to her pursed lips as she calculated. 'Hmm. I'll have to arrange it with the boss, so I won't be there till tomorrow evening.'

'Seriously,' Carmel said. 'I wouldn't plan your vacation time around this, and besides, it's awfully short notice.'

'Oh, that's alright,' Tina said. 'No problem there. If he doesn't give it to me, well, I'll just have to call in sick. I have loads of leave in my sick bank. And that's what it's for, right? Emergency leave.'

Tina was in an uncommonly good mood for the rest of the day, even gracing the tourists with smiles and chattiness. It took the regular habitués of the archives quite by surprise.

• • • •

Driving back to St. Jude Without that afternoon, Carmel paused the car and looked all around with a sinking heart. Tina was right – all sorts of things were happening in the cove.

Phonse had gotten his wish granted. The bouncy castle was being set up on Snellen's Field just down from where North Point Road Extension turned the corner of the mountain. The weather was still fine with hardly a breath of wind, and she could see the boxes of beer set down by the fence to help fuel the workers. The three of them were already well into the second dozen-case, and honestly, it seemed to Carmel they were paying more attention to the beer than to setting up the children's attraction. She watched as a couple of sheets of white paper slowly flapped off down the meadow toward the beach, and she suspected these were the set-up instructions for the children's attraction. But really, she told herself, hammering pegs into the ground didn't take a lot of brains, right? Surely they couldn't mess this one up.

Sid might have predicted the events which ensued in the following days, if he had bothered to stick around to watch.

Where she sat in her car, she could see that even the livestock were being put to work in Nate's grand plan. The small wild Newfoundland ponies in the meadow across from Snellen's Field had been press-ganged into service offering rides to small children who, never having ridden ponies before, grabbed them by their manes and kicked their bellies. Of course the ponies, never having been ridden before, promptly threw them off, but fortunately the meadow was soft and parents and relatives just laughed to see the unfortunates tumble onto the grassy land.

Even Clyde Farrell's farm was being turned into a petting zoo of sorts, with Clyde playing a reluctant zookeeper. She couldn't hear what he was yelling from this distance, but he certainly wasn't welcoming his visitors. She could only pray that Nate at least had the foresight to lock Clyde's guns away.

Carmel sighed and drove the rest of the way to her home. She was going to have to tell everyone what Laney was up to.

10

'Well, m'girl, and how's my book coming?'
The voice loomed out of the darkened hallway. Christ, what with everything happening she'd almost forgotten about Captain Jeremiah. He was real after all, or at least a very realistic figment of imaginary vapors.

The ghostly pirate was ensconced in her own comfy armchair. She would have to set some ground rules here, for this was her house after all, but for now she let it rest and sat herself on the old sofa that came with the house, settling unavoidably into the bum prints of generations of Ryans past.

'I haven't thought much about your book, to be honest,' she began. She'd actually been hoping the whole other-wordly encounter had been a bad dream, but the peculiar smell of sulphur and moldy earth was unmistakeably real. She stared at him with dismay. Yes, he was as real as it got.

'What with the murder and everything,' she added.

He raised a spectral eyebrow. 'Murder? Do tell! I am intrigued.'

'You don't know?' She looked at him, trying to ascertain if he was pulling her leg. Jem was unaware of the events of the past few days, of what was happening right outside his door. Well, technically and legally, it was her door, but it looked like she was going to be sharing the house for next little while till she got his story written and could set him in peace. But just outside that front door, St. Jude Without was becoming undone and the community was turning its back on everything it had held sacred for centuries, yet Captain Jem didn't have a clue.

'Don't you go out at all?' she asked. 'Are you, like, stuck here in the house, unable to cross through the walls?' Come to think of it, she did have a lot of questions about the laws governing ghosts. All she had as reference was fiction, and as authors tended to change the rules to suit their own stories, this wasn't a very reliable source. Surely there must be a set of natural rules for spirits, just like for gravity or the speed of light.

He looked affronted at her words.

'Go out? Of course I can go out, I can go wherever I want to go, whenever I choose,' he expostulated. 'If I wanted to. I just have never had a reason to.' He sat back and crossed his arms. She could have sworn that was a pout on his mouth behind the overgrown beard.

Phonse and Brigid had both talked about Captain Jem's ghost as if he existed. At the time, Carmel had thought they were testing to see how gullible she was, but it turned out they were just being matter of fact. But to choose not to leave the house, to remain inside these walls for all that time? What a dull, dull existence he must have led for the past two hundred years.

Well, it was time he learned what was happening in the cove he had founded. She had a feeling he wouldn't be any happier about it all than she was, and it cheered her to think she had someone on her side. Even if it was just a ghost.

She paused to collect her thoughts, then proceeded to tell him everything that had happened over the past few days from the death of Lars Andersen to the contest which had so seized the imaginations of Nate and the rest of the crowd. She spared him nothing.

'I just don't think this is going to end well,' she finished, shaking her head.

His reaction, when it came, was totally unexpected. The ghost put back his head and roared with laughter, his mouth opened so wide Carmel could see a glint of spectral gold deep within.

'What knavery is afoot, then? Are my little band of rogues planning to lift their wallets? Ah, the hoodwinking they will do. Mayhap I will go out to walk amongst my descendants and see the glory for myself.' He sobered up quickly and cast a wistful eye at the setting sun outside the window. 'Mayhap... tomorrow.'

His apparent reluctance lit a suspicion in Carmel's mind.

'You *can* go out, can't you?' she asked. 'I mean, it's not like you... you didn't pass away in this house. I heard that you... you breathed your last outside, on the old pine tree. I wouldn't have thought you were stuck in here.' Talking about Captain Jem's death to his face somehow seemed indelicate, rude even.

'What would you know about death and the afterlife? You're naught but a mortal creature. You have no idea of my powers.' He sneered at her.

'You're right, I don't, as I've never met a ghost before.' Carmel leaned forward, elbows on her knees. 'So can you go out of the house or not?'

''Tis not that simple a question,' he mumbled, after a lengthy pause, then looked up at her with defiance. 'I've never had to leave the environs, then have I? All the world comes to Captain Jeremiah Ryan, and my world is St. Jude Without.'

Carmel was beginning to understand. He'd never tested himself to see if he could exit the wooden house, not once in all that time. 'You mean you've never even tried to go out of the house? In two centuries, you've stayed at home like a ... like a feeble old woman, afraid of all the threats outside?'

'No,' he roared back at her, thumping his ghostly fists on the arms of her comfy chair. 'I've stayed put like a king in his castle! Like a buccaneer in his ship! You scurvy wench, are you suggesting that I, Captain Jeremiah Ryan, scourge of the Bermuda waters, that I fear anything at all?'

His outburst intimidated her only for a moment, then common sense took hold. He was after all, just an apparition, and a scaredy-cat one at that if she was reading the situation correctly. Jem might huff and puff about how awful and terrifying he was, but that was centuries ago when he was alive, and he hadn't set a ghostly foot out of the house since that time. If he threatened her, all she had to do was leave the house.

An idea was growing. Carmel had an inkling that she could use this ghost to her advantage if she played it right, for his kind had certain advantages over the living, if the stories were correct. First, though, she had to strike a bargain with him.

'You want me to write your book,' she began slowly. 'And I'm more than willing to do this, and I'm probably the only person you know who can do this for you, right?'

He sunk his chin onto his fist and scowled at her. She could see he was wondering where she was going with this train of thought. 'Well, you're the only person I have bestowed the honor upon, that is correct. Many would dearly love to do what you have been gifted with,' Jem answered, picking his words carefully.

'No doubt, there's lots of writers who'd like to hear first-hand from a ghost what their experience has been,' she said. 'However, you don't know them, and you won't get to know them if you don't leave the house, and besides I'm the one sharing my house with you. So in exchange for doing this for you, I'm going to need some help.'

'Bargaining? No one bargains with the renowned and feared Captain Jeremiah Ryan!'

Carmel's mind was working fast and furious on the many ways a ghost could help her. Captain Jem could possibly walk through walls, peer over people's shoulders unseen, perhaps even intrude on a murder investigation... She thought of Lars Andersen's lonely death on the breakwater. Murder or drunken slip? With the help of the ghost, she could maybe find out. And if she could get it done before the weekend, even better. If Captain Jem could listen to conversations between people and not be seen doing it, the possibilities were endless.

An uncomfortable voice niggled at the back of her mind. *And would Darrow be thrilled to enlist the help of this ghost in his murder and crime investigations?* She mentally shrugged that off, for that bridge could be crossed when she came to it. If she came to it. It all depended on the ghost.

Of course, a ghost's evidence would not be admissible in court, either. Inspector Laney would lock her up in the loony-bin if she suggested it to him. Carmel brushed aside these misgivings, excited by the opportunities at hand.

'This is all so new to me,' she said. 'Maybe we should see what you can do. You can walk through walls, right?'

Captain Jem was now wearing his rimless spectacles, the better to glare at her over them. 'I do *not walk through walls,*' he told her sternly. 'For the material world is not relevant to me. And I am not a performing monkey for your benefit.'

'Oh, sorry,' Carmel caught herself. 'But I'm thinking, this is not for my benefit so much as your own. Don't you want to find out everything you can do in this world?'

The glare turned into a blank stare. Right at that moment, he looked so much like Phonse, his great-great-whatever grandson, it was eerie. She could see that Jem would have been good-looking and charming in his heyday.

'I mean,' she continued. 'Don't you want to, you know, go out and explore, see what it's like out there? See what you're capable of? You're a ghost – not of this material world, as you pointed out. Think of the power you could hold over humans...'

His eyes lit up and the spectacles vanished. 'Oh, now you're talking,' he said as the idea took hold and blossomed inside his ghostly mind. 'We could get a ship and sail it to St. John's harbor, and wipe the Clerkwell family off the map, that scurvy lot of sliveens and hangashores. We'll take their whole shipping business and string them up from the topsail of their largest boat, starting with the priest.'

Carmel cleared her throat. 'Sorry to say, the Clerkwell's have been out of the shipping business for years,' she said. 'And all the ones you knew are long gone.'

Captain Jeremy had been press-ganged into working for the Clerkwell family when just a lad in the streets of Dublin. He still held a grudge against the whole clan, which was understandable in the circumstances.

'And,' she continued. 'You'll find that a lot of things have changed out there. But there's still a lot of sliveens and crooks out there, and you could make a difference.'

'Treasure?' he demanded.

She briefly wondered if ghosts could affect the stock markets or bank computers, and decided not to go that route. Ian, the musician and computer expert of the cove would no doubt lead him astray soon enough if he could.

'I'm sure we will find opportunities,' she replied. 'But first we need to figure out – what exactly can you do in the physical world? And can everybody see you, or do you choose when to be visible?'

The ghost shrugged and slumped back into his chair. 'Don't know,' he said. 'Never explored that.'

'In two hundred years you've never tried... I don't believe this.' She changed her tack. 'But I've never seen you before this past week, and I've lived here almost a year now in the house. How do you explain that?'

Jem thought for a moment, screwing up the side of his face as if it hurt, just like Phonse would do when required to perform mental effort.

'I wanted to talk to you,' he said. 'So I guess I appeared.'

'Try disappearing for a moment,' she suggested. 'See how that works.'

He squinted and grimaced and squirmed in the armchair, then cast a look of inquiry her way, the feather in his hat swaying.

Carmel shook her head. 'No, not working. I can still see you. Why don't you try thinking of being in the kitchen?'

He continued to sit in the chair, staring at her, looking much as if he was trying to have an uncomfortable bowel movement.

'Well?'

'I'm trying, damn you!'

She sat back and crossed her arms. 'Perhaps you need to try less,' she suggested. 'Don't think about doing it. Just close your eyes and imagine you're in the kitchen.'

He shut his eyes tight and remained before her.

'Stop trying so hard!'

His eyes flew open with a look of outrage in them, then he disappeared.

'That's great,' Carmel called out, clapping her hands together. 'You did it. Where are you?'

There was no answer.

'Jem? You did it, come back now.'

Carmel got up and looked tentatively around the corner into the kitchen, but there no one there, no sign of the ghost and she appeared to be alone in the house again. She sniffed tentatively, yes, he was gone and taken his smell with him. The air was clear.

But what wasn't clear was how she could solve the very real problem of Laney doctoring evidence of the very case he commanded. She could only hope that Nate and his friends would have some good ideas.

11

Inside the church-turned-bar-turned headquarters, Nate was flying high on adrenaline. Lights glowed through the tall church windows day and night as he drafted his plans to make St. Jude Without the most popular tourist destination in the province. Spurred to action, he ordered all the community to step up their efforts and the collective group were inspired by his energy.

He had less than a week to shine with this show, and was burning the candle at both ends. With so much to plan for in so little time, it was inevitable that something would be forgotten. Unfortunately, it was Sid's warning about the need for rules that flew out the window in the whirlwind of Nate's grand plans.

Yet give Nate his due, he had managed to do what no one had ever done in the whole history of St. Jude Without, for he'd tapped into the hidden depths of entrepreneurialism of the folks in the cove. The kind of 'get-up-and-go' that hadn't been seen since the days that Captain Jem breathed in the world.

Having finished putting up the bouncy castle, Phonse and the pool-players were now set to work stringing up an impromptu curtain made of old drapes and nylon bedspreads leftover from the 'seventies across the center of the church, allowing for Vee Ryan and her cohorts to open a tea-room in the part not used as Nate's center of operations. They served instant coffee and styrofoam cups of tea with the bag still in, canned milk and white sugar optional. For sustenance of the hungry crowds they expected, the women offered rock-hard tea-buns and baloney sandwiches, all good traditional fare. Vee sat hunched over the money box like a toad, hair perfectly coiffed and set in curls, and her best dress on.

Carmel watched all this with trepidation. Nate was in a frenzy, focusing only on the contest, and refreshing the FaceBook page every second minute, keeping a close eye on the likes. He could talk of nothing else, although she tried. Amazingly, Bell Island and St. Jude Without were running almost neck to neck for likes, with their cove behind just enough to keep Nate straining for more.

'We have to have another angle!' he roared out to no one. 'I need something to give us a boost over those friggers.'

He stopped his roaring when he became aware of Carmel standing in the large room, and a greasy smile dawned over his face. He leaned back and stretched and chuckled, a deep rumbling sound. 'I see Bell Island's page makes a big deal about how clean they all are, how booze and drugs are discouraged. I think someone needs to write a post about Lars and how drunk he was when he died.'

She shook her head resolutely.

'The blog you promised,' he insisted, pointing his cigar at her. 'We're going to nail Lars Andersen, tell everyone how he was so loaded the other day on the breakwater. That'll turn off the teetotallers and maybe even the Christians. At least we can get them to unlike Bell Island, that'll give us a fighting chance.'

'Uh, no!' She shook her head adamantly. 'No, no, no. I'm not spreading that kind of muck over the internet.'

'But it was true! He was so blind drunk he could hardly see.'

'And has the only witness to this told the police?'

'You're a journalist, you don't have to name your sources.'

'Not happening Nate. Besides I didn't agree to write a blog.'

'Well, Ian can do it. Ian!'

'Aye, Cap'n!' The Irishman looked up from the clothesline hook he was hammering into the wall.

'Stop what you're doing and write up a post about Lars being drunk. Make it juicy.'

'What, the blog under Carmel's name, then?'

'Yep.'

Ian glanced over to Carmel. 'That alright with you?'

'No! Don't use my name!'

'Don't worry about it, Ian, just do as I tell you.'

Ian shrugged at her as if to tell her it was out of his hands and left the building.

Furious and frustrated, she took a deep breath to calm herself and told herself not to mind the stupid blog right then, it wasn't not as if anyone would read it. Instead she cornered Phonse, for he needed to know Laney's plans, and she drew him to the bar in Nate's headquarter section of the old church. After he was seated on a stool and she had his undivided attention, she began.

'And he's going to doctor the video from last week, when you were at the fish and chip van, to make it look like you were there when Lars died.' She finished her explanation and sat back to gauge his reaction.

'He can't do that,' he said, his face as blank as his ancestor's when faced with something which required mental effort.

She shook her head. 'He can, and it's happening as we speak,' she replied. 'He's got someone working on it.'

Phonse flicked his curls back off his head in a superior manner, the silver threads catching the multicolored LED lights around the nave. 'That's impossible, sure,' he said with a hint of condescension in his voice. 'The video is date-stamped, isn't it, which means it's actually burned into the film. I'm telling you, it can't be done.'

He smiled at her generously for her gullibility.

'Phonse, it's not on film anymore,' she said. Where had this guy been for the past quarter century or more? 'It's all digital these days. And yes, they can manipulate it any way they want. They have access to the clips, and no one else does.'

It was his turn to shake his head. 'Nah, doubt it,' he scoffed. 'Besides, why would he want to go to all that trouble?'

'Something about you stealing his girlfriend twenty-five years ago?'

'Hah! At the dance in town that time,' Nate burst in. She hadn't realized he'd been listening to the conversation. 'You remember Sheila, Phonse, the blonde girl with the miniskirt?'

'Nope.'

'You know, the Protestant girl? She came to the dance with Laney, but ended up in the back alley with you?'

They gave Phonse a moment of space to cast his mind back. 'Um, nope.'

'Ah, what odds?' Nate seemed undisturbed by Carmel's news of Laney's treachery. He shrugged and took a swig from the dark liquid in his stained, chipped mug, then wiped his mouth with the back of his hand. 'He can't pin Lars death on you, you weren't there.'

And how would Nate know who was around when Lars breathed his last? The only answer that came to Carmel's mind was the obvious - because he had been present at the time of Lars' actual death, that he hadn't left him alive on the breakwater as he claimed. She bit her lip to stop the accusation from bursting forth.

'Well, we have to stop him somehow,' she said instead. 'And maybe, just maybe, there's a way.'

Nate's fedora was cocked at an angle over his face, leaving half of it in shadow, but his eyes narrowed as he looked at her.

'It's going to sound crazy, but perhaps not to you guys,' she continued. And it really was crazy, but she was clutching at a ridiculous straw. 'But...

She looked at them both to make sure she did have their attention and she took a deep breath. 'Captain Jeremiah's ghost...'

That caught the attention of both of them far more so than the news of Laney's treachery.

'Cap'n Jem?' Nate's eyes lit up and he pointed his stogie at her. 'That's the ticket!'

'You think he can help?' Carmel was relieved she hadn't sounded nuts.

'Help? He will put those FaceBook likes over the moon! No way Gen can compete against a ghost,' Nate said. He actually chortled with glee then relit his stogie and sat back in his chair. 'Why didn't I think of that? We can have haunted house tours. I'll get Ian on that right away.'

'No, not the contest, but with somehow getting evidence to clear Phonse from Laney,' Carmel said, outraged. But her protests were in vain, the guys had both tuned her out. She sent a beseeching look to the soon-to-be-accused – after all, it was his head which would be served on a platter to the justice system, so surely the stakes mattered more to him than anyone else. Yet Phonse had by now lost interest in the matter.

'Phonse, where're you going?' she sputtered.

'Gotta finish getting these curtains up, and...' He jingled the coins in his pocket, the first flush of income from the bouncy castle. 'Gotta spend this cash. This was the best idea ever! Do you know how much we'll rake in from this? Way easier money than, you know, other stuff.'

'Don't you care about what Laney's planning?'

He shook his head. 'Nah, I told you, I don't believe he can't edit film like that.'

She phhhted the air from her lungs in exasperation. 'How about the ghost, at least? I didn't tell you about the...'

'Now don't you worry your pretty little head about all that,' he interrupted as he turned away.

Pretty little head?

'The guys are in charge of all the details,' he added, tossing a patronizing smile over his shoulder as he walked away.

Yeah, the guys were in charge. That's exactly what the problem was, she fumed to herself as her fists clenched.

12

She stayed standing by the bar, her eyes boring a hole into the top of Nate's hat as he immersed himself back into the land of FaceBook. The guys were in charge, indeed.

'I can't believe that neither of you are worried about Laney's plan,' she finally burst out. 'He's going to frame Phonse just to wrap up the case!'

But Nate either didn't hear, or more likely didn't want to listen to her words.

Phonse, well, that was explainable, but Nate? She asked herself again how he could be so certain that his cousin hadn't been present at the time of Lars' death, and decided to take the bull by the horns and demand answers from him. She was still burning to know if Lars's death was connected to the contest, and hoping against hope that Nate hadn't been involved in it. She cleared her throat.

'Hey Carmel, you still here?' Nate glanced up from his renewed frenzy on the laptop. 'Another thing I've been meaning to talk to you about.'

She sat down at the table across from him. Despite the bright day outside, it was gloomy in here in the north facing transept of the old church.

'I need to talk with you too,' she said. 'And you need to listen to what I'm saying.'

'You've lived all over the world, right?' He ignored her interruption as he fixed her with a bleary eye. 'I notice you have a lot of international FaceBook friends.'

'Don't change the subject, Nate.'

'And I've also noticed,' he continued, putting up his hand to stem whatever she intended to say. 'You haven't done much promo to push the contest.'

She shut her mouth. Had he been creeping her on FaceBook? She now remembered accepting his friend request last week, back before all this had started. She had thought he just wanted to be able to boast he was friends with an almost famous author. She'd had a rush of new friend requests once people realized she might be becoming a person of interest.

His red-rimmed eyes burned into her, levering an accusation that she wasn't doing her part for the cove.

'All those people,' she said, hedging. 'It's not like I know them well, I don't even remember half of them. They're not interested in some stupid contest here at the edge of the world.'

'It's up to you to make them interested,' he said, leaning towards her, his breath rank with stale coffee and those horrible cigars he insisted on smoking. 'This is an opportunity we're missing! Just think of it. Five hundred people who have no connection with Newfoundland whatsoever, that's five hundred extra people. And if they pushed it, they could easily reach fifty thousand people between them.'

He'd done the math, sketchy as it seemed, but she was not going to inflict this ridiculous FaceBook contest on people who'd never heard of St. Jude Without and who had no intention of ever coming to Newfoundland as tourists. She could never ask them to be a part of this craziness.

Yes, she admitted to herself, she was a little embarrassed about this whole madness which had taken over her community, and she considered this whole contest thing beneath her dignity. Or at least, it was beneath the image she liked to have about herself. She shook her head firmly.

'All those people,' Nate was still talking. 'All those people that liked your post about the success of your short stories, and all the ones who commented. They are an untapped market of likes for St.

Jude Without. You have their attention already, now you need to exploit that interest.'

'No.'

'And by getting them involved, building their interest, you're also building interest in your book, right? This is an international opportunity.' He chuckled in his sleazy manner and sat back. 'Whether you like it or not, you as a writer are now inextricably linked with St. Jude Without and you might as well make the best of it, right?'

It was as if he could read her mind. She stared back at him. Nate was a smart guy – he had a PhD to prove it - and she was coming to realize that he wasn't just book smart. He understood people, and was showing signs of being a master manipulator. Nate O'Reilly would be a brilliant politician. Scary, yes, but very successful.

Unfortunately, he was also making sense. She hated this whole ridiculous contest thing, yet... A cross-promotion of her book and St. Jude Without was a natural and she might have thought of it herself if only she wasn't such a ... snob. Like any creator, she was proud of her collection of short stories, yet she had to face the truth. She would not be an award-winning author if it weren't for St. Jude Without and its happenings and its folklore.

'You owe it to us, Carmel,' he pushed relentlessly. 'You've used us, now it's pay-back time. You're a writer. So you don't want to do the blog, I understand. But it's no problem for you to whip up some promo and reach this whole new, untapped group of people. It's not like we even have to compete with Bell Island for this crowd.'

'Okay, okay, I get your point, I'll do it,' she said, anything to shut him up. She sat back and sighed, tracing the dusty beams of the ceiling with her eyes. Yes, for the good of her writing career, she had to look at the wider picture. The more interest they could drum up about St. Jude Without meant more possible sales for her book in an international arena. World-wide sales, perhaps translations? It was every author's dream.

And she only had to promote their stupid FaceBook page. It wouldn't take much effort.

But... it felt dirty, soiled, as if she was making a pact with the devil. This sort of shenanigans hadn't worked out well for Faust all those centuries ago, and she had a distinct foreboding for her own future.

Nate leered over at her as if he knew full well what was on her mind, and he waited.

Okay. She would do this, she would besmirch herself with the foolish contest. It would be over in a week, and then she could put it behind her and pretend it never happened. But before she agreed to anything, she had to know the truth from Nate.

'I need something in return from you,' she continued, determined to drive a hard bargain. 'I want to know about Lars. His murder.'

'Murder? My, that's a strong word,' Nate said. He got up from his chair and reached over the bar to pour another coffee. It was black as tar and almost as thick, having sat in the dirty pot since that morning. He wafted the pot her way in inquiry and she turned up her nose, shaking her head with vehemence. Nate shrugged and poured the remainder into his large mug.

'What do you know about it?'

'Shouldn't you be asking your boyfriend for details?' Nate asked as he poured sugar in a steady stream from the glass jar, then gave it a few shakes to loosen the lumps. 'Oh, wait now, we haven't seen him up here lately, what's on the go there? Lost interest in you, did he? Intimidated by your success perhaps?'

'No, he's away...' Carmel caught herself. 'None of your business where Darrow is. I asked you a question.'

'And why would I know anything about Lars' death?' Nate asked, raising his bleary eyes towards the stained glass above the bar which stood where the altar once lay. If he'd worn a black hooded cassock, he could be a modern-day overweight Rasputin. 'I believe he was drunk and fell over, smashed his head against a boulder. End of story.'

'Well, I'm not sure I buy that,' Carmel replied, shaking her head. 'It's a coincidence that you were the last person to see him. Phonse said he wasn't a drinker. That none of Gen's crowd are allowed to drink. And if you're so sure about it, why haven't you told the police?'

Nate ignored her last question. 'He wasn't on Gen's ground at the time, so why shouldn't he do what he wanted? There weren't any witnesses to Lars' death.' Nate slid his snake eyes over to Carmel. 'Were there?'

She stared at him, a chill creeping up her spine. She had suspected, no scratch that, she had been sure that Nate was behind the death of her boss, just two months ago. That he'd deliberately framed Carmel with the cold-blooded murder in order to gain access to Captain Jeremiah's treasure map. And just because it hadn't actually been Nate who'd committed the deed, or in fact had anything at all to do with the murder, didn't mean he wasn't capable of ruthless action to reach his goals. And he had ambition by the bucket load.

Nate admitted to have been drinking with Lars, and said that's when he found out about the contest. Did he make all that up? The man kept his ear to the ground, maybe, like Gen, he had prior knowledge of the contest. Maybe he came upon Lars by the breakwater, waiting for the ferry, thumped him over the head and emptied a bottle over the giant so the police would smell the alcohol, jump to the obvious conclusion, and not investigate his death.

It would have been easy to get away with, the fog had been as thick as a blanket, and the breakwater was directly below where the huge ferry docked. No one from the boat could have seen it. And

Nate was a big brawny man, could easily have overpowered the giant Lars if he crept up on him unsuspected.

Yes, perhaps Nate had had prior knowledge of the contest. But how would the murder of Lars Andersen from Bell Island further his ambitions? This kind of action required a far more devious mind than she wanted to give him credit for. In fact, perhaps she didn't want to get involved in this after all.

She clambered down from the bar stool in a hurry. 'I'll go work on that FaceBook stuff,' she mumbled.

Nate nodded. 'You do that,' he said. 'Remember, what's good for the cove is good for your book sales, right? Let's keep our eyes on the goalpost, and not get sidetracked by things that don't concern us.'

13

C armel let herself into her front door, pausing to sniff the air before she entered. Good, no stink of ghost. She was relieved because she really needed time to sit alone with her thoughts. Had it only been a little more than forty-eight hours since she'd stumbled over Lars' body?

So much had been thrown at her in that short space of time. She sat at her kitchen table to sort her thoughts, then just as quickly got up again, too restless to sit. Opening the fridge door from habit, she saw the whipping cream bought for the ganache for a new recipe, a special cake she'd been planning to make for Darrow because she was well aware of his sweet tooth. The cream would go off before he returned.

She sighed and looked up at the clock. The time difference between Toronto and Newfoundland was an hour and a half, so he would still be tied up in his conference and unreachable by phone. Might as well make the chocolate almond torte she'd been planning, at least for practice.

And it was easier to think when her hands were occupied. As she ground the almonds into flour, she fixed the order of events of the past twenty-four hours in her mind.

First, she had found Lars.

Wait, no, first she had seen Nate on the headland of Snellen's Field, singing into the fog. Breaking glass – presumably the bottle he'd either shared with Lars, or poured over the man's body to make it seem the giant had been drinking. Either way, that bottle was now smashed to smithereens on the rocks and the shards washed out to sea. There would be no recovery of that evidence.

She beat the eggs to a froth.

Next came the discovery of the body on the breakwater, the soft squish underfoot, then her zebra striped rubber boot awash in bright carmine. She shivered, but forced herself to search back in her mind to remember every detail of the surroundings.

The big ferry had left just moments before, its wake still boiling in the salt water below the boulders of the breakwater.

The almonds, the eggs, the sugar were almost perfectly mixed. She dipped a finger in to taste, and it was heavenly.

She had been alone on the paved breakwater, she was positive of that. Well, except for Lars, but dead men didn't count. And then, she'd made the call and Laney was there, right on the spot with the flashing lights of the police cars, the ambulance, the police van which was probably a mobile scene of crime vehicle, and all the attendant busyness that came about with an unexpected death.

And then, while she was still in shock, the ghost's appearance, demanding she write his biography. She shook her head. Yes, that had happened, it wasn't her imagination, because Cap'n Jem had shown himself twice, last night and this evening. But – get things in order first.

So after she'd gone to the bar next door and been abused by her friends, and had fought back, Nate had come in and switched on the TV for them to catch the news of the contest. Nate had known all about it, and had already been planning to use this as his jumpstart to fame.

He also said he'd known about it before Lars died, that the newly-demised man told him, but what was the truth? Nate refused to tell the police about what he claimed happened, and while Carmel could see his line of logic (for St. Judeans never willingly spoke to the cops), his mind should surely have been changed once she'd told him Laney was planning to frame Phonse, his cousin and oldest friend.

But no. Even the threat of Phonse's arrest for something he didn't do would not move Nate to tell the police of his meeting with Lars.

The batter into the pan, then into the oven. She shivered again, and wished that Sid hadn't abandoned the cove. She needed to get him back, in the hope that his common sense might overcome the madness that had settled over St. Jude Without.

This was all so inconceivable. How could the world have flipped one hundred and eighty degrees in such a short span of time? Carmel looked outside her window on to the road. She could see a single silhouette outlined in the church window, the shadow of Nate. And he appeared to be looking right back at her.

• • • •

She buckled down to her editing chores the next morning, shutting out the world as best she could with windows closed and curtains firmly pulled across. Yet the increasing noise levels still broke through, the unaccustomed sounds of cars and minivans on the roads outside, hammers banging and other unusual signs of industry in St. Jude Without, voices she didn't recognize braying and laughing and complaining. Carmel comforted herself with a slice of torte for an early lunch – after all, it had to be eaten, and it was so good she had a second piece for dessert.

It was noon before she stepped outside the door, and found there was a hint of the summer in the fresh air at last. The slop-ice had receded far, far off-shore, way past Bell Island up to the outer edges of Conception Bay, and the wind was from the south. She stopped to sniff the air. Coming down off the mountain the breeze was warmish and held hints of the green woods, the kind of day when you could take off your jacket and expose bare arms to the sun with barely a goose pimple raised. And she did so, loving the heat of the sun on her skin. Summer had finally, grudgingly, come to St. Jude Without.

Carmel paused after climbing down her front steps and looked around at the cove spread before her. From the vantage point of the pirate's original house, she could see almost everything. Her gaze went from left to right, from Phonse's bright red and yellow bouncy castle on Snellen's Field, past the ponies in the meadow by the wharf, and then along the bridge to Clyde Farrell's farm.

It all looked innocent enough. Now that school was out, there was a growing crowd of visitors, families were streaming in from nearby St. John's and the suburbs to take in the delights of the impromptu fun fair that St. Jude Without was becoming. Pony rides on the point, Phonse's bouncy castle swaying in the breeze full of laughing children, Ian fiddling across the road as he busked for dollars with his electric violin. A bright orange extension cord ran through the open window of the Bridget's house to his sound system, and the volume dial was turned up loud.

Yet to Carmel's eyes, the whole scene was fast taking on an air of creepy carnival, with the murder of Lars Andersen hanging over it like a dark cloud. The sun shone harshly on the water, showing the tawdriness that lay behind the cove's attempt to present itself as a fun family kind of place. Looking at the scene closer, she could see the white pony's mouth opened wide in a grimace as he turned to nip the arm of the youngster who had just dismounted. From this vantage point she watched the guys behind the bouncy castle on a quick smoke break as they hacked up their lungs and drank surreptitiously from brown paper bags, unaware of a fight that was breaking out inside amongst the kids. Far over to her right at the very end of the cove, Clyde Farrell was stalking with murderous intent in his eyes the family of five who were hugging a struggling goat, his cane raised threateningly behind their backs, and over it all rose the sound of Ian's single frenzied violin playing the whirling dervish of an ancient gypsy tune, painting a picture in sound of the madness that had overtaken St. Jude Without and the greed of its inhabitants.

The minute she walked out onto the road she saw that Nate and his crew must have been busy into the wee hours last night, for there was a new billboard erected right at the top of Snellen's Field where it would be visible from Portugal Cove and from across the bay. It had started life as a warped 8 x 4 sheet of plywood, and had been cut to a profile of an imaginary pirate's face complete with feathered cap. The face was painted in lurid pinks and reds with bulging blue eyes. She suspected Brigid's artistry here, it had the look of her pottery cups. The rather long nose pointed out over the water, towards Bell Island, and a wooden cut-out arm had been mechanically fitted so that it waved as if beckoning people to come on in to the community.

She nearly tripped over a smaller sign, hammered into her front garden like an election placard.

Haunted Cove Ghost Tours! It proclaimed. *$10 per person. Get yore tickets at the Tea Room.*

'What the hell?' she said aloud. She wasn't happy about this, and strongly suspected Cap'n Jem would have something to say about it too. 'Nobody, but nobody, is getting into my house.'

She missed the calm common sense of Sid and his gang of bikers. Even with the skulls on the backs of their leather coats, they were a lot less creepy than what was happening in the cove right now.

She missed Darrow even more.

14

J ust as Carmel was striding over to the church to demand the Haunted House sign be removed, Tina's bright red little Fiat pulled up in front of her house and came to a screeching stop, gravel spitting everywhere. Carmel stopped as her friend climbed out of her vehicle. The other woman was newly spruced up, her bobbed hair gleaming and a new short summer dress on with high heel sandals obviously bought to match. Her eyes popped with color behind her glasses and bright pink lipstick glistened on her lips. How had she gotten so tanned in such a short time? Tina must have been very busy since they last saw each other just the day before.

'You're early,' Carmel blurted without thinking. 'I figured you wouldn't come by till this evening. After work?'

'Ah, I blew them off,' Tina replied airily. 'This is too important, y'know? I think we haven't got a moment to lose.

'Dr. O'Reilly needs the help, you said,' she added, seeing Carmel's look of incomprehension.

'Oh, right, Nate,' Carmel replied, slowly. He'd been in a state last night, and probably hadn't slept or washed since then. One look at the man and Tina would be hightailing it out of the cove as fast as her little Italian car could take her. 'Well, my, don't you look nice today.'

Tina giggled and patted her hair. 'A girl's gotta make an effort, you know,' she replied, then looked around at the village. 'Quite the happenings going on here, hey? Lots of bodies and action.' She went back to her car and lifted out a large suitcase bag.

'What's in the bag?' Carmel had to ask. 'Are you planning to stay?'

'Ya never know your luck, right?' Tina gave an exaggerated wink. 'If I play it right with Ignatius. But also I was thinking about what the cove needs, so I brought along some things.'

'Well,' Carmel said. Tina's dramatic new appearance had really put her at a loss for words. 'Well, let's go then. See if Nate needs any help.'

Carmel cut through the lilac hedge and into the side door of the church leading directly to Nate's impromptu office. Although an overhead light burned, the bar where he'd set up shop was empty except for the growing number of pizza cartons and dirty coffee mugs, along with the addition of some empty beer bottles. Carmel looked around with satisfaction. Good, she thought. Nate should be in prime form by now, and Tina would see what he was really like.

'They must all be outside,' she said aloud. 'Let's go through.'

An electronic scoreboard was now set up in the parking lot, borrowed from a local hockey arena by the looks of it. She assumed the 'Home' score was St. Jude Without and the 'Away' team must be Bell Island.

Tina homed right in on Nate who stood by a picnic table, hovering over his laptop while he kept up a running commentary to complement the scoreboard. It looked like he'd made no effort to clean himself up since Carmel last saw him – his hair was even more unkempt and his flannel shirt was stained and unbuttoned in the front, the untucked ends flapping in the light breeze. Tina stood closely to him and smiled brightly up at him.

'Hey Nate, how's it going?' Carmel caught up to them. 'You remember Tina?'

Nate glanced up from the laptop. 'Hey,' he said briefly in his gravelly voice.

Carmel poked her index finger firmly into his side. 'Tina's offering to help the campaign,' she said. 'She's a great organizer.'

'Oh, yeah, that's great,' Nate said, briefly looking up again. 'The more the merrier, huh? Did she vote yet?'

Another like for St. Jude Without came in on the FaceBook page. Nate roared and entered it into the board with a flourish. A cheer grew up among those clustered near over the electronic fiddle music.

'We're only fifty behind those Bell Island bastards now!' This was yelled right in Carmel's ear. She winced.

Tina moved even closer to Nate and placed her hand on his shoulder. 'I know where there's a whole bunch of votes which haven't gotten involved yet,' she said, her voice pitched seductively and her mascaraed eyed glancing coyly at him.

He responded like Pavlov's dog at a bell, all attention on Tina now. He liked the sound of what she offered, and he evidently liked what he saw in front of him too, now that he'd bothered to look.

'Hey,' he said, his eyes sliding over her dress and down to her orangey legs, smooth and sexy in the high heels. 'Heh heh, you must tell me about these unused votes. Why not come back into my office?' He placed his arm around her waist.

Tina made a delighted 'OMHFG' face at Carmel. She snuggled into the burgeoning beer gut that fit nicely around her own curves, a huge smile on her face.

Carmel really didn't want to watch the seduction of Nate, or of Tina for that matter, and turned her face away.

• • • •

It turned out Tina was a wonder at organization when she put her mind to it, and she had a sharp mind when it came to finding new avenues of advantage for the cove. Within a space of two hours she had claimed her spot as Nate's latest significant other, along with which came the acknowledged title to being second-in-command to the cove's commandant.

'So what we need,' she said as she stood in front of the assembled crowd in the erstwhile headquarters. Everyone was tired after a full day of being pleasant to strangers, and they were beginning to realize just what hard work their new venture was. Tina however, being fresh on the scene and unflappable, was determined to show Nate her value and would not let them flag. 'What we need is to create a CFA atmosphere.'

'What, Come From Away?' Phonse groaned and bent his head to peer into his empty beer bottle. 'Don't we have enough of them here already?'

Tina snapped her gum. 'No, I mean like the Broadway show? You know, the big hit about how friendly Gander was during 9/11 to the Americans?'

Blank stares greeted her all around.

She chewed her gum viciously as she looked around. 'Well, the mainlanders love that stuff. So what we need to do is open our homes to visitors.'

'Oh no, they can come to the tea room for refreshments, and pay for it,' Vee Ryan grumbled. 'I'm not giving them anything for free.'

'No,' Tina said, losing patience with these ignoramuses. 'I mean, invite them to stay. As *paying guests*.'

Heads perked up at these words.

'You see, we'll rent out all the spare bedrooms in the cove,' she went on. 'So then we have a captive audience, and everyone'll make a little money on the side.'

The faces around her were much brighter now, the hard graft of the day being forgotten as they saw new ways to increase their revenue.

'Doesn't sound like too much work,' Vee said, considering. 'They'll just be sleeping there, right? We don't have to feed them or do their dishes.'

'You could maybe throw in some toast and coffee for breakfast,' Tina said. 'But seriously? Yes, you can charge a fortune for the rent, especially you, Vee, down by the water like you are.'

'But Ma, you don't have a spare room,' Phonse objected.

'You can bunk out on the boat,' Vee snapped over at her son. 'Same as you do when you come home late and drunk.'

Carmel had to speak out. 'Wait a moment now, Tina. Just how is this going to work? I mean how are we going to advertise this? It's way too late to get in the government tourism publication.'

Tina winked. 'No worries, I have that covered,' she said. 'I've set up everyone with an Air B&B account. You'll get the text notifying you when the visitors are arriving, and I've emailed everyone the website links. But you don't even have to respond, I'll look after all that for you. I've entered everyone's details, photos of the cove, all that, and promised a real authentic CFA experience.'

'Everyone?' Carmel looked with dismay around the room. 'Uh, I think I'll opt out, if it's all the same with you.'

She'd only just gotten rid of Ian, and she wanted the house to herself and Darrow when he returned. Besides, there was still the matter of the resident spirit. 'No, I definitely can't have guests,' she added, shaking her head.

Tina stood with her hands on her hips and a pugnacious look in her eyes. 'We all have to do our part, Carmel.'

'What part? I wrote the stories, didn't I? And it's not even your cove! Who are you to tell us what to do?' Any soft feelings she may have had for Tina were quickly evaporating.

'I'm working on behalf of Nate!' Tina threw back at her 'He's the real organizer, the only real brains in this cove.' She straightened her blouse and looked back over the room. 'Just one last thing...'

She pushed her glasses up her nose. 'Like I said, we want to create a real CFA atmosphere here. Now, the tea room, the bouncey castle and hot dog stand – they're all good. But we need more. We want fun and entertaining. Think of Disney Land – we want costumes.'

She checked the clip board in her hand.

'First off – Phonse, and you guys doing the kids section. We need to be more kid friendly. I have some clown costumes here, I'd really like to see you wearing them, it'll cheer the kids up, make it feel like a real circus and fun time.'

Carmel could feel Phonse start and out of the corner of her eye saw that he was trying to get her attention. She refused to look over, for if she did, the sudden bubble of laughter forming in her throat might escape. Tina reached into her suitcase and tossed out an assortment of wigs, striped pants and oversize boots.

'Mrs Vee – yeah, you're alright for costume, you got the 'fifties housewife vibe happening there, I love it,' Tina continued, oblivious to the small dramas playing out on the floor. 'Now Ian, I was rootling around the costume section of the Archives today, and I've got you this.' She removed from the plastic bag at her feet a tall, slightly ratty top hat, yet the silk glistened in the light of the sconces which lined the walls of the old church. The room let out a collective sigh. Ian's dark eyes lit up with pleasure. Phonse, on the other hand, was looking slightly disgruntled as his eyes moved from the fine hat to the orange wig in his hands. 'Look after it, they don't like to lend their stuff out. But it's perfect for your busking and Haunted Cove tours.'

'Just one more thing.' She looked up brightly from her papers. 'In order to really get the CFA atmosphere, you know, the genial and generous Newfoundlander-vibe – I've started to write a script for a dinner theatre, something that will really bring the crowds in. Who here can sing?'

But with this last request Tina had pushed the cove a little too far, and the group en masse suddenly realized all the pressing things that had to be done, and the building was emptied within minutes.

'Wait, come back!' Tina wailed after them all. 'This is going to be fun, goddam it!'

Carmel shrugged at Tina as she too closed the front door behind her, the last rat to leave the ship.

She shook her head as she made her way to her home next door. Her plan to dissuade Tina of her crush on Nate had obviously backfired, for her friend appeared to be even more enamoured of the man and was not bothered by his lack of personal hygiene.

'I have to admire her get up and go, though,' she thought to herself. 'If she put half that much energy into her job, she'd be running her section by now.'

She'd just reached her front steps when her phone buzzed with the suddenness of a swarm of wasps on a September day. Carmel automatically took it out of the back pocket of her jeans to check the new text. It was from a number she didn't recognize.

Brendan wants to stay with you!

15

She stared at the text, puzzled. Who was Brendan and why would he...

Then it struck her. This was the Air B & B that Tina had set up just that afternoon. Oh! She quickly flicked to her email, and scrolled through to Tina's link to the main website. Yes there was a request from a man called Brendan. He wanted to come the next day for a week and he was prepared to pay an exorbitant sum, a whole monthly mortgage payment, for the privilege.

Carmel suffered a moment of complete petrification as she realized the enormity of what was to happen. A stranger, coming to stay in her house. If she accepted.

She scrolled through his profile, but there was little there. Brendan lived in Ontario and was new to the Air B & B site, so he had no reviews from previous hosts. She studied his photo. He looked harmless enough, sort of her age-ish, a little soft and definitely balding. She could barely make out squinty eyes behind the glare of his glasses, and his mouth was rictured into a square which must be meant to be a grin.

He probably wasn't an axe murderer, right? Not if he lived in that little suburb outside of Toronto, the odds had to be against it. And all that money for nothing, really, except to clean her house and keep it that way while he was here. Her visitor would no doubt be gone all day and just come here to sleep. This would delay her work with Captain Jem, but think of the money. She could do it. Her royalties wouldn't be coming through until the end of the quarter, so she had to do it.

As she thought about it some more, she realized she was getting paid to clean her own house, which was a strange incentive but it worked like magic. Despite the late hour, she immediately hauled out the vacuum cleaner and filled her only bucket with hot water to get a start on the long overdue spring cleaning. The house very quickly took on an unaccustomed air of lemon cleaner and even dustlessness in one room, and the innards of the fridge glistened whitely. She was quite proud of the results so far. Another piece of torte was in order as way of celebration of her industry.

Her pride was reaching the point of smugness at her hosting, and all the while she added sums in her head as she dreamed. This could turn out to be a lucrative sideline, no doubt, with her mortgage paid from a single week of rent, every month. Forget toast for breakfast. Carmel's house would become known for the quality of her offerings, with pastries and gourmet coffee. Carmel McAlistair could be the hostess with the mostest with an impeccably clean house. And all these dreams of her new money-making venture and pride had given her a space where she could forget all about the awful things that were happening in the cove around her.

• • • •

Darrow's phone call brought her back to reality.

'The course is exactly what I expected,' he said crisply when she inquired. 'New protocols to be rolled out ASAP, with quarterly audits on the effectiveness. I foresee a massive amount of paperwork in my future, but fortunately we all know this will be dropped within the year when they hit on another great idea as priority for the force.

'But never mind my woes,' he continued. 'How are things in the cove? This Lars Andersen, have they figured out what's what with him?'

Where to start? More to the point, what had she decided not to tell him? Nix to the existence of the ghost in her house and its' demands on her. She could hardly still believe that herself, and she knew she might come across as crazy if she shared this with Darrow.

She also hadn't told him about seeing Nate at Snellen's Field just before stumbling across Lars' body, as she had truly believed at the time that Nate couldn't have had anything to do with it all. The situation had changed since then, true, yet she still found herself holding back. If Darrow knew about Nate and Lars sharing a bottle, then he would demand she inform Laney or even worse, would feel duty-bound to tell him himself. And then Laney would... God knows, he'd probably charge the lot of them with withholding information, and then truss Nate and Phonse up both with his edited video.

Carmel looked at the phone in her hand for a moment before replying. The video footage. Only Darrow could prevent that.

'Well,' she began. And she told him about overhearing Laney and his cohort down by the breakwater, about how Laney had stated he would doctor the evidence to frame Phonse because of a grudge held since high school. That, at least, was believable.

'No,' Darrow said. His voice sounded incredulous and she imagined he was shaking his head on the other end of the line. 'No. Laney is an Inspector of the RNC. He would not mess with the evidence. Tell me again the circumstances under which you overheard this?'

'I was hiding in my car, I'm pretty sure he couldn't see me,' she said. 'They blocked me off so I couldn't move, and Laney was complaining about not being allowed to smoke in the squad car.'

'So you're telling me he undoubtedly saw your car.'

She hadn't thought of that. 'Yeah, but...'

'You're aware that your vehicle is, ah, shall I say, quite recognizable? The rust and mismatched paint job make it stand out from all the other dark blue sedans in the vicinity.'

Sometimes Darrow's logic could be annoying, but she agreed. Again, reluctantly.

'He was having you on,' Darrow said, a hint of a laugh in his voice. 'At the worst, he was attempting to scare you, and in turn all the other residents of the cove, perhaps to turn you against each other and flush out the wrong doer, if one exists, which, based on what I've learned, is unlikely.'

Carmel's face began the slow burn of embarrassment. She'd been taken in by Laney, and believed what he'd said because... well, because Laney was a horrible man. She had never doubted for a moment that he would mess with the evidence as he claimed he would. And all along he knew she was hiding in her car, and he was stringing her along. It probably made for a great story at the Police Bar.

'So what else has been happening up there?' Darrow asked. 'I caught the local Newfoundland news on cable, and have seen some odd reports from your neck of the woods. Something about a contest for the most tourist friendly community, and St. Jude Without has actually entered?'

'Oh, that,' she replied glumly still feeling the hurt. 'It's crazy here, just nuts. Nate has this idea we can win over Bell Island, and he's gotten everyone onboard with his plans. There's a bouncy castle of all things, and a hot dog stand, a petting zoo...'

Even as the words came out of her mouth she realized how ludicrous it must sound to Darrow. He snorted with laughter.

'But,' she continued in a brighter tone. 'I'm now an Air B&B hostess. I have someone coming tomorrow, my first guest. Do you know what people pay to stay in your home? I mean, the guy is giving me my entire month's mortgage payment just for a few nights in the spare room.'

The laughter abruptly turned to dead silence.

'Really,' she coaxed. 'It's a good deal. Visitors are vetted by the site, it's all above board.'

She heard him draw a breath. She knew that tone of breathing – he was trying to find the words to tell her, to convince her, that he thought this was a very bad idea.

'It's just for the summer,' she rushed in. 'Maybe just for this month, who knows, I mean, who knows where this will go?'

'I don't want to rain on your parade, but I can give a good guess,' Darrow said, his voice dry. 'If it was organized by your friends in the cove.'

'I really wish,' he said, then he sighed.

'I know,' she said. 'You think I should move out. But this is my home.'

'Yes,' he replied. 'But do you not have a bad feeling about things this time?'

· · · ·

The ice had just as magically disappeared from the waters and all of a sudden it was summer. The temperatures rose to double digits on the Celsius thermometers, the dandelions popped up in a blaze of yellow in the ditches on the sides of the road while the trees were suddenly clothed in bright spring green as Carmel came down her front steps, intent on heading to the Portugal Cove mini-mall to get the best delicacies and baked goods before they were snapped up. But in St. Jude Without, the change in the weather went largely unappreciated as the village was gearing up for war, with Nate as the Commander-in-Chief and everyone else caught up in the excitement.

The front entrance of the church opened as she walked past, and Tina came out stretching and yawning and blinking into the morning sun. She held her strappy sandals in her hand. Carmel's inner level of disgust was rising.

'Really Tina – Nate?' She thought to herself, but didn't say aloud. She didn't want to encourage the other woman to give her any details.

'Where do you get a decent coffee hereabouts?' Tina was looking around at the cove spread before her as if searching hard for a Starbucks, or at least the comfortingly yellow glow of a Tim Horton's franchise.

'There's a cafe out in Portugal Cove, above the ferry terminal,' Carmel replied. 'Other than that, you'll have to go into town.'

'Mmmh,' Tina grunted. She didn't look too bad, considering the night she must have had. Nate was a hard partier, it would have been a late night with lots of booze, but Tina's eyes were clear and her skin was fresh and her hair was gleaming.

'You were serious about taking your vacation this week, eh?'

'Eh, I can be spared,' Tina answered. 'They have a bunch of university interns there for the summer, they can handle it. Besides, there's no real work happening at the Archives right now, the professors are all on summer leave. It's only tourists looking for their roots, and you know how boring that is.'

'So, what are your plans for this unexpected time off?'

Tina smiled with satisfaction. 'I'll be sticking round here,' she said. 'Helping Nate with his campaign. Not a moment to lose, you know.'

Carmel now knew the meaning of feeling her heart sink. It was a visceral feeling, one of impending doom. For she knew Tina, and Tina was like a dog with a rat in its mouth. She would wring out every last FaceBook like and organize the place like a battlefield. Yesterday's organization was nothing compared to what could come, and there would be no talking Nate out of the competition now.

Once he had gotten the ball rolling with the FaceBook competition, with Ian's help of course, the buzz had started and didn't seem like it would ever end. The likes for their tiny community had grown exponentially, as did the on-line promises to return to the mother-cove. Camper trailers were sprouting up on any available flattish land – down by the point, the ponies had to share their meadow with a fast growing trailer park.

The local media were excited by it all too, for St. Jude Without was a dark horse in this race, a newcomer which rose from nowhere to give the other communities a run for their money, and bets were flying as to who would win the great contest. Bell Island across the water was the traditional favorite – they always won anything that required the participation of the thousands of ex-Bell Islanders existing throughout the known world.

But it was quietly rumored that Bell Island was becoming concerned about the competition. The death of Lars Andersen hadn't helped, for whispers of murder and alcohol tainted the image of Gen's total control over her forces.

Carmel didn't make it to the next cove over as planned, though, not right away, for she could see that a visitor was heading towards St. Jude Without, speeding across the Tickle in a direct beeline from Bell Island. This was an unprecedented occurrence as there was so rarely traffic between the two rivals. Like everyone else in the cove she hurriedly made her way to Phonse's wharf to see what was happening.

The unofficial flag of Bell Island flew proudly above the white shining launch, the 'Coal Chimney'. It depicted a smoking brick stack, harking back to the glory days of the island when Bell Island coal had heated every home and had fired every steam engine in the land and beyond. That was before global warming and climate change of course, but the islanders remembered those glory days with fondness. A tiny figure stood under the flag in the prow of the launch.

As the launch drew closer, a murmur spread through the small crowd.

'Is that the famous Gen?' Carmel whispered. She was standing next to Brigid.

'The mayor of Bell Island,' the redhead said with respect in her voice. 'It must be serious, it's been more than fifty years since she's come here to St. Jude Without.'

'We've rattled her,' Nate said with glee, standing just behind them on a boulder on the rocky beach by Phonse's house. 'She knows we're a threat and that she's not going to win the money!'

16

G en was the matriarch of Bell Island, the woman who would probably continue to be proclaimed mayor even after her death, for the Islanders were loyal like that. She ruled the island with an iron glove, and it was rumoured she had become a millionaire by investing in CostCo in its early days, that and a few Tim Horton's franchises scattered around the nearby city of St. John's. Yet, Bell Island itself was surprisingly free of franchises and junk food, for Gen didn't like them for her own people. The only deep-fried food available on the island was the fish and chips shop down at the ferry on the island. Gen's brother's family owned it, so it never did get shut down.

And so Carmel got her first sighting of the famous Gen. The petite figure could now be seen clearly as the launch docked, wrapped in a large neon green puffy coat with the hood pulled tight against the ocean chill. A short man, who looked tall in comparison to Gen, helped remove her coat once they were in the shelter of the small harbor, and she stood before them in a bright red fleece, elasticated black polyester pants and olive green rubber boots. Every wrinkle on her face had a story to tell, but large sunglasses and a baseball cap pulled low obscured her eyes. She couldn't have stood much taller than four foot eight, yet every eye in the cove was focused on her, for Gen had an aura about her, a glamor like a Hollywood movie star. Gen was the stuff of legends, and everyone crowded closer to see.

She stepped out of the launch without aid to stand on Phonse's rickety wharf. The man who stood at her right hand made to get off the boat with her, but she turned and gave him a hard stare.

'Get yourself back, Roland,' she said to him. 'I'm still in charge. I may be old, but I'm not dead yet.' She chortled at her own joke and stared around, forcing everyone to chortle with her in agreement.

Roland didn't laugh though, as he stepped back onto the launch. His eyes gave only a hinting flash of resentment before he put his shades back on, and he remained on the launch the whole time, his arms crossed before him and feet planted firmly. Although he was not tall of stature in comparison to Phonse, say, or Nate, he was built like a brick house and his broad shoulders strained through the black hoodie he wore. From where she stood, Roland looked to be a little bow-legged, like an old-time sailor. He faced the crowd head-on as if daring them to mock him after Gen's treatment of him. His face fell easily into a scowl, the lines on his face showing this was an expression of habit for him. Yet his black eyes still burned, and the writer in Carmel wondered at what thoughts ran through his mind.

Gen sniffed as she looked about her with her hands on her hips, and spoke in a voice that was itself evidence of a hard life of booze and cigarettes, no matter the whispers of her abstinence. 'Who the frig's in charge here?'

Nate jumped off his boulder and skipped forward to the front of the crowd, doffed his fedora and bowed.

'Dr. Ignatius O'Reilly at your service, ma'am.'

'Doctor, is it? What, ye crowd got no mayor?' She hawked a goober onto the rocks.

A speculative look came into Nate's eye, an ambition to be stored until it could be examined more fully at a later date. 'At the moment, ma'am, we are a collective organization without the need of a hierarchy.'

'Like I thought. No mayor,' she replied with a nod, and shared a satisfied glance at the crowd before her. She turned back to Nate. 'You and me need to have a talk.' It was meant as an order, not a request.

'That would be delightful,' Nate replied, still with Clyde's fedora in hand. 'Why don't you step up the hill to my headquarters?' He indicated the church at the top of the road.

'I'm not walking up that hill,' Gen said decisively. 'We'll talk right here.' The sunglasses were turned full force on to Nate, daring him to disagree and ensuring that everyone knew Gen was in charge here.

Vee stepped up to the plate. 'Sure, Gen why don't you step up to my house right there? I'll make you a nice cup of tea to warm you up,' she simpered.

'This isn't no social occasion,' Gen sneered, and Carmel was gratified to see her arch enemy in the cove quail before the shriveled octogenarian. 'I wouldn't step past your front door, dirty trollop that you are, and you always have been, Vee Ryan. This is business pure and simple. Mister Doctor and me'll talk right out here in the open. I'll say what I got to say right here so there's no misunderstandings.'

She thumped her walking stick onto the rickety wharf. The gray weathered wood creaked and juddered under the force. Roland had remained on the launch the whole time, his arms crossed before him and feet planted firmly. Although he was not tall of stature in comparison to Phonse, say, or Nate, he was built like a brick house and his broad shoulders strained through the black hoodie he wore. From where she stood, Roland looked to be a little bow-legged, like an old-time sailor. He faced the crowd head-on as if daring them to mock him after Gen's treatment of him. His face fell easily into a scowl, the lines on his face showing this was an expression of habit for him. Yet his black eyes still burned, and the writer in Carmel wondered at what thoughts ran through his mind.

Nate replaced the fedora, cocked it at a jaunty angle to show he had no fear of the tiny old woman and with a few strides came up almost to the wharf. Even with the raised wooden structure he towered over the diminutive figure as he crossed his arms and planted his feet firmly on the rocky beach.

'Alright then Gen,' he said, his voice pitched at its most gravelly. 'Say what you need to say.'

She scowled up at him. 'I realize that you and your motley cove are tryin' your hand in the contest,' she said. 'And I got no quarrel with that, you can fill your boots with your measly attempts.' She flung her hand up at the village.

'Bouncy castle. So-called tea room.' She sneered at Vee when she said this. 'Even your made-up ghost stories. Good luck with it.'

Gen leaned closer to Nate, not in the least intimidated by his size, and she shook her stick at him. 'But you overstepped the line, Mister Doctor, when you publicly defamed Lars Andersen. Our Lars was no more drunk than I was that Sunday afternoon.'

'I got news for you, Gen,' Nate leaned down till the two were almost nose to nose. 'Your Lars was loaded. Pissed to his eyeballs. Couldn't see straight. And...'

He straightened his back the better to see the effects of his next words. 'I happen to know for a fact that he was planning to leave your employ.'

Amid gasps from the guys manning the launch, the tendons on the crone's neck tightened and her shoulders clenched and Carmel could have sworn the little old lady grew four inches as she barked up at Nate.

'You... You... Liar!' The spit flew over his flapping flannel shirt as her face grew dark red.

'Not so sure of yourself now, are you, Gen?' Nate was trying too hard to give a good show of chuckling. 'Better watch that blood pressure.'

'You tell your blogger to remove that post.' This was in a mean and vicious voice.

'Or what? What're you going to do if we leave it up there for all the world to see the truth of it?'

'Or you'll be sorry. Every single last one of you,' Gen snarled, then she took in the whole crowd of St. Judeans thronging at the wharf, pausing when her sunglasses rested on Carmel. 'Especially that blogger.'

The blog written by Ian, the one that had Carmel's name and photo emblazoned across the header.

Carmel stared back at the woman, caught in the glare of those dark lens like a cornered quarry in the headlights of a truck, until all she could see were the huge black circles like a spider's eyes, and she was paralyzed by the threat that lay therein.

She couldn't move or break away from them, although she tried to speak and defend herself, to say it wasn't her that put the words up, but all that came out was a squeak.

Gen nodded, satisfied.

'Hit it, boys,' she told her men. Roland hurried to wrap her in her puffy coat again, while the others started the engine and untied the launch.

She turned again to face Nate who hadn't moved, just stood there with a peculiar smile on his face, much like the cat who just found the butter dish left uncovered on the counter. 'This is friggin' war, you know,' she shouted at him, shaking her yet again. 'And if I find out you had anything to do with Lars' death, you're in for it!'

Nate bowed again towards the matriarch, then straightened and lifted up his fedora. 'Bring it on, Gen!' His deep rumbly roar carried over the engine's noise and Gen's figure visibly flinched as they disappeared back over the waves to Bell Island.

Yet for all his bravado, Nate was shaken and noticeably paler when he turned to walk back up the hill. He said not a word as he climbed the road back to the old church at a faster pace than Carmel had even seen him move.

Carmel, too, felt unsettled as she made her way along the road to Portugal Cove. She'd just been threatened by a tiny octogenarian. She hadn't even written the bloody blogpost, but her name was on it.

Unsettled and shaken, yes, but she was also totally pissed at Nate and fed up with his schemes.

17

Later that day, Carmel found herself having to explain the concept of Air B&B to the ancient ghost as she unpacked the goodies from the pastry shop.

'It's just one person, and he's only staying for a week. He'll hardly be around at all.'

'You'd turn my house into a common hostel then? Let any traveller stay here?' Jeremiah sounded furious, yet he was barely visible where the sun cut through the window. 'What's next, a bawdy house? I suppose you can place a red light over the door with your electrickery. Have a beacon, calling them in from far and wide.'

'It's not like that! I'm not... And any guests are thoroughly vetted by the website,' she said, hoping that was true. 'It'll be fine, and it's money coming in.'

Captain Jem disappeared, leaving an extra huff of sulphur to show his distaste.

'Oh, be like that then', she muttered. She still had cleaning to do and she better get started. Brendan said he'd be here by two o'clock and she still had to wash the hall and kitchen floors. A quick sniff of the air told her she'd better get some air freshener in too. Jem might not be visible but he sure could leave his stink hanging around in the air.

'If t'is money you're wanting, I can think of a better way,' the ghost said, reappearing suddenly before her as she heaved the bucket of hot water from the sink. She didn't like the glint she saw in his eye.

'Look what you made me do!' Carmel bent to mop up the spilled water. Might as well start cleaning here since the hot water was on the floor already. 'And where are you going to get money from?' she asked as she got on her knees and started scrubbing the old linoleum. She always forgot how bright the red and white of the tile pattern was, and she was pleased to see it emerge again. Perhaps she should do this more often.

'I have means,' he retorted, sounding a little put out that he hadn't grabbed her full attention.

'Your treasure, or should I say Eliza's treasure, is long gone.' She splashed water over by the ghost's foot, just to see what would happen. The water went right through the ghostly boot, but Jem squealed and jumped back nevertheless.

The treasure she spoke of had been the dowry of Jem's wife Elizabeth, the intended bride of the Clerkwell son whom Jem had stolen away along with the ship as he began his pirating career. According to legend, he'd never spent that treasure, choosing instead to hoard it, keeping it hidden in a chest buried near the shore by Snellen's Field. The chest remained there underground until it was blown up by the British navy during WWII when they were aiming their guns at the German U-boat which had attacked the coal boats leaving Bell Island. The treasure had long been dispersed to the waves. Or so it was believed.

'Pah!' Jem said, dismissing the lost treasure with a sniff and a toss of his feathered hat. 'There's other funds to be found for those who are bold enough to follow the path.'

'And probably illegal,' she replied. 'Save that for Phonse and Nate and the rest of the gang. I have no intention of ...'

'My biography!' Jem interrupted her. 'You're wasting time in cleaning when you could be writing about me. That's where you'll find the money is!'

His voice was cut off by the cacophony of a car horn close by. It continued, not in the regular rhythm of a security system going off, but in an erratic series of short and long blasts.

'What the heck is that, now?' Carmel threw the rag back into the bucket and stood up. Jem had beaten her to the front door, where he was peering out the window.

'Tis your visitor, announcing his arrival,' he said. With that he disappeared again, leaving her to manage on her own.

She dried her hands on the sides of her hoody, thinking as she did that she really should remember to use the rubber gloves next time, and opened the front door. The loud blasts continued from the red rented mini-van parked half-way in her driveway and half on the road. The sun on the windshield hid the occupant.

But it must be Brendan, far earlier than he'd promised. It was barely ten o'clock in the morning, and he'd said he would be here after lunch. He bounced out of the drivers' seat with a wave.

'Carmel?'

'Hi, yeah, come on in,' she said, opening the door wide.

'Let's go, gang , we're here,' Brendan called back inside the vehicle, then he slammed the door and made his way to the back of the van.

Gang? Brendan had booked for a single person.

The passenger side door opened, and a short woman with a frizz of curls heaved herself out without greeting Carmel. She proceeded to slide the rear door open and bawled at the occupants therein.

'Get your butts out here! Pick up your mess first. You can go to the bathroom now.'

Carmel watched in horror as the woman unloaded not one, not two, but three snivelling mop heads from the rear seat of the van. Small, medium and large. Medium was crying over something, she couldn't pick out the words through the whine.

There must have been a misunderstanding. Her house had only the one extra bedroom, with just one bathroom. And Brendan had said there was just himself. Didn't he? She racked her memory.

He beamed up at her with his shiny cheeks, one arm around his wife and the other holding a suitcase.

'This is Melody,' he said. 'And that's Tyler, Tiffanee and Joss.' The youngest at about two or three years old, may have been male or female, she couldn't tell, but it wasn't happy to be here judging by the snotting and bawling coming out of its mouth.

'Are you.... all planning to stay here?'

'Yeah?' He blinked up at her through his glasses.

Melody shrugged off her husband's arm and pushing Tiffanee ahead of her, charged up the steps. They would have bowled Carmel over if she hadn't neatly sidestepped out of the way. 'Where's our bathroom?'

'It's upstairs...' They were quickly gone into the house and out of sight.

'Uh, Brendan, I think there must have been some mistake,' Carmel began. She stared down at Tyler who was staring right back up at her, finger up his nose. 'Can I speak to you? Alone?'

'Sure,' he said, turning back to the vehicle. 'Want to give me a hand with this stuff?'

She came down the steps and followed him to the rear of the mini-van.

'Wait now, before you unload the van...'

'Hey Tyler, you're a big boy, want to take this bag for Daddy?'

Tyler stared at his father as if he didn't understand the language, then stared off toward the ocean, his finger still exploring the depths of his nostril.

'Kids today, eh?' Brendan said, smiling still, as he hoisted the bag back over his shoulder.

'No, wait, don't take out the suitcases yet.'

'Hey, baby, get out of the road!' Brendan dropped the luggage and swooped over to snatch the youngest up in the nick of time as a yellow bus careened past the house with a church group full of kids on the way to Clyde's farm.

'Dangerous place you've got here,' he reproached Carmel, squinting through his glasses as he hugged the youngest close. 'I thought this was supposed to be a quiet get-away, not a major road.'

'It's usually pretty dead around here,' Carmel started to excuse the village, then shook herself. 'But listen, we need to talk. I thought there was just you coming, not your whole family.'

'You don't like children?' His tone was shocked, as if she was probably the kind of person who kicked puppies, too.

'No, I... I was under the impression there was just a single person coming to stay,' she reworded her objection. 'Believe me, there's only room enough for one person, two if you squish in.'

The window above them was flung up with a screech. 'Brendan, this place is filthy. The sheets aren't even changed or the bed made.'

'That's my room!' Carmel shouted back at Melody. 'Get out of my bedroom!'

18

'Where else are we going to stay?' the petite woman yelled back at her. 'There's only one bathroom in the whole house and just two bedrooms.'

The racket of the woman's strident voice was attracting a crowd of idle watchers along the road, folks out for a day in St. Jude Without yet it was too early for the amusements to be started. This show promised to be better the bouncy castle, though. Carmel looked up at the red-faced Melody hanging out the open window and then to Brendan who was still looking accusingly at her with the bawling Joss in his arms.

'Just get in the house and we'll straighten this out,' she said to him. She grabbed a handful of bags off the ground and led the way up the steps.

Inside the house, Melody was stomping down the stairs. The two women glared at each other, then the intruder pushed past Carmel on her way to the kitchen.

'Can't you at least offer us a cup of tea? We've been traveling all night to get here. Some hospitality this is.'

The youngest was still crying at the shock of being rudely grabbed by his or her father and Tiffanee was blubbering at the upset of her mother yelling.

'Tyler, get in here!' Carmel demanded. Surprised no doubt at being spoken to in such a manner, Tyler sullenly and slowly came up the steps. She dumped the bags by the living room door. 'Tea is in the cannister,' she said over her shoulder at Melody as she slammed the front door against their audience. 'Help yourself.'

When the adults were fairly settled into the kitchen and the children occupied with juices and brownies and bags of chips from the family's cooler, Carmel stood above them by the doorway and crossed her arms.

'Now, we need to get this straightened out,' she said, trying to pick her words carefully. She was far outnumbered here in her own kitchen. 'There's been a misunderstanding – I thought there was only one guest coming. If you read the ad, you'll see there's only one bedroom. So just one guest. Not five. Did you read it through?'

Brendan slurped his tea, then shrugged. 'I figured you wouldn't mind if it was a couple, and the kids don't take up too much space, so...'

Melody's eyes crinkled and started watering. She hiccupped. 'What are we going to do? I came all this way for the home-coming, and I can't even get home. There's nowhere else to go.'

'You're from St. Jude Without?'

'No, Bell Island,' Melody said.

'So why don't you take the ferry and go over there?'

'I can't go there,' Melody replied. Her face crinkled up again. 'I was bullied too much. I was traumatized, I could never return to that place. And besides that, I'm terrified of crossing the water now!'

Carmel stared at her. What, was she a witch or something, unable to cross water? And also, come to think of it - they were presently on the island of Newfoundland and the only way off or on was by water or air. 'How did you get here from the mainland?'

'We flew, of course,' the other woman sniffed.

'And how did you expect to get to Bell Island from here?'

But this question only set Melody off blubbering more, which set off a chain reaction with Tiffanee and the baby. Brendan sat there amid the noise, munching on brownies and being no help at all.

Carmel could hardly make out the banging at the front door with all the racket in her kitchen, but when she recognized the extra noise for what it was she was glad to escape. On her way to answer it she was accosted by Captain Jem as he lurked in the living room.

'Get those people out of here,' he hissed at her. 'I can't stand the noise. What were you thinking?'

'I'm trying my best,' she retorted. 'Why don't you do something?'

'I'm a ghost, it's not my job.'

The thought must have struck them both at the same time, and they stared at each other for a moment. The banging on the front door only increased in volume.

'Yes, it is. It *is* your job.'

He nodded reluctantly and hunched his shoulders. The feather in his hat quivered. 'I'll try my best.'

Slightly relieved that the problem was on the way to being solved, she opened the front door only to find another problem waiting. Inspector Laney lurked outside with a scowl on his face.

'This is really not a good time,' she began.

'I'll decide when a good time is, Ms McAlistair.' He sneered as he looked her up and down, and jangled the handcuffs clipped to his waist as if itching to use them. 'This is a murder investigation. Best let me in unless you want this interview to be on You-Tube.' He flicked his head behind him. The crowd had actually grown now, attracted by the sight of the police car, and phones were held out filming Carmel and Laney.

Carmel swore under her breath and opened the door wider for the two officers.

'Murder?' Tyler had finally found his voice and was staring up at Laney with what could only be adoration.

'Who the hell is this? Get this kid out of here.'

'Sorry,' Carmel said. 'It's complicated. Tyler, why don't you go back in the kitchen with your parents?'

'Are you a cop?'

'Yes kid I'm a cop, what do you think? Go on, now.'

'That your car?'

'Yeah, it's my frigging car.'

'Can I go for a ride in it?'

'No, get out of here, I said.' Laney's face was turning red by now. He wasn't the most patient of all cops.

'Oh my God, what are the police doing here?' Brendan filled the doorway, mouth agape. Tiffanee, her tears forgotten, peered round his legs, her mouth open like her father's.

'What is this?' Laney turned to Carmel. 'Your family?'

'No!' Carmel was quick to disavow any connection to these people.

'You running an illegal boarding house then?' Laney's eyes narrowed. She could see the wheels turning in his head. He hated Inspector Darrow with a passion, and ever since Laney had found out she and Darrow were an item, he had transferred that hate on to her too. A blow against Carmel was a blow against his rival in the Royal Newfoundland Constabulary. She wasn't quite certain of the legalities of running an Air B&B out of her home, but she was pretty sure it was a gray area within the law. To make it worse, the baby now started up its caterwauling again in the kitchen.

'Mister! Mister!' Tyler was now pulling on the handcuffs on Laney's belt. 'Mister take me for a ride in your police car?'

'Now Tyler,' Brendan said. 'Don't bother the nice man. I'm sure he's here for a good reason?' Brendan stared at Carmel while he spoke, his brows drawn together in suspicion.

'MISTER!'

'Christ,' Laney muttered, trying to shake the kid off his leg. 'What a friggin' mad house. Can't you shut that kid up?'

Tyler was almost climbing up Laney's stout length to get the police officer's attention.

'I got to get out of here.'

'Oh?' Carmel said, as innocently as she could. 'Didn't you have something to ask me?'

'I'll call you later.' With that, Laney and his partner turned tail and fled out the door. Some guys were kid-people, some weren't. Herb Laney definitely wasn't.

'What was all that about?' Brendan demanded. 'Are you in trouble with the law? What murder was he talking about?'

For a split second, Carmel considered her options. She could tell the family about finding Lars' murdered body, and perhaps scare them out of her house. On the other hand, Tyler for certain would be thrilled and demand to stay, and his parents were awfully indulgent towards him. Best hold off for now, she quickly decided. They'd find out the grisly details soon enough, and she had every confidence in Captain Jem's ability to scare them out.

'No, really, he just stopped by for a chat,' Carmel dismissed Laney. 'Come on, why don't we all return to the kitchen? What were we talking about before Laney arrived?'

'Someone got murdered! Was there any blood?' Tyler had now turned his attention on to Carmel.

Melody and Brendan shared a significant glance. 'Not now, Tyler, darling,' his mother said to him.

'I wanna know if there was any blood! Did they catch the killer? Missus, did they find the murder weapon?'

'Tyler dear, be quiet now. You don't need to know about that,' Brendan spoke with treacly patience to his son.

'Did you do the murder, missus, was it you? Was that why the cops were here? Are you a killer?'

'Tyler shut up right now!' Melody had quite the voice on her for such a small woman, and it was effective for the moment. 'Take your sister and go outside to play.' She took the two oldest kids and hurriedly pushed them through the back door. Shutting the door behind them muffled most of the little girl's renewed bawling at being yelled at.

Carmel thought to warn them about the ravine not too far away through the graveyard, the steep and unexpected drop to the rocks below, but Melody was pressing for details on the murder.

'There was an unexpected death,' Carmel agreed, reluctant to get into it. 'In the next cove over, nothing to do with St. Jude Without.'

'What happened?' Brendan was staring at her through his owly glasses.

'A man was found dead on the breakwater, the police think it may be a suspicious death but the common consensus is he fell and bashed his head in on the rocks when he was drunk,' she replied, hoping that was enough information to satisfy them.

'Who was it?' Melody asked, leaning forward so as not to miss a word.

'Some guy from Bell Island, actually,' replied Carmel, realizing now that it might be someone Melody knew. Perhaps a family member even? 'Lars Andersen.' She looked at the other woman to gauge the effect of the name.

There was no reaction from either of them except to press for more details.

'How did he die?'

'Was there a lot of blood?'

'Who do you think did it?'

They really were ghouls, the whole family, and Carmel was already heartily sick of them all, even though they'd just arrived. Perhaps one of the kids would fall into the ravine and sprain a wrist, nothing too serious of course, but it would get them out of here. Hopefully.

And where was that damn ghost?

'The death of this man has nothing to do with anything,' she said in a firm voice. She had full intentions of insisting they move their stuff out, that she could not have five people staying in her house, and she even began a spiel to that effect when Melody was seized by parental remorse and realized she could no longer hear the two oldest through the open window. She grabbed the baby in her arms and they all had to go outside to look for the abandoned brats.

19

The children were found on the other side of the cove, way down by the bouncy castle in Snellen's Field, arguing with Phonse about being allowed in. The general rules of this structure was that an adult had to be present outside the castle before a kid was allowed in, but that wasn't what was deterring Phonse. Dressed in his clown's outfit, complete with red nose and oversize shoes, he firmly blocked the entrance of the castle, refusing to let Tyler and Tiffanee inside.

'No money, no bouncy,' he insisted, shaking his finger at them. 'Them's the rules. You can snot and bawl all you want, but I'm not budging.'

'Come on kids, let's go away from this nasty man,' Brendan collected his children while Melody's eyes shot daggers at Phonse. 'Look, there's ponies over there. Let's go for a pony ride.'

'Want bouncy castle...' Tiffanee sniffled as she was led away.

'Damn kids trying to rip me off,' Phonse grumbled as he cupped his hands against the wind to light a cigarette. His handsome bone structure was lost behind the painted clown grin.

'Should you be smoking around here?'

'I'm outside aren't I?' He scowled at her as he spoke around the smoke. 'Not going to pollute the little darlings' lungs.'

The cigarette smoke was hardly noticeable against the smell of exhaust from the generator which kept the castle buoyant, but that wasn't really her point.

'I mean, around the castle,' she clarified. 'It's made of plastic. It could catch fire or something worse.'

'I'm careful.'

'Do you have insurance?' It was a silly question and deserved to be ignored as it was.

120

'You know, Inspector Laney's trying to fix Lars' death on St. Jude Without,' she said, drawing closer toward him, away from the little ears inside the castle.

'No one witnessed the death,' Phonse spoke with certainty.

'How do you know that?'

He stopped to take money from two ten-year-olds, waiting impatiently as they dug in their pockets for change.

'Shoes off before you enter the bouncy castle!' he barked at them, then stuck his head inside the castle. 'You guys, there, yes you! Time's up! Get out.'

In answer to the loud groans from within, he pointed his cigarette at them and drew his eyebrows together. 'Don't make me come in and get you!'

'This is a lot of work, you know,' he complained to Carmel.

'You're self-employed, aren't you?'

'It's not all it's cracked up to be, life as an entrepreneur,' he said, shaking his head. 'Do you know how much it costs to rent this thing? And the kids – don't get me started.'

'Sort of a hazard in this line of work, huh?' She got back to the subject of Lars. 'How do you know no one witnessed his death?'

'No one has come forward, have they?' he said simply. 'We'd 'a heard if they did. And Laney wouldn't be sniffing around here if he had someone to pin it on.'

'You saw him up at my door, did you?'

'Hard to miss, him and his goon going around in a cop car at the top of the rise. The whole cove could see him.'

'Something else I wanted to discuss with you...'

He flicked the cigarette butt away from the tent, down towards the shoreline. It landed in the tall grasses lining the rocks.

'Phonse, that's still burning! Aren't you going to put it out?'

'What, you think I'm going to cause a forest fire?' He looked around at the field, bordered on one side by the road and the other three by rocks and ocean with not a tree in sight, and snickered at his own joke.

'You won't be laughing if the field catches fire and burns your castle down,' Carmel reminded him, her hands in her hoody pocket. The wind was rising and she brushed her mess of curls out of her face. 'You'll have to reimburse the rental company for the cost of it.'

'Damn.' They both walked down to look for the butt, kicking aside pebbles and clumps of grass. Phonse's over-sized clown shoes made the going difficult for him.

'Captain Jem,' she said, hesitantly. 'What do you know about him?'

'Founder of the clan,' he replied. 'Built the first house here in St. Jude Without. What else do you need to know?'

'Do you remember last summer, how you asked me if I'd seen his ghost?'

'I was only messing with your mind. You didn't think I was serious?'

'Hard to tell sometimes with you,' she replied making a face at him. 'But I have. I've met him.'

'You've seen Captain Jem?' He turned on her, and grabbed her shoulders with both hands. His eyes were wide. 'When? Where? How?'

She eyed him with suspicion to see if he was having her on. After all, he was the one who'd tried to scare her last summer when she was new to the cove with his stories of ghosts and witches, and the fairies in the graveyard behind her new home.

'Holy God,' he said, stopped in his tracks. He wasn't playing. 'I need to let everyone know. This is huge.'

'What do you mean?' But she was speaking to his back for Phonse was now headed back up the slope of Snellen's Field.

He stopped at the bouncy castle long enough to clear it of children.

'Everybody out! Right now! Time's up.' He held the flapping door wide and quickly shooed the reluctant children out, then tied the flaps tight. 'And don't let me catch you in here while I'm gone or I'll come after you, you little rats.'

He tore off up the field to the road, clown shoes flapping and sliding on the meadow. Carmel glanced back to where he'd thrown the cigarette end, but there was no sign of a grass fire, so she ran after him.

'What's the big deal?' she asked him, catching up as they hit the gravelled road and jogged along beside him. He was breathing heavily by now.

'Cap'n Jem... only shows himself... when the cove is in danger,' he huffed. His hat and wig were loosening as he ran towards the church, so he ripped them off and stuffed the lot into the large front pocket in his costume. 'That's what the legend says. The last time... was during the war.'

Phonse stopped suddenly, bending over from the waist in true marathon fashion. 'Damn, I should cut down on the smoking,' he said.

'What does this mean?' Carmel slowed down to his walking pace, almost afraid to hear the answer. Captain Jem hadn't seemed upset or scary, not at all the picture of doom.

He stopped a moment to look at her. 'I don't know what it means,' he said. 'And I'm not sure I want to find out.'

· · · ·

The air in Nate's quarter of the church was thick with the stink of tobacco, and old coffee mugs lay scattered all along the bar amid the papers which held Nate's notes. Nate himself looked as though he hadn't slept in a week. His carefully dishevelled appearance of before was now truly rank, his flannel shirt bore the coffee stains and sweat of his labor, but his red-rimmed eyes burned fiercely as he listened to what Phonse and Carmel had to tell him.

Nate drummed his fingers absently along the granite bar, staring into the stained glass above his head as if lost in prayer, but the wheels were churning inside his head.

'Captain Jeremiah, huh?' He nodded as if having made a decision then turned to Phonse and Carmel. 'As you know, this isn't a good sign. Our generation has never seen him, because we've kept under the radar like we're supposed to. He didn't seem upset or anything, no rattling of chains, not moaning warnings??'

'No,' Carmel said, remembering back to the ghost's demeanor. 'Not at all. He's an odd duck, but he doesn't seem to be a harbinger of bad news. But what do you mean 'like you're supposed to'? That's the first I've heard about this.'

'That's a long story, haven't got the time to fill you in right now,' Nate replied. 'But we're going to use him to our advantage. If St. Jude Without is going down, we're gonna go down with a splash and win that contest, if it's the last thing I do.'

20

'So Captain Jem – does he leave the house at all?' Nate directed his question at Carmel.

'No, we were going to work on that,' she said, wondering where he was going with this. 'But first I want him to scare out that family of visitors that have taken over my house.'

'Who are they?' Nate barked at her.

'It's my Air B&B,' she said. 'I thought there was just going to be one person staying, but he brought his wife and whole family. Kids included.'

'They mainlanders?' Anyone who wasn't from the island of Newfoundland was, by default, from the 'mainland', and thus a different breed of person.

'Yeah, the husband is,' she replied. 'But his wife's from Bell Island originally.'

Nate thought again, then nodded to himself, a small smile forming on his haggard face.

'Perfect! In fact, even better if she's from over there. You work on scaring them,' Nate ordered. 'They'll set up the alarm and spread the word. Phonse, get Ian in here. Pronto!'

Phonse flapped his way out the smoker's entrance and out to the road where Ian had last been seen busking outside the house he shared with Brigid.

'What are you waiting for?' Nate was scowling at Carmel.

'Just wondered where you're going with this,' she began. 'And also, there's the matter of the threat to me because of the blog!'

'Never mind all that,' Nate said. 'Can't help it if you can't keep up. Go. Go go go!' He made a shooing motion with his hands. 'We have to get this thing in action. There's only another few days for the contest, not a moment to lose! We have to take advantage where we can. Where's Tina?'

• • • •

Back at her home, she was prepared to spend the night on her old lumpy sofa. The family was not budging out of her house despite all her pleas, and it just wasn't worth it to put up with their complaining about the lack of sleeping arrangements, so she grudgingly changed the sheets and comforter on her own bed and allowed the three horrid children to sleep in her space. Melody assured her there would be no bed-wetting.

Jem obviously hadn't come through for her yet so far, either. She suspected the ghostly equivalent of stage fright was the cause, but he wasn't showing his visage for her to argue with him.

But even the living room was no longer a private domain. Although the rest of the family was upstairs by the time she got home, Brendan was still sitting up, ensconced in her favorite armchair, reading a book by the light of a single lamp. It was a new book she'd bought the previous week, one she hadn't yet had a chance to read.

'Hi,' she said roughly, not bothering to put a false note of cheer in her voice at the sight of him.

He looked up with a start, peering at her through his glasses. 'Hello, Carmel,' he replied. 'Hope you don't mind, but I've helped myself to one of your books. You sure do have a lot of them.'

'I'm a writer,' she said shortly, as she flapped the sheets out noisily, laying them on the sofa. 'I read.'

He wasn't taking her hint that she wanted to go to bed. Instead, he turned down a page corner in the murder mystery paperback to save his place. 'Melody doesn't like me reading in bed, she can't sleep with the light on,' he told her. 'In fact, she hates me reading at all.'

'Why would she care?' Her voice was flat and bored as she fluffed up the single cushion that still looked relatively unravaged from his children's play, the one that didn't have peanut butter smeared on it.

He laughed cynically. 'She says it scares her. That I shouldn't read mysteries, because it might give me ideas.'

Carmel shrugged. She would love to write a mystery with Melody as the victim, it would give her great pleasure to rid the earth of the woman's presence, even if only on paper.

'But you had a real life murder here, didn't you?'

'I think it was an accident. He slipped and fell off the rocks.' She dismissed the idea as she flicked the single quilt over her makeshift bed.

'That's not what the cops are saying. I saw the TV footage on my laptop,' he persisted. 'The Inspector said it was murder. That someone hit him over the head with a rock and killed him.'

'Maybe,' she snapped.

'Who would have done it? They say it was someone from here. Do they have any suspects?' His eyes were avid with curiosity.

Brendan was too concerned with the affairs of the cove, and she was already sick of this family of ghouls. 'I don't know,' she barked. 'And I don't want to talk about it. Right now I just want to go to sleep. Here.'

At last the man took himself off and lumbered up the stairs to his own bed. It took Carmel a long time to get to sleep that night. The sofa was uncomfortable and her thoughts resentful. Where the hell was that ghost?

• • • •

She remembered to stop by the bakery for breakfast items on the way home after work the next day. As Melody had pointed out that morning, she was running an Air B&B, and breakfast was written right into the contract. Spotting the bag of day old croissants marked at half-price, she grabbed it. That would be good enough for the family of intruders, perhaps the staleness of the offerings might encourage them to move on to friendlier pastures.

When she got back home, she saw that Captain Jem still hadn't done his work yet. The family were not in the house when she got back, but had left the evidence of their encampment all over the place, and had even taken over the living room again, spreading their toys and half-eaten sandwiches all over the floor and the sofa where she was now forced to sleep.

Carmel sighed as she collected the mugs and plates and tetra-boxes, scrubbing at the dried orange juice and sweeping up the cookie crumbs. Good grief – the family had hardly been in her house for twenty-four hours, and look at the mess they'd made.

There was nothing to eat for supper in the house, she saw as she surveyed the fridge. All the milk was gone, even the peanut butter jar had been scraped clean and left on the counter. But there, at the back of the fridge, gleamed the foil covering the chocolate torte.

'Best consolation prize ever,' she said aloud, and reverently removed the pan and laid it on the counter. Knife in hand, she tore off the foil wrap to find nothing but crumbs and a single almond rolling around the bottom of the pan. Even the chocolate ganache had been wiped clean by a tiny finger, and possibly a little tongue.

They'd eaten the whole thing and replaced the empty dish back in the fridge as if she wouldn't notice. This was a step too far. This was war. Captain Jem better get his act together.

Speaking of whom, where was that ghost?

'Jem?' Her tone was menacing to match her mood. 'You around? Get out where I can see you.'

There was no reply. She tentatively sniffed the air, but not a tang of the spirit at all.

'Listen up! We need you,' she said to the empty air around her. 'I know you're here, you don't leave the house.'

A spasm of air wavered, hesitated, then the ghostly form of Jem slowly became visible. The atmosphere was permeated with a taste of his trademark sulphurous tones.

'There you are,' she said with relief. It struck her, as she stared at the outline of his form, she was the only person in living memory to see this apparition. This might be an honor, perhaps, but not if his appearance was a harbinger of doom for the whole cove. She really hoped Nate knew what he was doing with his hastily thought up plan. Whatever it was.

The ghost looked back at her gloomily through his haze. 'You called?'

'I have a lot of questions for you, a lot! But first... have you given any thought on scaring the family yet, how you're going to do it? We need to get rid of them, and fast.'

He sighed, giving off the scent of the grave as he did so. 'Yes, about that,' he said. 'I don't think it'll work so well.'

'What do you mean? We need you to do this, whatever it takes to rid of them.'

'I have told you before, I am not a performing monkey,' Jem told her as he drew himself up, looking for all the world like a character from a Gilbert and Sullivan opera as he looked down his spectral nose at her.

'We're not asking you to be... an ape,' she said. 'I just need you to be a scary ghost and get those people out of my house. Uh, I mean our house.'

'It can't be done.' He shook his head with melodramatic regret.

'Why not?' Nate's sense of urgency had infected Carmel, to say nothing of the intrusion of the family's bags strewn around her hallway. 'You don't need to do much, just show yourself. No need to put on the Jacob Marley act with clanking chains, because you'll be scary enough as you are.'

Not to mention the stink he carried with him when he materialized, that would chase anybody away.

The ghost wavered a little, then his outline grew stronger. 'I know not if I can appear to these people,' he said sadly. 'I am out of practice, you know.'

'But you had no problem showing yourself to me, remember?'

He nodded reluctantly. 'Ay,' he said, sitting down heavily at the kitchen table as if he had a world of weight on his shoulders. 'But that was out of my control. Took me quite by surprise, I must say, when you reacted to my presence.'

'Why was it out of your control?' Carmel had a sinking feeling about this. Perhaps what Phonse said was true – the pirate was only able to show himself when the cove and its inhabitants were threatened. Maybe Jem had nothing to do with the procedure. Carmel drew closer so as not to miss a word.

But she was out of luck at that point as, with the slamming of the front door, the ghost evaporated into the air just moments before and Brendan and company rolled into the kitchen.

21

The children had been out all day, apparently, and were now hungry, tired and very quarrelsome, and the parents weren't much better. They were quickly running out of things to occupy the kids in St. Jude Without, and the whole family was picking at each other.

'Why don't you take a trip over to Bell Island?' Carmel asked Melody as she poured hot water into all the mugs. She would soon be out of tea bags. 'You're from there right?'

'There's that little matter of being afraid to cross water,' Brendan reminded her, a sneer in his voice. 'A pretty odd thing for someone who supposedly grew up on an island.'

'Brendan you know I've tried,' Melody said, tears in her eyes. 'I just can't do it.'

'This is why we never come back here,' Brendan said to Carmel. 'It's not because I don't like her relatives, like they all say. It's because we get here and then we're stuck and we don't see anyone.'

'You can fly over water, though, right?' Carmel said to his wife. 'You came here from Toronto on a plane?'

She sniffed and nodded. 'I just hate being ON the water. I almost drowned the last time I left Bell Island, you know, all those years ago. Fell over the side of the ferry, and no one even noticed. I could have died!'

'That must have been traumatic,' Carmel said. She looked for a tinge of sympathy inside herself for the woman, but by now the two older children were in a tug of war with the throw cushions from the living room, and her nerves were stretched taut to their limits. 'Give it up!' she hissed at the youngsters, snatching back the cushions from their hands. This set them up to crying even worse.

'Yes, it was traumatic,' Melody said, turning to her husband with her blubbery face. 'I was traumatized, that's the very word, and no one seems to understand.'

'Have you ever thought of hiring a helicopter to take you over the Tickle?' she asked the adults over the screams. She tried her best to keep a smile pasted on her face.

'Do you know how much that costs?' Brendan said in a horrified voice.

'And you don't think I'm important enough to pay for it!' Melody was in full stream now and her upset just made the kids worse.

God, Carmel might pay for the helicopter herself just to get rid of them.

'Hey,' she continued in a falsely bright voice as if she'd just come up with the most fabulous, the most fantastic of ideas. 'They're having a barbeque outside the church this evening. Why don't you take the kids over there? They sound like they might be hungry.'

Anything, she thought. Just get out of my house and leave me in peace for a moment.

As if on cue, the smell of burning hot dogs wafted through the open windows, drifting over from the church parking lot. It worked. Taking the last box of tissues with them, the family departed en masse.

Finally. Blessed peace. She sighed and looked around at the destroyed living room which she'd already cleaned up once that day, but that could wait. There was more important work to be done.

'Jem?' Carmel demanded. 'Get back out here where I can see you.'

The air quivered slightly to Carmel's left, as if the ghost were tentatively feeling the temperature of the atmosphere, reluctant to fully submerge.

'More. Look me in the eye.'

He materialized further, hesitant.

'Now,' she said, crossing her arms. 'That was easy enough. Why can't you do that in front of Brendan and his family?'

He sat heavily on the closest kitchen chair. 'They scare me so,' he confessed. 'The children are so loud, so horrible.'

'They scare you? But you're the ghost,' Carmel reminded him. She stared down at his bowed head. 'It's your job to be the scary one.'

He said nothing, just looked down at the old oak table in his ghostly shame.

'You had kids once upon a time, didn't you? Eliza and you had a whole brood of them.'

'That was many years ago,' he replied, shaking his head. 'And a different time. These children – they're demons, I tell you! They have no rules, I'll bet you they've never even been introduced to the belt in their lifetimes. Those parents – they have no control. It is unnatural, I tell you.'

He had a legitimate point. The parenting style of Brendan and Melody was inconsistent, at best.

'And do you know what the devils were doing upstairs? The lad was burrowing into your closet, and the female child was painting her face with your rouges.'

'They what?' The kids had gotten into her make-up and clothing. That took the cake. 'Okay mister, that does it. You'd better muster up the courage and the ectoplasm to show yourself. Or... or... I'll offer to sell the house to them as a summer home!'

22

Outside the clouds were finally settling to roost, all pink and gold in the still blue sky, while the sun was nearing the horizon way over at the western edge of Conception Bay, the larger body of water of which the cove of St. Jude Without was such a tiny part. But between here and there loomed the bulk of Bell Island, its large shadow cast on the water as if the night had already begun.

With the contrast of sun in the eyes of the St. Judeans, it was no wonder the flotilla of tiny boats on the Tickle went unnoticed as it silently travelled in the ferry's path from north-west to south-east. All the St. Judeans were at the church making the most of the free beer and edibles, and no one thought to look around. The small water craft pulled up to the Phonse's wharf and the occupants of these Bell Island boats soon interspersed with the general movement of bodies along North Point Road Extension, a large exodus into the cove, for one of the beer companies had brought down a load of free beer to help with the festivities and word quickly spread.

The cove was already feeling frayed along the edges. Carmel cut through the body of the church and through Vee Ryan's tea-room. In the sparse light coming from the windows, the room looked dreary and uninviting, the tables unwashed and mug rings all over. On an impromptu buffet table made from a wooden door placed over the pool table and covered by a vinyl table cloth, the unsold tea buns and wilted sandwiches of the day sat under plastic waiting for a second chance tomorrow.

In the parking lot the carnival atmosphere in the cove had been taken up a notch further, with lots of life, noise and bright lights. The sound system blasted a local FM station with all the hits from the seventies and eighties, forcing folk to shout to make themselves heard over it. The scoreboard was now perched precariously on the roof of the church, the better to be seen. The red flashing bulbs showed numbers for 'Home' and 'Away', but the last word had by now been painted over to read 'Bell Island' in a direct nose-thumbing to Gen's visit the other day.

Someone, most likely Ian, had somehow connected the lit board directly to the laptop, and now it automatically refreshed every ten seconds. It was a close competition, and every time the numbers changed a roar sounded through the crowd.

But not all were paying attention to the board, of course, not when there were free beers and Purity Syrup on hand to go along with the hot dogs. Even Ian had lain down his fiddle to fill up, as the food was provided at no cost for the inhabitants of the cove. The outrageous prices charged to the tourists helped cover the expenses, and Vee was keeping a watchful eye to make sure she wasn't being cheated. The beer was free for everyone, of course, which contributed greatly to the festive atmosphere.

Someone handed her a can of beer and she opened it absently, her eyes idly scanning the crowd. The beer was flowing, the crowd were growing ever louder by the moment. She recognized a lot of the faces here – Phonse, with his clown make-up half smeared off by now, the pool players whose names she never could get straight. The young teenage girls in their short skirts and too much make-up, surreptitiously sharing beers and cigarettes between them and thinking no one saw through their cleverness. Tiffanee and Tyler had found other tourist children, and were running off their sugar and nitrate highs with loud screams and shouts.

The only people not appearing to enjoy themselves were her unwelcome guests, Melody and Brendan, who lurked at the edge of the crowd looking miserable and out of place. They stood next to each other but apart, holding themselves stiffly upright with Joss in between like a buffer. Her face was set in a petulant frown. The uneaten hotdog was held distastefully between her fingers as if it was a bag of doggy do, while Brendan resolutely stuffed his face with the wieners and buns like he was determined to get his money's worth. What a strange couple they were, Carmel thought idly, they didn't seem to actually like each other at all. One might think that the only thing they had in common, besides their offspring, was the constant tension between the husband and wife. It was the single chain linking them, like a heaviness forged from years of grudges and animosity and welding them solidly together. But then again, Carmel could only speak as a single woman, and surely no marriage was perfect.

Nate and Tina had relaxed their determined vigilance for the evening. In between refreshing the scoreboard above their heads, they spent their free moments necking in the shadow under the church roof. With a wince and a shudder, she quickly moved her gaze on.

There were many faces she didn't recognize, probably tourists, by the looks of them. She could always tell who wasn't from these parts, for they wore winter coats and hats in June against the frigid evening breeze, as opposed to some locals who were determined to pretend summer was here and still wore the shorts they'd had on in the daytime.

Her eyes paused on one figure. She could have sworn it was Roland, Gen's son, but it was hard to tell in the dim light and the press of the crowd. Like many others, the man had the hood of his black sweater pulled right up over his face against the evening chill, but those bow-legs and the boxer's body under the hoody couldn't belong to anyone else. Carmel laughed to herself. Free beer and a barbeque was a great equalizer, and sure enough this was drawing a crowd even from overseas. He was probably hiding his face to avoid recognition, for if Gen found out any of her people were socializing in St. Jude Without, she wouldn't be happy.

And then there were other bodies she didn't recognize who didn't look like tourists but who were definitely new faces. The word must have spread through FaceBook about the free beer and these might be townies come out for the party. There was still no sign of Sid and his bikers, though, and it bothered Carmel that they were avoiding the cove. Somehow, despite his outlaw habits, Sid was the voice of reason in St. Jude without and without his calming presence, the whole place had the feeling of a train about to run off its tracks.

She tried to shrug off that niggling feeling of doom – after all, everyone except Melody and Brendan looked to be having fun. In fact, there were hundreds of happy people were milling about the crowded parking lot and the party spread out onto the road. Lots of the partiers were recording their own fun times with photos and selfies, and all these pictures would be posted on FaceBook, leading to more promotion for the cove's competition ratings.

Yet something just didn't feel right in the cove. A warning bell was sounding deep inside her gut. She scanned the crowd again, trying to figure it out. Perhaps it was the glance she intercepted between two of the hooded figures, the tenseness in their stances, the way the hooded figures separated and deliberately spread throughout the crowd.

It was at that very moment that the brawl started up. It was skirmish with no center of action, she couldn't see where the first shove happened, or where the first punch landed.

And there was no time to figure out who was responsible or even why it started. This became a brawl like no other the cove had seen, unless it could be compared to the lynching of Captain Jem all those years ago. Certainly not like the Mummer's Affray which took place every year in the days before Christmas when all the rogues and lads from miles around dressed up as mummers in their mother's old dresses with bras on the outside, with brin bags or masks to hide their identities, and they all collected on Snellen's Field for the express purpose of beating the hell out of each other. Everyone understood what to expect on that day, and that was just a bit of fun, really.

But this brawl. This brawl had a quality of meanness to it, and there was no single source of the trouble. Like a sudden summer squall it blew up and swallowed everyone in its path. Innocent bystanders were caught up in it, those who were just there for hot dogs and fellowship and free beer. In the long shadows of the setting sun with only the red flashing lights of the scoreboard above them to show who was where, fists were flying and feet were kicking. Mothers screamed and clutched their children to their sides, fathers defended their broods from whoever came close enough to threaten. Vee Ryan stood behind the barbeque and squawked her outrage, brandishing the barbeque flipper at anyone she didn't recognize.

'Nate!' Carmel screamed over the racket as she pushed her way over to him, ducking a fist or two. 'What's happening here?'

Nate, caught in mid-seduction, was struck dumb as he looked up from Tina's chest to see that the whole place had exploded around him. His overwrought brain, fueled only by coffee and other stimulants over the past few days, was still quick enough to register the melee and what it could mean for him. All he could focus on were the cameras flashing, lighting the downward path for all his ambitions as photos were immediately uploaded to Facebook, Instagram and other social media for the world to see. He panicked.

'Stop it!' he yelled as he grabbed the flipper from Vee and crashed into the crowd, arms flailing and long hair flying. He showed no fear – Nate's brain had clicked into berserker mode at this threat to his plans, and with his height and brawn he single-handedly quelled the center of the crowd from where the fighting had broken out.

And as quickly as it had begun, it ended. People were running away along the main road towards Portugal Cove and down the lane to the point and, with the last of the sun in their eyes as they stood at the top of the hill, Nate and Carmel couldn't recognize any of them. But in the leftover light after the sun had disappeared behind

Conception Bay, they all saw the small launches leave Phonse's wharf and hastily creep back to Bell Island.

23

Everyone who was left on the parking lot made their way into the bar to regroup and patch up. Carmel helped make tea, the universal panacea which was a holdover from the British colonial days, and Vee broke out the stale raisin buns and bandages.

Their stunnedness soon turned into anger, for all had witnessed the little boats heading back to Bell Island, and there was not a single soul in St. Jude Without who was under any illusion as to who had started the fights and why. It had been a deliberate attempt to undermine St. Jude Without's chances at the contest. The islanders hadn't chanced relying on the ferry to get them out of the cover safely and in a timely manner, so they had brazenly snuck over and used Phonse's own wharf to tie up their launches. Nate stepped up to bat and showed his true leadership qualities, even strung out as he was on lack of sleep.

'I saw Roland here,' Carmel said. 'And those other guys I didn't recognize were probably with him.'

'The whole thing stinks of Bell Island treachery,' Nate answered her, shaking his head.

'Frig this,' Phonse said, his clown wig off and his natural blond curls going every which way. The make-up was just about worn off his face by now, although it was hard to tell with the black eye that was forming and the bruises coming out on his cheek. 'I just want to go over there and murder that lot.'

'They can't do this to us!'

'No!' Nate called out in his loud voice. 'I hear what you're saying, but we will NOT hit back in kind.'

He paused and looked around at each of them in turn. His eyes were reddened still but a manic light shone through.

'We're going to act very carefully, and plan each step of our revenge,' he said slowly. 'We will fight them on social media, we will fight them on FaceBook, we will use every resource we have to win and we never never stop until the battle is finished.'

While Nate was channelling Winston Churchill, Tina was busy checking the damage on the laptop.

'Hoo boy,' she trilled out. 'Not looking good.'

'You ask – what is our aim? Our aim is victory, pure and simple,' Nate continued. He was now clutching the lapels of his sports jacket with his fedora at a jaunty angle as he paced the room. He even had his habitual cigar in his mouth, although it was unlit. 'This is the final countdown. This, my friends, is the final war, the war to end all wars!'

It really wasn't a bad speech, considering it was impromptu, even if it did borrow heavily from other sources. Perhaps Nate would make a politician yet.

'We're getting unliked!' Tina wailed from her corner of the large room.

'What?' Nate broke off his self-indulgent spiel and spun round to look at the laptop. 'Let me see that.'

It was true – St. Jude Without was actively losing likes as the photos of the brawl were being uploaded onto their competition page. The accompanying comments were just as damning, and sometimes outright lies.

Tourist friendly? I don't think so... was attached to a photo of children huddling in fear against their mother's side.

'IT' got nothing on the scary clown in St. Jude Without! marked a photo of Phonse snarling, his make-up smeared and beer in one hand as he swung out wildly with his other fist.

And on it went. The uploaded pictures didn't stop at the mysterious brawl which broke at the barbeque – no, Gen's gang must have been surreptitiously infiltrating the crowds all day and snapping pictures of everything and anything that could show St. Jude Without in a bad light. Of course, there was Clyde Farrell with his stick upraised, it looked like he was about to beat his own goat, which was inciting the animal huggers on FaceBook, of which there were many. Another long shot showed the garbage accumulating along the ditches, which was no one's job to clean up. The accompanying post didn't point out that this trash was purely from tourists.

And there was a shot of Nate at his most greasy, taken as he swivelled his head with eyes narrowed and the stogie in his mouth, heavy bags showing under his eyes. *Mayor of SJW? What a shyster!*

And on and on it went, sparing no one and nothing, and all of these pictures being shared across the world by every ex-Bell Islander who still breathed. The likes were rapidly diminishing.

'This is it,' Nate roared. 'No holds barred. Everyone has to step up their game.'

24

Despite it all, the brawl and the terror, the family wasn't budging from Carmel's home, although Melody was loudly complaining about the violence and unlawfulness in the streets of St. Jude Without while they hogged the TV in the living room.

'Streets?' Carmel mumbled to herself, huddled in her kitchen in the dark, unable to go to bed until the family left the room. 'A gravel road and a laneway. It's hardly Detroit in the nineteen-seventies.'

The tension between husband and wife was palpable as they bickered over the noise of the blaring cartoon channel. The kids weened and whined, unused to being ignored and not having their parents hovering closely over them, and were not cheered at all by the antics of the garish figures on the screen, the volume up on bust to cover up the bitching between the adults.

A cheerful sound pinged from her phone.

Be back soon! Darrow wrote. *How're things?*

Inspector Darrow of the Royal Newfoundland Constabulary. Her boyfriend. He must be missing her – he actually used an exclamation mark. A burst of joy spurted through her, but was just as quickly quenched.

How in God's name could she answer that question truthfully? Apart from the shambles that was her home village at the moment, there was also the peculiar happenings in her own house.

She imagined his reaction if she told him about the family of aliens who had made roost in the house.

'Bloody hell, Carmel,' he said to her in her imagination. 'What are you thinking of? Get them out. It's that simple. How could you have let this happen?'

He would think her absolutely insane, as crazy as them, if she told him about it. Which she might, after they were gone. It would even be a funny story. Some day.

But of course, there was the presence of the ghost in the mix. No, Darrow wasn't going to hear about this one. She had a lot of clearing up in her life before he returned. She had momentary panic attack at that thought.

Great! She answered. *Pretty quiet here as usual! When are you coming back?*

Back on the Rock in two days, he answered immediately.

Two days. She could do it. They could do it, her and the ghost.

'Jem?' she whispered, and waited. 'Where are you? Get out here, would you?'

The air across the table shimmered and the shadow in the unlit kitchen grew darker as he showed himself a little. Like the Cheshire Cat, but all could she could see of him was a ghostly scowl.

'These people are horrible,' he hissed at her.

'Yeah, no kidding,' she replied. 'You need to up the attempts to get rid of them.'

'They scare me,' he whispered, shuddering.

'Wrong answer,' she shot back, forgetting to lower her voice. 'You're the scary one. They're not going to leave until they're forced to. I've even offered them all their money back but they won't go. And Darrow's going to be back soon...'

'Who you talking to?' The oldest child, Tyler, had gotten bored with his parents and wandered into the kitchen.

Jem looked with horror at the midget and disappeared in an instant.

'Was that a ghost?' Tyler asked. His voice was excited, avaricious, thrilled even. 'Where'd he go?'

Dammit, the child should have been scared of the apparition, but that wasn't terror she saw on his face.

'Holy cow, a ghost! Can you make him show himself again?' His squinty little eyes were bugging out of his head.

This really wasn't the result she had hoped for.

'Mom! There's a ghost here!' Tyler had taken off to the living room, yelling at the top of his lungs to be heard over the TV and his parents.

But then again, this might be it – the straw that broke their inexplicable resolve to stay here in her house. Her mind raced through possible scenarios. If she admitted there was indeed a ghost in the home, these helicopter parents might up and leave, worrying as they did about their poor darlings' safety. That would be good.

On the other hand this tactic might backfire – Brendan and Melody were so stuck on staying here that they might decide since Carmel had met no harm from the ghost, they wouldn't either. It would be a great story to tell back home, their week in the haunted house in Newfoundland.

If she denied all knowledge of a ghost – what then? She thought quickly. Yes, that was the route to take.

Carmel approached the living room.

'There's no such things as ghosts,' Melody was saying, trying to pitch her reasonable voice over the sound of the TV and Tiffanee who by this time of day was totally exhausted. The news of the ghost was not welcome to this little one. At five years old, she understood enough about the nether world to know that her ineffective parents could not keep her safe from things outside their ken, and so she wheened and wailed against the uncertainty of life.

Brendan, meanwhile, was staring at Carmel with what looked like suspicion behind his round lenses, but the dancing light from the television bounced off the glass and hid whatever he might be thinking.

'I saw it, just its head. I saw a ghost,' Tyler stubbornly insisted. 'It disappeared when it saw me. Missus, you know I saw the ghost, you were talking to it!'

All of them turned towards Carmel now, even the baby. She pretended to be thinking hard about the matter.

'No,' she said finally, shaking her head. 'No ghost here. I must have been talking to myself again, I do that sometimes. You only imagined you saw a ghost. Perhaps a trick of the light, the shadows?'

'You were, like, having a conversation,' Tyler insisted as he stamped his foot on the hardwood floor. 'I heard him talking back to you.'

The certainty of her son's conviction brought doubt to Melody's eyes.

Carmel gave a tight smile to the parents, one that protested innocence. 'Children have such vivid imaginations, don't they?' she replied and gave a little titter. 'No, no ghosts in this house.'

'He seems pretty sure, though,' Melody said in a doubtful voice, still looking at her son. 'He must have seen something.'

Brendan let out a loud breath of impatience. 'Don't be ridiculous, Mel,' he said. 'There's no such thing as a ghost.'

'True,' his wife answered. The poor woman, Carmel could see that Melody didn't know which side of the fence to sit on when it came to the supernatural. On the one hand, her natural inclination was to disbelieve anything that wasn't believable in her narrow mindset, but that would mean agreeing with her husband against the protestations of the apple of her eye, her firstborn child. And she really wasn't too happy with Brendan at the moment.

'Though of course,' Carmel quickly added in a casual voice. 'There have been rumors...' She slid her eyes over to Brendan and Melody to better judge their reactions.

'Those are just made up stories to get the tourists in,' Brendan said, disgust filling his voice. 'Newfies are a bunch of ignoramuses to believe something like that.' This was said with the assurance of a man who had lived in solid suburbia all his years and knew the inherent superiority of an unimaginative life.

Whoah, Carmel thought, her eyes widening. A mainlander using that word was like waving a red rag in front of a bull, and practically suicidal when done here on the island. It held a lot of history, did that seemingly innocuous endearment, and had come to mean a lazy ne'er-do-well, a hangashore. Did Brendan not know this?

Melody's face twisted. Carmel watched in fascination as first anger ripped across the woman's face, then bitterness, and then a decision was made.

'I've told you never to use that word in front of the children,' she hissed. 'And you think I'm lazy? You try spending all your hours looking after three children. I would love to have a paying job, but you knocked me up before I could go for my nurses training, remember?'

'You got pregnant on purpose,' he spit back at her. 'You made me quit university and take the first job that came along. If it wasn't for you, I could have been someone, instead of being stuck in the insurance business. It's all your fault, you selfish bi...'

'Hey! Cut it out,' Carmel said, stepping between the two like a referee, although she had the uncomfortable feeling she was merely playing a part in a well-rehearsed scene. She lowered her voice. 'The kids are right here.'

Melody's eyes glittered as she pulled visibly herself together for the sake of her children and without losing a beat continued with the previous conversation.

'There's no ghost here, my sweetie,' she said to Tyler in an overly kind voice. 'You want a cookie before bed? Let Mommy read you a story.'

Tyler scowled at her in outrage. 'You haven't read me a story in three years! I'm too old for stories.'

'And you're also too old to believe in ghosts,' Brendan pointed out. There was the tiniest twitch in the muscle under his left eye. 'Besides, you're scaring your sister. Now, it's bedtime for all of you.'

'And Mommy's family are coming over tomorrow,' Melody added. 'Won't that be fun to see your auntie again?'

'She'll believe me about the ghost,' Tyler said, pouting truculently. Yet he'd already forgiven his parents, for they were adults and didn't know any better. Besides, he now had had something exciting for the other kids visiting the cove, something to make them forget his disadvantage of being a mainlander.

Melody looked up at Carmel, her face as bland as she could make it. Her eyes didn't leave Carmel's as she dared her to make a fuss after the inconveniences of the street brawl and ghost sighting. 'Hope you don't mind,' she said. 'Since I can't make it over to the island, my sister and her husband are coming over here.'

All five unwelcome guests trooped upstairs, leaving Carmel with the detritus of their existence and a sinking feeling deep within. Did Melody mean her family was coming here, to her house? Which meant there were more of them.

Carmel was now feeling so frustrated she could cheerfully murder each and every one of them. What would it take to get rid of these people from her home?

25

Things changed in the cove after that night, although the tourists still came in even greater droves, attracted by the rumors of dark happenings in St. Jude Without in the same way ghouls are attracted to a car wreck where blood has been spilled and lives lost.

Carmel stood at her living room window overlooking her village, watching as Ian led a crowd of folks through his haunted tour spiel. He wore the dusty top hat atop his mess of black Irish curls, and pattered non-stop as they walked through the cove. It was a short tour, beginning with Snellen's Field where Rev. Wilson had been brutally murdered last Christmas time, then down Phonse's lane to where the pirate gold had supposedly lain for hundreds of years. After that, a quick hike up the ravine to show where another unnatural death had occurred, then past Melba's cottage with a quick aside in hushed tones about the witch, and the rumored fairies in the graveyard behind.

The grand finale of the tour was of course Carmel's own house, and she listened as Ian pointed out the stump of the pine tree from which Captain Jeremy swung then told the entranced crowd about the pirate's ghost which could be seen at night, gazing over the sea mournfully, keeping eye on his lost treasure.

Ian was making all of this last bit up, of course. Being Irish, he loved nothing better than to enhance a tale for the enjoyment of his listeners. As far as Carmel knew, only she and now Tyler had ever seen the ghost.

'Is that the ghost?' A woman shrieked upon seeing Carmel standing at the window.

'Doesn't look like a pirate,' someone said doubtfully.

Carmel resisted the urge to stick out her tongue, and merely moved herself out of sight. There was no privacy for her anywhere, these days, not even in her own house.

By now the children were awake and milling about the house, beginning to grouse for their breakfast, but except for a plate full of crumbs and half a glass of orange juice on the counter, there were no signs of their parents. No way was she going to act as a babysitter, that wasn't in the hostessing contract, so she left through the front door while the kids were in the kitchen. Their hungry wails would soon rouse the lazy sods from her spare room.

But meanwhile there was nothing left to do but go into the city to buy groceries. Do something, anyway, to give her an excuse to get away from the cove and its neighbors.

St. Jude Without had a tattered look to it. It was the litter that did it, making the place look messy. Bright red pop cans lay amidst garish orange chip bags discarded by the side of the gravel road, and eeuh! Was that a used diaper peeking out from behind the shrubs in her front garden? The cove didn't have the necessary infrastructure in place for this influx of visitors. Perhaps if Nate won the contest they could put in public facilities, if there was any money left over after the massive party.

The ferry gave its mournful toot in the distance, warning the small dories and fishing boats to get out of its way as it made its way back across the water to Bell Island. Melody's family might have landed already, so it was definitely time for Carmel to get out of Dodge

She pulled up at the wharf, and got out of the car, watching the ferry on the water. From here, she couldn't see the build-up of salt and grime and rust on the body of the ship – it gleamed white and the sun sparkled in its wake.

Carmel asked herself why was she here, revisiting the scene of Lars' gruesome death, but she already knew the reason.

A greeting stopped her short.

'Hey.'

She looked up to see one of the pool players. The pudgy, balding guy with the comb-over – he was either Pat or Mike or Len. Why could she never remember their individual names? She'd known them all as long as she'd known Brigid and Phonse.

'Hey,' she replied. He was standing by the ticket booth, his arms crossed, just standing as if he had been planted there. A frown was on his face.

'What are you doing?' She had to ask him. He didn't look like he was there for fun.

'I'm keeping guard,' he said. He sort of lowered his head after he spoke the words, as if hearing them aloud brought home how ridiculous this situation was. Who was he to stem the hordes from Bell Island if they chose to come to St. Jude Without?

Carmel nodded as if in sympathy. Inside her head, she was screaming for it all to end, just end, right now, the whole stupid farce. Nate was now posting guards on the ferry?

'I see.' She paused a beat. How could she put this tactfully? 'Nate... he's really going over the top, isn't he?'

'I dunno... I mean, he's doing his best,' Pat or Mike or Len said, shuffling his feet. 'It just feels like... maybe this whole thing is getting out of hand?'

'I can't disagree with you,' she replied. 'Is this FaceBook contest really that important, do you think?'

He shrugged and thought about it. 'We don't need a new jukebox, really. Sid's stereo has done us for years. And the pool table is fine, just a few rips in the felt. It's always been like that, and no one's ever complained before.'

The man lifted his head and stared toward where St. Jude Without was hidden behind the curve of the mountain. Only the red and yellow of the plastic bouncy castle was visible from here, sticking out from the natural landscape like the trash collecting along the road in the cove.

'Yeah,' Carmel said, following his eyes. 'I hear you.'

Even the pool player was getting tired of the whole FaceBook thing and the upset it was causing to the community. And if he was, then others probably were too. Which meant, glory be, perhaps they could all convince Nate to give it up. And then she just had to work on getting rid of The Family.

But the death of Lars. That's why she had returned to this spot, the scene of the giant's demise. Not to look for evidence – that would all have been washed away in the rain. But she had to see for herself if Nate's story was possible, or even likely.

Carmel walked right to the boulders at the edge of the breakwater and climbed up one that was set lower than the others. This would be the natural path to take. Peering over, she saw the ledge where the two would have sat, a protrusion of rock over the water. Not the safest place to be on a wet and foggy night, but both men would have been climbing rocks and cliffs from a young age and would not have found it challenging, even if they'd been loaded drunk. But she had to test it for herself.

From this ledge, she found she was quite hidden from view, so neither of the men would have been seen from the ferry that afternoon. They would have had only fog before them, and after she stood and clambered back onto the breakwater, she looked up and realized no one would have seen them exit the spot, either, for the large ferry would have towered over them. Due to its bowed sides, they would have had all the privacy they needed.

Privacy enough for murder? She shuddered. It could have been possible, but was it true?

'Re-enacting the murder?'

Carmel whirled around. Brandon stood before her, his eyes wide and avaricious behind the glare of sunlight on his glasses, and his mouth agape in a square rictus.

26

'What are you doing here?' Her voice wasn't kind. 'You found him, right? Where was he lying?' Brendan looked all over the boulders at the edges as if he might spot something the police had missed.

It was as she feared, the ghoul Brendan had come down to inspect the site of Lars' death. She sighed and pointed reluctantly. 'It was over there.'

'Here?' He moved where she indicated. 'Right where I'm standing?'

Carmel stared at the man. 'Brendan, why are you doing this?'

He looked up as if hurt by her tone and peered at her through his spectacles, pushing them up his nose as he did. 'I'm just... curious, I guess. I've never been this close to something this exciting. Ever.'

'Death isn't exciting,' she tried to explain. 'It's shocking, it's horrible to come upon a dead body, whether it's murder or natural death.' She shivered and looked away.

Brendan looked down at the spot where she'd found Lars in a pool of blood, and he scuffed the pavement as if trying to unearth some dried blood. 'But if it wasn't an accident,' he said softly. 'If it was murder, how was it done?'

'It wasn't murder! He was drunk and fell, and, oh I don't know, probably smashed the side of his head on the boulder. Now give it up.'

Brendan rubbed the side of his head. 'The side of his head, like, his temple, maybe?'

'That's the most vulnerable part of the skull, yes,' she replied, turning away and leaving him without another word.

What was it with people that they were so fascinated with the macabre? First the murder tours in St. Jude Without, now Brendan attempting to be an amateur sleuth. She hated it all, but she had to admit – Ian in his silk top hat had probably at last found his true calling. There was money to be made in death.

· · · ·

H er obvious choice of action was to find Sid and beg him to come back to the cove and set things right. Only Sid could have the power to convince Nate to drop his course of action, and once he'd returned and voiced his objections, the rest of the cove were ready to follow him. But where would he and his biker friends be on this fine June morning? Asleep in their beds still, probably, and she had no idea where they all lived.

Carmel drove into St. John's without the first clue as to where she would track down Sid, and then drove aimlessly around, looking for their motorcycles. Water Street by the harbor was blocked with traffic and there wasn't even a place to park the car, so she headed back up the hill to the coffee shop just down from the Royal Newfoundland Constabulary headquarters. If Darrow was here, he would know in an instant where to track down the missing motorcycle gang, but Darrow was still in Toronto and Carmel was on her own.

It was eleven o'clock before she sat down at a table with an extra-large paper cup of black coffee in front of her. Her doughnut, bought as an afterthought, remained in its bag. She took out her notebook and pen – sometimes it helped to scribble while she thought.

The coffee shop was almost full. In the far section sat the old guys, the same crowd who came in every day, long retired all of them. They knew a lot of what was happening in the town, but they didn't seem the types to be up on biker activities.

The cops at the next table though – they would know if anybody did. She didn't recognize any of them, but lay her pen down and sat back, trying to overhear the conversation between them. That was a bust though, doubtful if she'd get anything out of them. They were all discussing the upcoming rugby tournament this weekend.

Then Herb Laney swaggered into the shop with his usual sidekick, voice loud as if he owned the place. Carmel withdrew her ear, put her head down and pretended to be entranced by the squiggles she had written in the largely empty notebook. She really didn't want a run-in with that oaf this morning.

'Mind if I sit here with you?'

Carmel gave a start and looked up to see, not the menacing figure of Laney but a ragged little man, a harmless man, standing beside her table. She nodded and gestured to the empty seat.

'Sure, go ahead,' she said, just a little uncomfortable at the intrusion. In the year she'd been back in Newfoundland, she'd already lost the big city veneer that came with the enforced rubbing of shoulders with strangers. Here in this province, there was so much space to spare that everything was spread out – houses, roads and green spaces – in fact even where she was sitting, she could look out the window and see the beginning of wilderness across the harbor on the South Side Hills, minutes from the heart of the city itself. And likewise personal space was redefined in this great land. Newfoundlanders might have a reputation for friendliness, but they didn't like to get physically close to people they didn't know, and that included sharing tables with strangers.

She gave the man a little smile and nod to show it was okay.

He removed his shabby gloves and nursed a small coffee in front of him with shaky hands, then began to speak out of politeness.

'Got the cheque today, you know, the cheques come in every two weeks on this day,' he said.

'Mmm,' she replied, trying not to encourage him as she bent her head back down to her notebook.

'Bars don't open till twelve, right,' he said. 'Dying for a beer.'

Bars. Could Sid and company have found a new bar to hang out in? She looked up at her companion.

'Course, there's always the Fiddler's Green down on George Street, they opens at nine, but I can't stand the crowd that goes there,' he informed her. 'I likes the Paddle, myself. There's always a good bunch there on cheque day.'

'Do you happen to know any bars where bikers might hang out?' The little man appeared to be knowledgeable about the seedier bars in the city.

'You don't want to be going there, missus,' he said, affronted. He moved his face out of the glare of the sunlight through the window. 'They're a hard crowd, they are. I don't think you'd fit in. Might want to try one of the nice places, down on Water Street.'

'It's not that I'm looking for a place to drink,' she explained, giving a small smile to show she was neither offended nor implying that there was anything wrong with wanting a bit of alcohol before noon. 'I'm really looking for some bikers, I need to get hold of them, and I don't know where to find them.'

He shook his head. 'I dunno about that,' he replied. 'You shouldn't be at it. But if you really want to know, there's the Sports Bar over on Boncloddy.'

Carmel racked her memory of the winding St. John's streets. 'Is that over off LeMarchant Road?'

'Yup,' the man said on his inhale.

'When do they open, do you know?'

'Sure they never closes,' he said, tapping his nose with his index finger. 'They're a... private club. They might let you in, they might not.'

She stood up, taking her coffee in hand. The bar was not five minutes' walk away, and surely there would be someone who might know Sid's whereabouts. She could leave the car in the parking lot where it was.

'Don't forget your doughnut, missus,' the little man said wistfully.

'You can have it,' she said. 'I'm not really hungry.'

27

S he put her sunglasses back on as she walked outside the coffee shop onto Harvey Road. The sun was hot on her arms even here up on the crest of the hill where it would usually be windy, and the brightness glared off the concrete and pavement with hardly any trees or greenery to soften it. She found Boncloddy soon enough, a tiny residential street except for the discreetly run-down sign of the Sports Bar in the middle of it.

The road was empty save for the small blank faced row houses perched right at the sidewalk's edge. No one was about, not even a stray cat. A chip bag flapped listlessly though there was no wind.

The blinds were drawn in the single plate glass window of the Sports Bar, and the neon sign unlit so early in the day. No motorcycles littered the pavement in front – this was not good. She grasped the door handle anyway and pulled. It opened smoothly.

The first thing she saw on the inner porch glass door was a sticker depicting a skull and wing, placed right at eye level so there was no missing it. Damn – was this a real Hell's Angels stronghold? She'd heard about the mainland biker gangs moving into the province but never dreamed they would be so bold as to have such an obvious presence in the city.

She paused. What was she doing here? Sid and his friends, well she called them a biker gang, but that was only because they all drove motorcycles and wore leather jackets. With their own insignia, true, but they weren't real bikers, not in this league. She had just that moment convinced herself to leave, to turn and flee, when the inner door opened and a man in leather pants and vest fixed her in his gaze.

'C'n I help you?'

She forced herself to look up, way up. Jeez, this guy was tall. And skinny, except for his round pot belly. This was not the hardened killer she was expecting. Her shoulders lost a bit of their tension.

He must be sixty years old at least and looked more like an out of shape college professor than a hard-assed biker. Yeah, he had a beard, sort of, a goatee that was pure white and looked soft like Santa's beard should be, sort of fluffy. His eyes were soft too, a kindly expression behind the round tortoiseshell frames and the wrinkles at the corner looked like he laughed a lot. She felt herself relax, and she placed a bright smile on her face.

'I don't know,' she replied. 'If you can help me, that is. I hope so. I'm looking for Sid.'

He continued to look at her pleasantly. 'Sid,' he said. 'Does Sid have a last name?'

Now he had her stumped. The crowd in St. Jude Without didn't really go for last names in their introductions. Phonse and Brigid were both Ryans, and everybody in the cove was related somehow, so she took a chance.

'Ryan?'

'Sid Ryan...' The man appeared to be thinking, then shook his head. 'Can't say I know him.'

So that might not be his last name. She tried again. 'A little shorter than you, dark hair, long moustache...' Carmel twiddled her fingers around her cheeks to demonstrate Sid's magnificent handlebars.

'Oh, Sid!'

How many men with motorcycles and leathers were named Sid in this town, for God's sake? It wasn't that common a name.

'I don't know where you'd find him at this hour,' the man continued. 'But you can come in and wait if you want. He'll be along at some point in the day, I'm sure.'

He held the inner door open to welcome her into the private bar.

'I haven't really got all day to wait around for him,' she hesitated. 'But perhaps I could leave him a message?'

'Yeah, yeah, no problem,' he said. 'Come on in though, don't stay out in the porch.'

She followed him in to the dark interior. Lit only by the fluorescent lights above the bar, there wasn't much to see except for bottles lined up by the mirror, and the scarred wooden bar itself that ran along the length of the room. She had a dim impression of tables and chairs scattered in the depths.

'My name's Dave, by the way,' he said. He walked through the opened half door and placed himself behind the bar. 'What'll you have?'

Carmel shook her head and held up her half-drunk paper coffee cup. 'I'm good, thanks,' she said.

'Hey, come on! The sun's over the yard arm somewhere,' he wheedled. His voice was surprisingly high-pitched for such a tall man.

'No really, I'll just write out a message for Sid, if you wouldn't mind passing it on to him,' she replied, laying her paper coffee cup on the bar before she hauled the notebook out of her purse.

'I make a wicked martini,' he said coquettishly as if she hadn't spoken.

Jeez, was he flirting with her and trying to get her drunk?

'Seriously, no,' she told him in as firm a voice as she could without sounding rude. In the harsh yet inadequate light from the fixtures, she began to write. But what could she say? *The cove is falling apart and we need you back.* Yeah, that was sure to appeal. Sid had already warned them this would happen. Okay, then. *You were right, please come help us clean up the mess.* That wouldn't work either, would only send him running in the other direction.

A writer should be able to handle this simple task, but she was conscious of Dave looking at her book and trying to read upside down. Carmel realized she wouldn't be able to write too much on the note, for this guy would no doubt read it before handing it over to Sid.

'So,' Dave said as he leaned his elbows on the bar, far too near for comfort. 'You seeing this Sid?'

Carmel glanced up at him quickly before putting her head back down. 'No.'

His breath was rank, as if he subsisted on coffee and hard liquor and not much else. He moved even closer.

'No ring, though, you're not married,' he noted. 'Got a guy, or are you in the market?'

Oh God, he was leering at her! This was too much. She brought her notebook closer and hunched over it. If he was her only possible contact with Sid she didn't want to piss him off, but she was just about ready to throw up.

'Could take you for a ride on the hawg someday,' he continued in his suggestive manner.

Carmel suddenly became aware that they were no longer alone in the bar, sensing movement in the corner of her eye and feeling the hot presence of bodies surrounding her. They must have slipped in the back door.

She glanced up, wildly searching for Sid in the press around her, but she was out of luck. The new people, these bikers, were the real thing. She was surrounded by hairy guys in leather and denim, and they looked out of sorts to find a stranger in their midst.

And they were all really big men, like middle-aged jocks gone to seed through hard living and long nights. What had she gotten herself into? Now, right now, was the moment Sid and his buddies should walk casually in through the door and save her.

But it didn't appear to be happening. Carmel was on her own, there no cavalry riding to her rescue.

So she did the most sensible thing she could think of. Carmel leaped off the bar stool and ripped the note from the book. She hurriedly scribbled Sid's name on the back and stuffed the book back into her purse. 'I gotta go now,' she said in a rush. 'Pass that on to Sid, would you? Thanks-see-you-later.'

She barrelled through the first opening she saw, a space of light between two burly shoulders and was amazed to see them part and let her pass. The daylight suddenly grew brighter as the inner door opened. She aimed for it only to be brought up solid against the bulk of not Sid, but Inspector Laney himself.

'What have we here then?' Carmel found herself staring at Laney's chest, the tie askew and the shirt grubby. Above his collar there were bristles missed by his morning shave. 'Now what are you up to?'

The darkened room went totally silent, all eyes on her. She was really sunk now. Not only had she infiltrated the bikers' lair, she must have been followed by the cops and led them right to the Hells Angels headquarters. Crap. This morning was not going as she planned.

'Friend of yours, guys?'

'S'alright, she's with me,' Dave said, his small lips pursed smugly behind his fluffy white goatee.

'That so?' Laney said. 'Very interesting. Ver-r-ry interesting, wouldn't you say?' He turned to his cohort, who laughed back in a nasty way.

'Inspector Darrow would find that interesting,' he agreed, being too unimaginative to find a synonym.

'He hasn't turned his back for a week, and she's already in the arms of the Hell's Angels,' Laney observed. 'Wait till Darrow hears about this one.'

'I'm not...' Carmel was ready to scream with frustration.

And so she did, as there appeared to be no other action to take. Clenching her fists and letting her vocal cords loose, she screamed. Every single one of the men quickly stepped back, even Laney, all of them staring at her with dismay and with the common thought that this one was too crazy to mess with.

'She's not with me,' Dave said, shaking his head. 'She's nuts.' She heard a murmur of agreement from the other men behind her.

Carmel took a deep breath and plunged past Laney and into the bright glare of the sunshine outside, then ran, ran back towards her car in the parking lot, crossing streets against the lights and in front of buses, not seeing anything in her path, just like the crazy woman they must all think she was.

In the safety of her car with the doors locked and the windows up, she could now pause for a breath. Damn! She'd left her coffee there. Well, she certainly wasn't going back for it.

What had she gone and done now? Carmel had merely meant to look for Sid, to plead with him to return to the cove and talk sense into the crowd, to Nate, to get them to drop this whole stupid contest before it erupted into all-out war between them and the neighboring Bell Island.

But she'd managed to get herself tangled up with Hell's Angels, of all people, and led the police right to their door. Never mind Laney getting back to Darrow to tell him she was now a biker's moll or whatever they were called.

What with Gen's threats against her, she wondered who wasn't out to get her now?

And it wasn't even noon yet. She banged her head against the steering wheel, but that only set off the car horn, drawing even more attention to herself.

28

Back in St. Jude Without, it was gearing up to be another touristy day full of fun and scams as the cove's inhabitants picked themselves up from the detritus of the large brawl and put renewed vigor into salvaging the contest. The fiasco hadn't discouraged visitors, instead, they streamed into the village as if to see for themselves how bad it really was there.

There was nowhere for her to park in front of her house, for her private driveway was taken up by a vintage pickup truck dating from the early nineteen-seventies, green in color. Old, yes, but in perfect condition. Gleaming in the sunlight as if it were freshly buffed and polished, it hearkened back to a gentler time, an easier time, an age when all the kids and dogs and neighbors would be loaded into the back, never mind safety or seatbelts, and the whole group would chug off to a relaxed day by the sea. Although the back of this truck was fitted out to be a camper, the really old-fashioned kind no longer seen these days with the bed sitting over the cab. It was a big rig, designed to hold the perfect family.

Melody's kin had arrived from across the water, and it looked like they were here to stay. She stared at the vehicle hard, as if by mere force of desire she could wish it away, but it remained solidly in place.

Carmel paused on her path to the front steps and looked wildly around the cove. Was there no one around she could speak to in order to avoid going home? Brigid? Phonse or Ian? No, they were at their businesses, busking and clowning. And there was no way she would interrupt Nate and Tina, whatever they might be doing, she shuddered to think.

It was her own house, dammit. Why shouldn't she just go up those steps and clear them all out? She girded her loins and strode up the few steps. The whole packing lot of them – they had to go.

The wooden front door was open, with the screen door clasped to allow the breeze into the house but keeping insects out.

'Hi, you must be Carmel! I'm Nancy,' said a voice behind her screen, then it opened silently, its usual squeal noticeably absent, and the owner of the voice beamed out of the space.

Carmel did a double take. She could have been looking at Melody, if her guest had lost fifty pounds, dressed quietly and turned her mouth up instead of down. The same blonde hair, but hers was neatly trimmed in a bob, not fried from a bad perm. The same stature. The resemblance between the two was astounding, but served to make the differences stand out even more.

'Yeah, we're twins,' Nancy said as she laughed. 'She didn't warn you? I really want to thank you for letting us all meet here. We'll be out of your hair the minute we get the kids' mess cleaned up!'

Carmel breathed deeply, the better to give her rehearsed speech evicting them all from her home, but she had to pause, for the unfamiliar smell of citrus filled her nose. Someone had broken out her lemon cleaner and even stranger, not a thing was out of place in the living room. The room was tidier than it had been in two months, and dustless. It was all sort of shiny, like a home you might actually want to live in.

She ran a finger along the glowing wooden shelf in the porch. Nothing came off on her finger. The spot where Phonse had signed his name in the dust last month had disappeared.

'Hope you don't mind,' the woman said. 'Just gave the place a quick go-through.'

'That's okay,' Carmel replied, still staring at her dirt-free index finger. 'You can come round anytime.'

Nancy laughed, a silvery chime. 'I had to do something while waiting for that lot to get up and have breakfast and get washed up! Your house isn't that big.'

Nancy leaned in to whisper. 'Look, I know her kids can be a bit of a handful. I really want to thank you for putting them up. It means so much to all of us.'

Gratitude and house cleaning? Nancy could move in here, Carmel decided. Without her extended family.

'Mel, you got those dishes washed yet?' Nancy sang into the kitchen.

Carmel walked through the short hallway to see Melody at the sink washing and rinsing. She was performing it grumpily, but doing the chore nevertheless. Brendan and the kids were nowhere in sight. She looked up from her task to meet Carmel's eye.

'What sort of place doesn't have a dishwasher?' she demanded in a low voice, glowering at her host.

A man came in through the back door as Carmel entered the room. He was medium height with brown-gray hair and wore jeans and a denim shirt with press lines down the sleeve. He was so clean-cut he shone, and he smelled like fresh laundry.

'Glad to meet you, I'm Boyce,' he said, holding out his hand with a large grin. He was as warm and lovely as his wife. 'Hope you don't mind, I put a bit of oil on all the door hinges while the girls were cleaning up, and I fixed the dripping tap. You just needed a new washer and I had some kicking around the truck.'

She found herself giving thanks again, and then her attention was caught by the shiny gleam of the kitchen window. She was still stunned at the transformation of her home in such a short time. 'You guys... you didn't need to do all this, although I have to say it looks wonderful.'

'Are the kids all ready?' Nancy asked as she bustled into the kitchen.

'They're outside,' Melody told her reluctantly, drying her hands on the last clean tea-towel. 'Probably catching their deaths of a cold.'

LIZ GRAHAM

'It's a gorgeous day, the breeze will blow the stink right off them.' Nancy answered cheerily. 'They're looking a little pale from being inside so much. Video games and TV are such a time suck. They need more fresh air.'

Melody's body tensed and her mouth grew a deeper frown, if that was possible, but she didn't respond to the implied criticism of her parenting skills. 'I'll call them in.'

'No, tell them to come round the front!' Nancy said. 'No sense them trooping all their muck back in here when I just mopped the floors.'

Boyce held the back door open while Melody stomped through, and they both left went in search of the children.

'You even cleaned the floors?' Carmel thought guiltily back a few days. She had been in the middle of doing that when her guests descended and, well, just hadn't gotten back to it.

'No problem,' Nancy told her, then paused and took a deep breath. 'I understand that Melody and her crowd can be a little... difficult. Thank you for putting up with them.'

Carmel found she couldn't stop staring at Nancy. She found it amazing how the two women could be so similar yet different. 'You guys must be identical twins, the resemblance is astounding...'

'Yeah, though we've gone our separate ways in life,' Nancy agreed. 'We're not so close these days. Not since she moved away and married... Brendan.' Her face shuttered for a moment as she turned away.

'So, what happened to your sister?' As soon as the words were out, Carmel realized how rude she sounded. 'I mean, you guys are so very different,' she added quickly.

'That's what families are like sometimes,' Nancy said, not in the least bit offended. Instead, her smile seemed to grow cheerier. She took a cloth in her hand and re-wiped around the sink where her sister had just cleaned. 'I was the popular one, always getting top marks, always had a pile of friends to hang with. Melody, well… she's different, as you say, and she's been like that all her life. Mom and Dad didn't know what to do with her.'

So Melody had been pushy and whiney all her life, according to her twin sister. The woman had demanded to be the center of attention since she'd arrived in the cove – look how she even made her sister come over to see her, instead of simply getting the courage up to face her fears, hopping on the ferry and going back to her home town. No wonder she'd been bullied all her early life as she claimed.

'And what's this about not going over water, anyway?' Carmel casually sat herself at the table. She did feel the tiniest bit uncomfortable at being so nosey, but the writer in her was fascinated by the strange family dynamics that were emerging, and Nancy appeared to be willing to talk.

The other woman gave a martyred sigh, probably not for the first time in her life and took a chair across from Carmel.

'Oh, that girl is so clumsy! She fell over the side of the ferry the last time she left the island, and hasn't been able to get back on a boat since,' she said, then leaned over to whisper. 'She won't admit that it was her own fault she fell. It's all part of the attention seeking, you know? We just work around it. I had to come out to see the kids, I miss them so much!'

'They're really lucky to have you in their lives,' Carmel suggested. 'Family is important.'

'I agree.' Nancy straightened up, then heaved another sigh. 'But Melody is so jealous, she's worried about them liking me more than her.' She looked up at Carmel, her pale blue eyes wide and luminous, with a suggestion of tears around their edges. 'And… you know what's really unfair?'

Carmel shook her head. There was definitely a lot of dysfunction happening there, and Carmel was beginning to have doubts as to whether the problem had stemmed from Melody after all.

Nancy bit her lip. 'Me and Boyce, we can't have children. We've tried every route, but it's not happening. Yet Melody, she can pop them out like puppies.'

She leaned in toward Carmel again, and her eyes were round with disbelief. 'I don't think she even wants them,' Nancy whispered.

Carmel tried to keep a neutral expression on her face, but alarm bells were ringing in her head. This was too much information, it was unnatural for Nancy to make confessions of this magnitude when they'd only just met.

'Those kids probably won't have much of a chance to turn out normal. I try my best. But Melody... there's always one in the bunch, isn't there,' Nancy continued, keeping her voice low. 'Our family would have been so ... perfect, but for Melody being so weird all the time. And her husband – well he tries, but what can he do? He's just a little ineffectual, wouldn't you say?'

'Hmmm,' Carmel said. Yes, there was definitely something off about all, something unsettling. True, she didn't like Melody or Brendan from what she'd seen so far, and she resented their continued presence in her home, but this was the woman's own twin sister badmouthing her to a virtual stranger and no matter how Melody acted, this wasn't right. 'I think they're waiting for you outside.'

Nancy trilled again, that tinkley, silvery laugh, like shards of glass falling. She flashed her bright white teeth at Carmel. 'That's a change, it's usually me trying to round up all of them! Better go before they all disperse into the four winds again.'

And with that she strode confidently out the door.

29

That was one strange family. If she didn't know better, and if she didn't so heartily dislike Melody, she would say the woman was the victim of family scapegoating. Maybe even worthy of her sympathy.

Carmel shivered. 'Sometimes I'm glad I have no family,' she said aloud.

'Speaking of families, they're still here,' a voice hissed in her ear. 'You're not doing anything to get rid of them.'

She whirled around, but Jem wasn't visible. Not even a whiff of grave in the air. 'Where are you?'

'I am always present,' he replied, this time sounding like he was over the kitchen sink.

'Show yourself.'

'Nay, I will not.'

'You did the other day.'

'Not with the demon one here,' he replied.

'Melody and the kids are all outside. Besides, didn't we agree it was your job to chase them out of the house for good?' Carmel said, getting impatient with him. She cast her eye around her shining kitchen, and sniffed the fresh lemony goodness of the air. 'Although, maybe it's not so bad. Nancy cleaned my house, and the family's only going to be here for a couple more days. I could live with this, I think. And if you don't show yourself, it actually smells good in here.'

'Oh, woe...'

'Give it a rest, will you? It's only a few more days,' she scolded him. 'Don't put the scary ghost act on for me. Besides, what do you know? You can't even go outside the house.'

Silence greeted her. 'Well?' But he was no longer answering her.

• • • •

The sun was beating down on the rocks outside in the cove, yet it didn't feel hot because of the strong breeze off the water. This was the time of year when people sported sunburns, achieving them unexpectedly because the air felt cool yet the sun's rays were sneaky and brutal to exposed skin, unexpectedly burning through the cool wind.

There were kids everywhere in St. Jude Without today, set loose in the perceived safety of this isolated cove with only one road leading out of it. The parents meanwhile sat back on the boulders and grassy fields and in Vee's tea-room, anywhere they could find to get out of the constant wind bearing down on them.

Carmel ducked inside the church to speak with Nate, to check up on him. She hoped he had found time to sleep, for last night he'd looked to be burning the candle at both ends.

She found only Vee in the building, standing by the long church window by her table with the strong box and staring vacantly off down over the cove.

'What's up, Mrs. Ryan?' Carmel asked her. 'You don't look well.'

Vee turned her head and met Carmel's gaze. The past week hadn't treated her well and, like the rest of the cove, she was becoming frayed around the edges. Her hair was back into its constant rollers, yet these were not fixed in tightly and the curls were escaping into frizz. Her once white apron was stained with blueberries and tea. Vee Ryan looked as if she had aged ten years since the beginning of the FaceBook competition.

'I can't do this anymore,' she said in a listless voice, and sat herself down in the nearest chair.

The front door of the church opened and a family of ten trooped in – mother, father, a couple of grands and a slew of kids. They looked around and spotting the only clean table, swarmed over to it. Vee didn't even register their entrance.

'I've had it,' she continued dazedly. 'I'm not getting anything else done – it's all work work work here. When the cafe's closed, I have to spend my time making more teabuns and buying bread and baloney – and why? They're only going to gobble it all down again. There's no end to it. Phonse got neither clean shirt to wear, sure he'll have to go to Walmart to get more underwear for himself.'

Forty-five year old Phonse still lived with his mother, and she did all the chores of daily life for him. Including washing every bit of laundry he wore and cooking every bite he put in his mouth.

'Don't you have help here?' Carmel was sure Vee had organized the tea-room with her cronies from down on the point, but they were nowhere to be seen right now.

Vee flapped her hand. 'They all took off,' she replied. 'Said I was too bossy and ordering them around, and it wasn't no fun for them anymore. Plus I wasn't paying them enough, they said.' She gave a half-hearted sneer. 'They weren't worth what they were getting, let me tell you.'

She noticed the family of guests for the first time. Hard to miss, for they were waving their arms for her attention, but her eyes glanced off them like teflon.

'Sure, someone had to organize it all,' Vee said to Carmel defensively. 'Never knew there was so much too it, this business stuff. Nate said the money would roll in, all we had to do was stand around and collect it.'

Carmel remembered having a conversation much like this with Phonse just the other day. 'Yeah, business is like that,' she said. 'You have to keep putting something in, in order to get something out.'

'Well shag all this,' Vee replied. 'I'm going to have to start buying tea-buns from the bakery. I just can't keep on top of it all.'

'It's only for a few days,' Carmel said, and searched inside herself for the wherewithal to find kind words for the woman. 'Then the contest will be over, and everything can go back to normal. Just keep telling yourself that. You can do it.'

She pasted an encouraging smile on her face. It was killing her to be nice to Vee Ryan after all the rotten things the older woman had said about her behind her back and even to her face. The pair had a short but unpleasant history together, even after Carmel insisted she didn't want to marry her son and become the second Mrs. Ryan.

'I don't suppose you couldn't look after those folks over there, could you?'

'No,' Carmel said quickly. 'Sorry, no. This is your baby. Like I said, it's just for a couple of days, then you'll be free. Although, it wouldn't be such a bad thing to end all this foolishness. It's tearing everyone apart.'

This got Vee's attention and rose her from her stupor somewhat. Any opportunity to disagree with Carmel was a welcome one, even if in her present state she could only summon up a half-hearted response. 'We're not quitters,' she told her, crossing her arms across her considerable bosom. 'I'll see this to the end, even on my own. Think of the money I'll have. I won't be sharing it with the likes of you, neither, so don't go thinking I will.'

'I don't want your money, Vee,' Carmel said. 'Or your son.'

Vee looked outside again. 'My, that Tina's some girl, isn't she?' she said, still totally ignoring her customers. They were getting a bit impatient, and some in the party were preparing to leave again. 'She's like a whirlwind, don't know where the lass gets all the energy. She should get to know my Phonse better. Bet she keeps a clean house.'

Even in the midst of her doldrums, Vee couldn't help making snarky remarks to Carmel. 'I think Tina has her eye on Nate,' Carmel replied. 'Anyway, if you don't move fast, you're going to lose those customers. And their money.'

'Ohhh,' Vee groaned as she hoisted herself off the chair. 'Not like I have anything to serve them, just some Campbell's soup from yesterday. Better see what they want.'

Carmel watched as the older woman reluctantly stomped over to the table. It wasn't just Vee who was feeling the stress, and Carmel didn't know how much longer they could keep this up. Something had to give, and soon.

30

She found Nate behind the make-shift partition which curtained
off the tea-room from his headquarters. Things were a bit livelier
here, but it was because Tina was still fairly fresh to the whole
business and hadn't burnt herself out yet. She bustled back and forth
between the computer and printer, barking out orders no one
listened to, totally in her element and loving her new purpose in life.

Nate was in much the same state as Mrs. Ryan by this point. Too
many days of no sleep, too much coffee and other substances had
worn him down to listlessness. He stared off into the distance, his
coffee cup turned cold by his side.

'Nate,' Carmel said, then had to repeat herself. She shook his arm
to bring him back into the world. 'How's it going?'

He heaved a sigh, and pushed some papers on to the floor from
the nearest chair so Carmel could sit. 'I don't know about all this,' he
said. 'That fight the other night at the barbeque and all those photos
published on FaceBook – that really brought the likes down. Those
Bell Islanders are killing us.'

'Yeah, the whole cove is hurting from this,' Carmel noted. 'Do
you think we should just all call it quits? Before someone gets hurt, I
mean.'

Nate was back to staring off in the distance – she wasn't sure he'd
taken in her suggestion. Or perhaps he did and was agreeing to it,
deep down inside his mind.

'Who's being a 'Negative Nellie', then?' Tina had certainly heard
her. 'None of that kind of talk here, Carmel, if you please. We're
going to win this competition, and that's just the beginning.'

She set a hot coffee in front of Nate and whisked the stale cup
away. 'Drink this down, babe. You've got to give a rallying speech in
a bit. Don't want the troops to get discouraged.'

Nate groaned and brought the mug to his mouth.

'Now the other night was just a bump in the road,' Tina continued. 'You'll see, people will realize what the crowd across the water have done, and there'll be lots more likes as the day goes on. We just have to show the world we're not down for the count yet!'

She turned away. 'I'll just go out and make sure the sound system is up and running.' She left the church through the smokers' entrance.

Carmel quickly turned to Nate. She only had a couple of minutes before the dragon fiend returned. 'Look Nate, we have to stop this craziness,' she said.

'It is crazy,' he agreed. His eyes were reddened and tired, and the coffee wasn't doing much to revive him. 'But you heard the dame, we can't stop now. The train has left the station and can only go forward.'

'More of a train wreck, if you ask me,' she replied. 'I don't have a good feeling about all this. It's time to call it quits.'

His head perked up at the sound of that.

'What, just drop it all?'

'Yeah,' Carmel said, drawing nearer to him. But not too close, for Tina hadn't quite managed to get him fully cleaned up yet. 'Just... let Bell Island win the stupid competition, what odds? We can go back to being quiet little St. Jude Without, living our lives in peace.'

'Peace...' Nate stared off through the transept window at the sparsely treed mountain behind the church.

'Now Mr. Mayor, you got that speech rehearsed yet?' Tina had returned, and winked at Carmel as she said this.

'Mayor?!'

'Just our little joke,' Tina said. 'Nate here is destined for big things, you know, and I'll be behind him every step of the way.'

'That's a bit... sudden,' Carmel said, looking from one to the other. 'When did these plans arise?'

Tina placed her hands on Nate's shoulders, firmly claiming her territory. 'We discussed it in great detail last night,' she said. 'Among other things, of course.'

'You guys just met three days ago.'

'We've known each other for ages,' Tina retorted, a tad defensively. 'Remember, at the Archives in the spring? That was, what, two whole months ago.'

'Right.'

'Anyhoo,' Tina continued airily. 'You can't fight love, right? And my Nate'll be going places, just you watch and see. He can do anything with me behind him.'

Carmel sat back to better judge the effects of Tina's words on her new boyfriend. Nate had always been a rough character, an independent kind of guy. Sure, he had plans, but they were mostly conceived in a haze of marijuana and alcohol, like any of the misbegotten plans of this cove. He was no more ready to settle down and be led by a woman than Phonse was.

Nate rather sheepishly met Carmel's eye and reached up his hand to cover Tina's. He looked a little dazed, but slowly nodded his assent.

'Now Nate,' Tina continued briskly. 'You have a speech to give. I've got it all written out, don't stray from the main message. Remember, we have the press out there, you have to shine. Go give it to them, babe! Tell them how we're winning the contest.'

She inspected him from head to foot, then tucked in the loose shirt tails and, reaching into her pocket, withdrew a tissue which she spit on and scrubbed at a spot on his face.

He winced and drew away.

'There, you're gorgeous again. Go on, now, I'll be right behind you.'

Both women watched as Nate lumbered to his feet. He set Clyde's fedora on his head and headed out of the building.

'He doesn't look too hot,' Carmel murmured. 'I think he needs a break. Sure you're not pushing him too much?'

Tina turned on her, the light sparkling off her oversize glasses, almost spitting as she spoke. 'He's fine!' she said with vehemence. 'He can do anything with me by his side.'

She must have caught the expression on Carmel's face at this outburst, for then she visibly relaxed her shoulders and tried to lighten the mood again.

'Of course he's tired, but it'll all be worth it in the end,' she continued, then a slow satisfied smile crept onto her face. 'He'll thank me for this, because I can see his dream, and there's nothing going to get in our way.'

Tina held her head high and made to follow Nate outside, but then she paused turning to fix Carmel with a beady eye.

'By the way, your visitors are not happy.'

'Brendan and Melody? Tell me something I don't know,' Carmel said with feeling. 'She's been complaining since the moment she got here. I really wanted to discuss this whole business with you...'

'Did you know she's threatening to sue the cove?' Tina broke in. 'She's claiming that we endangered their lives because her people from Bell Island caused the brawl. And because her kids got sick on the hot dogs.'

'Sounds like Melody.'

'You need to solve this issue, Carmel, or they'll ruin all our work so far.'

Solve the issue? Carmel was fervently hoping the ghost would do something, anything, to get rid of the family.

'If you don't take action, I will.' Tina's face was unreadable as she turned to follow her lover out the door.

Carmel also left the church but by the front entrance. Passing through the tea-room which was now buzzing with customers again, she saw that Vee must have gotten her second wind and was managing quite well single-handedly. Perhaps she was only kept going through pure spite at Carmel's words, but still, it was working and she was holding the fort down, dishevelled and stained and crabby as she was.

Outside the wind had not abated, but this hadn't discouraged the crowds. Perhaps the fiasco of the other night had peaked people's interest even more, and they were coming in swarms to see the cove of ill-repute. Gen's plan to scupper St. Jude Without's chances may have backfired, for far from discouraging people to visit the cove, it seemed like everyone and his dog had to come to see what the fuss was about and hopefully witness another incident.

The press was out in full force too of course, a couple of TV vans blocking the only road. Their reporters and camera crew stayed well on the fringes of the massed gathering, under strict orders to keep their expensive equipment out of the crossfire. One intrepid reporter that she recognized, however, didn't have such restrictions, and was right in the midst of the crowd, clicking his camera at every angle.

'Hey, Josh,' she said casually, coming upon the young man she had last seen outside her house on the news. 'You're not with the TV crowd anymore?'

He flicked his head in recognition. 'Them?' he sniffed. 'There's no room for me with all those egos,' he said. 'I've switched my career direction. I'm a free agent now, I can go where the news takes me. I find the news.'

'Ah.' She nodded, immediately understanding. 'You're freelancing. Well, good for you. Getting lots of shots, I see.'

'Yeah.' His face took on a wistful look. 'Wish I'd been here for the brawl, though. I could have sold that story five times over.'

And then like a dog chasing a squirrel, Josh found something else photo worthy and he dashed off into the crowd to capture the events.

'Well, stick around, you never know what might happen,' she called out after him, only half-joking, not realizing how prophetic her words would turn out to be.

31

B ut the mood was not a happy one, Carmel could sense as she
stood near the church door overlooking the cove. Hordes of
disgruntled people were milling about, looking for and not finding
some new entertainment. They herded together to avoid the sharp
wind, which only served to concentrate the ill-feelings and the
mutterings, and there was some loud talk of wanting their money
back.

The ponies down on the point of land past Vee Ryan's house
had reverted to their feral state, she could see. They ran and kicked
in their enclosure, not letting anyone close, and they gnashed their
teeth at the children who lined the fence, shivering in the sharpness
of the breeze and crying with disappointment that they could not
have their promised pony rides. Even from up here, Carmel could see
the whites flashing in the ponies' eyes.

Along the road, the large sign with the image of Captain Jem
had suffered too. Perhaps it was the wind which had damaged the
mechanism of his arm beckoning a welcome into St. Jude Without,
or perhaps it was simply the result of lackadaisical jerry-rigged
workmanship, but his bent arm had caught on the pirate's long nose.
It looked like good old Jeremy was leering down at the people while
picking his nose.

But nobody was paying attention to that.

And suddenly she found herself face to face with her nemesis.
Her guest. Melody.

'I'm calling the police!' Melody threatened her, wildly waving
her Iphone in front of Carmel's face. Melody's hair was mussed and
her pink lipstick smeared across her cheek. 'That old goat bit me!'
She was pointing back towards the farm.

'Clyde?' Carmel asked, trying to fit her mind around this new
catastrophe. She'd seen the farmer threaten to shoot, or beat with his

walking cane, but had never heard of him biting before. Besides, she was pretty sure his perfect pearly yellows were false.

'The goat!' Melody screamed at her, then turned to show the rip in her green jeans with the white of her undies showing through.

'Oh, the *goat* goat.' It was a small relief to know that Clyde had not turned feral along with the ponies, but that was short-lived.

'I'm calling the cops on him! They have to put that animal down. What if I get rabies?' She began to punch in the numbers.

Her husband appeared by her side, grimaced at Carmel then grabbed for his wife's phone. 'He didn't draw blood, Melody,' Brendan yelled at her. 'Stop making such a fuss!' They tussled for a moment, the taller man looming over his short wife.

Their noise was drawing a lot of attention from the hither-to bored crowd, and people began to press forward, hoping for more action. And it was all getting recorded for later consumption on social media.

Melody held her phone out of his reach and her plaintive cry rose over the crowd. 'That crazy old man had a gun, and he was going to shoot Tyler, I swear. All my boy wanted to do was play with the goat. We need the police here!'

A woman in the crowd gasped. 'Shooting a child! Oh my God, a child's been shot!'

'No...' Carmel began to shout out, to deny there had been bloodshed.

'Maybe if Tyler did as I told him, the dog wouldn't have knocked him down,' Brendan said to her through gritted teeth. 'You have those kids so spoiled, they don't listen to a word I say.'

'Maybe there's another reason they don't respect you!' Melody shouted at her husband. 'Ever think of that? Maybe you don't deserve their respect, huh? Look at you, you're a fat slob, and you're weak!'

Brendan's face was blood red behind his spectacles, and if steam could erupt from his ears, it would. Their three offspring were now huddled slightly apart from their parents in the sheltering arms of Nancy, all three screeching their own discontent.

Nancy shook her head and grimaced around at the people watching on the scene domestic disharmony, as if to say, what could she do? Not her fault the pair were such lousy parents. Just another scene in the life of Brendan and Melody, but she was doing her best with the kids.

'Mommy and Daddy don't mean to be so angry,' she told them in a voice pitched loud enough to carry. 'They can't help themselves. It's not your fault.'

Finally, loud feedback from the mic filled the air, drowning out even Brendan's shouted words at his wife and diverting the attention of all around.

'Whoa, that's loud! Attention, one two three,' Nate's voice filled the air of the cove. 'Can you hear me?'

With Tina's help, Nate had pulled himself together admirably. She must have placed the tie around his neck and buttoned up his suit jacket against the wind.

Melody had gotten clear of her husband long enough to dial 9-1-1. 'Police?' she shouted over the noise of the electronic feedback. 'I'm calling to report a murder attempt in St. Jude Without!'

'Hey, you two down there,' Nate said from the platform erected by the side of the church, talking to Carmel's guests. 'Button it, would you? I'm trying to speak here.'

His voice echoed across the cove, bouncing down from the cliffs of the granite mountain above them and down the point, out to sea. Melody looked up from her phone call and met his eyes, outrage on her face.

'I'd like to welcome you all here to St. Jude Without today...'

'This place is a sham!' Melody screamed loud enough to be heard even over the loud sound system. 'You guys couldn't run a hen-house! My little boy was almost killed at the petting zoo!'

'And that tea-room,' she continued as she whirled and faced the crowd. 'That old woman's filthy and the tables haven't been cleaned and all they serve are rock-hard tea-buns! I could make better than that!'

Vee Ryan, standing at the door to the church, clutched her pilled acrylic cardigan over her apron and looked like she was ready to jump into the crowd and wrestle Melody to the ground for her words. No one, but no one, ever dissed Vee Ryan and got away without a fight.

The attention of the crowd was shifting back away from Nate and to Melody and her outrageous claims. Nate, being a natural politician at heart, worked the crowd and the hecklers.

'Sure, there's only a goat and a couple of cows at the petting zoo,' Nate spoke genially into the mic, smiling at everyone in turn. 'No lions or bears there! Nothing to cause harm.'

'The old man!' Melody's voice was hoarse as she tried to project over the sound system. 'He almost shot my boy, and then he was attacked by a huge black dog!'

Loud gasps came from the crowd gathered by the church, then the murmuring started, spreading through the assembled group like the inexorable ocean tide.

Tina was keeping a grim eye on the altercation, and she reached over to turn up Nate's volume a notch. She gave a hard look at Melody and Brendan, and if they'd been paying attention to her, it might have struck fear into their souls. Nate's voice grew to a pitch almost unbearable as he poured his oily deep rumble onto the raging waters.

But Melody now had the crowd in her hand. Only those closest could hear her wild allegations, yet those few passed on and expanded her words to the people next to them, and so the rumors grew and spread like a grassfire in the thirsty crowd.

Clyde appeared at the edges of the mass, a stick in hand and black dog by his side. Without his fedora, his sparse hair stuck off in all directions, and he searched the crowd furiously. Melody, because of her disadvantaged height, was not seen by him, and probably just as well, for his eyes were sparking and he looked ready to rip at someone.

Nancy stood by, the kids almost forgotten by her side and a tiny smile on her face as she watched her sister's moment in the spotlight. Melody's allegations grew, her arms flapping wildly, as she spoke of ghosts and demon ponies and rabid goats in the cove of St. Jude Without. The TV cameras had swivelled away from Nate and were fully trained on her now.

Nate looked over to Tina, a panicked expression on his face. She made a slicing motion with her hand and shook her head. Crowd control was needed, but neither of them knew what to do.

Carmel poked Ian, who was standing right next to her with his fiddle in hand, dumb-founded at the scene playing out before him.

'Can you play that thing?' she yelled at him. 'Get up there and provide a musical interlude or something!' Carmel pushed him toward the stage.

The Irish man seized his opportunity for the spotlight, leaping up onto the makeshift platform and adjusting the mic so as to get the full effect from his fiddle. Tina, seeing what he was about, quickly turned the sound level up even more in an effort to drown out Melody's high pitched screams which were by now not making any sense. Another ear-splitting feedback sounded and then the cove was filled with frenzied gypsy music.

Some people at the back of the crowd, who hadn't yet heard all of Melody's accusations, well, they started dancing, because the music coming from Ian was loud, crowding out any conversation and it grabbed them. This was all part of the entertainment, and when music played one must dance to show what a good time was being had by all. So they danced, weaving in and out and back and forth and grabbed others to join their reel.

And so the dancing spread throughout the mass of people congregated before the old church, urged on by the devilish tunes played by Ian. Shouts and cries of encouragement sounded, egging Ian on to play faster and faster.

Only Melody and her family weren't dancing. And of course, Clyde and Vee and the rest of the inhabitants of St. Jude Without.

The kids down in the meadow by Vee's house had by now given up all hope for the ponies and a movement had began with a trickle, then as they saw their peers moving on it, became a mass streaming towards the bouncy castle where Phonse stood guard with his stop watch and money box. He hadn't bothered with the clown get-up today, because he realized it was an unnecessary accouterment. The kids were coming for the bouncy castle not for a clown, and it advertised itself by being visible from every spot in the cove. His stained white t-shirt echoed the story of Vee's woes.

Melody's children were bawling at the top of their lungs by this time, fed by the unhappiness and anger coming from their parents. Nancy grabbed the littlest sprog in her arms and shouted to the others in a fake happy voice. 'Come on, let's join the other kiddies in the bouncy castle!'

Melody, of course, had refused them entrance to that dirty, germ-laden place, which had made it all the more appealing to their little eyes. Auntie Nancy had to have been aware of the ban, yet she tore through the crowd and headed down to Snellen's Field, trailing a growing mass of children in her wake and joining the other stream of little ones coming from the pony field until she looked like a very short and modern Pied Piper.

Melody and Brendan left off their screaming match as they watched in horror as the children, their own offspring in the lead, quickly poured their way down the gravelled road and into the field where Phonse stood hunched over his cigarettes and brown paper bag.

'Look what you've done!' Melody shouted at Brendan as her short chubby legs set off to follow the children. 'They can't go in there! I forbid it!'

Brendan's face was more infused than ever as he too took off, hurling incomprehensive abuse at his life partner. It was as if he'd been storing up a decade or so of resentment and anger, and it had finally reached a breaking point and he could no longer hold back the tide.

The rest of the crowd, those who weren't caught up in the crazy dance, they set off too, just because it seemed that's where the party was going. And once they started, the rest followed, dancing their way down the potholed road and into the tramped down grass of Snellen's Field, and thus the trickle became a full-fledged river of bodies heading toward Phonse and grimy red and yellow bobbing castle.

And Ian's music hurried them on their way in the frenzied outpouring which covered the cove like a miasma of evil vapors. He nudged the volume dial up to eleven with his foot, delighted to have full control at last and no one to yell at him to turn it down. His electric notes ran up the mountain and down again, filling every crevice and spreading out to sea, perhaps over to Bell Island only to bounce off the rocky cliffs and down the shore again. Weeks later, once the events of the day had solidified into local legend, people swore they heard the music that day out in Bay Roberts, on the other side of Conception Bay.

Tina's eyes were set hard, not leaving Melody, the one who had started today's furor, as she stepped down from the stage and cut through the river of bodies, never wavering from her target. Clyde and Vee were heading down to the field, too, Carmel saw, neither of them aware of the others. Even the large black dog hurried down the road, following a trail only his nose could see, leaving splashes of drool behind him. They'd reached the sign of Captain Jem, picking his nose as he swayed in the rising breeze. And still Ian played, as if whipping the wind to ever stronger furies.

In trepidation, Carmel headed down there too, grabbing Nate's arm as she hurried them down to Snellen's Field. She had a terrible feeling this was not going to turn out well.

She watched from a distance as Phonse's cigarette dropped out of his mouth as he realized the tidal wave of people that was now heading his way. He quickly took his stance at the entrance of the inflated castle, legs firmly planted and arms crossed, determined none would get in without paying the entrance fee. And with the size of the crowd bearing down on him, the ticket price was probably rising exponentially in his mind.

But he was swarmed by the children and as one side of the castle was entirely open, he couldn't police all of the flow. He ran from side to side as the kids jumped in behind his back not bothering to remove their shoes.

'Get out of there you little rats!' he roared. 'You there, where's your money? Take off the GD shoes!' He hauled one small girl out of the castle, only to find her place taken by three more as they squeezed past him.

'I'm going to sue you and the whole community!' Melody was screaming at Phonse and she took his arm and held on and refused to let go. By now, he was angrier than Carmel had ever seen and he swung round with his free hand and swatted. It might have knocked her out if he'd connected but her lack of height saved her from the blow. As he shook her off she screamed again.

Nancy gleefully helped the littlest ones in, shouting encouragement all the while. 'You deserve some fun kiddies!' she called. Her eyes were shining.

Finally Phonse leaped into the castle himself, determined to shake every red cent out of every tiny pocket, his brawny shoulders pushing the tiny tots out of the way, those who had no money being tossed bodily out of the entrance, only to be pushed back in by Nancy. She cackled as she did so.

In the midst of the melee and the music and the roar of the wind through the telephone wires, no one heard the rumble of motorcycles at the bend in the mountain, no one saw the Harleys pause with Sid at the helm as he quickly sized up the situation in Snellen's Field, his hand automatically reaching to smooth his luxuriant moustaches. His eyes were narrowed under his German helmet. There were more bikers in the herd than the four or five habitués of the cove, for Sid must have recognized Carmel's panic and brought reinforcements. At the flick of his arm, all the bikers jumped off their steeds, leaving them in the road and they too swarmed down to the action, but their large burly black leathered bodies only added to the confusion.

Meanwhile Ian played on to the few left dancing, all lost in the spell cast by his notes.

By the time Carmel and Nate reached the mass of people surrounding the bouncy castle, the storm was rising. The wind roared down the cove and Captain Jem's image was creaking, loosening from its nails. The sudden easterly wind brought with it dark clouds and the light changed in an instant from the bright sunlit day to an ominous, overcast gray. Hurricane blasts of icy fingers coming straight from the North Atlantic Ocean crept down the exposed necks of the people, yet nothing chilled this feverish crowd.

'Do something!' She yelled at Nate over the whistling wind. An ominous creaking filled the air, ropes and wood bending in the gusts, unable to hold. 'You started all of this – you have to fix it before someone gets hurt!'

Nate could only stare dazed around him like the magician's apprentice, unable to stem the flood he had started.

Josh was in his element, his camera clicking as he dashed and dodged through the crowd. His reporter senses were on high alert, and he knew, just knew deep inside him, that this afternoon might make his career, never mind that he'd missed the fight the other night. He clicked on relentlessly, capturing the tears and the screams, not stopping to help a soul.

Nancy was no longer to be seen at the entrance, and Phonse himself had stepped out of the vibrating inflated castle, giving up the battle and conceding defeat. He'd been outnumbered and he knew when to cash in. Pausing only to check that his pockets were full of coins and none were leaking out, he stumbled his way through the mass of people, shoulders bowed and not watching where he was going. His self-preservation instincts which had gotten him this far in life were on full alert, and he had no intention of being found on the spot in the aftermath.

Melody was also nowhere in sight, but no one noticed. In the sudden darkness caused by the low racing clouds overhead, little could be seen. In these strange shadows, no one was recognizable.

And up on the road, their way blocked by motorcycles and minivans and SUVs parked any which way on the gravel, three police cars whooped their sirens and flashed the red and blue. They'd been sent to the scene by Melody's panicked phone call prior.

All the while, the wind rose, and rose some more, until with a final furious paroxysm, the storm gods blew and the portrait of Captain Jeremiah Ryan finally loosened from its inadequate moorings and sailed over the heads of the crowd, catching onto the red turret of the castle, where it lingered, fighting the air-filled plastic until the heavier weight triumphed. The steady force of the gale blew against the plywood which acted like a sail and it dragged the castle with it, straining the ropes which held it down until the castle gave up the fight and submitted to the wind's dominance, the trapped air inside the inflation straining to join the wild feral airs outside the plastic confines.

Almost everybody ducked at the moment the ropes finally snapped and the loosely hammered-in anchors burst free of the three inches of topsoil of the field. The wooden portrait of Captain Jem, the damage done, clattered off brokenly to the side as the castle, loosed from its moorings, began its slow graceful slide down the meadow. Like a stately galleon in full sail it majestically skimmed over the wild grasses. People ran to get out of its inevitable path while others stared in disbelief at the sight, and nothing could stop the plastic castle with its cargo load of children as it headed down to the beach.

This only lasted for a moment of course, as the hoses keeping it inflated broke away from the machinery and the generator, and as the red and yellow castle sailed down Snellen's Field it deflated quickly on its journey.

Sid's leather-clad army ran toward the flailing ropes but they arrived too late and were unable to catch them. Everyone in the field watched as the drooping castle gently slid with barely a shudder onto the rocky beach and came to rest half in, half out of the white-capped waters of the cove.

A cry of anguish rose up from the innards of the castle as the children, thoroughly doused by their dip into the cold June waters of Conception Bay, realized that the game was over. The plastic castle writhed as if overtaken by alien worms as the children squirmed to find the exit.

And the storm blew itself out as suddenly as it had risen, the wind dancing back out to sea taking the clouds with it. Peace and sunlight suddenly reigned over the cove once again with only a light breeze ruffling the treetops. The squad cars up on the hill had by now ceased their whooping as the police, also too late, ran down on to the field. Ian, having reached the finale of his demonic composition, paused and realized he had no audience left, for even the dancers had been drawn into the drama in the field below.

The new silence was broken only by the cries of the gulls circling overhead like they did when the fishing boats came back to shore, laden with the day's catch. They were always drawn by smell of fresh blood in the air.

The static of police radios cut through the air as everyone stared at the red and yellow deflated castle lying half submerged in the bay, clinging onto the land by the plastic caught on the boulders of the beach. Within moments though, the sound of helicopters filled the space above St. Jude Without – large Cougars, air ambulances, even a small private copter belonging to a former Premier, for the airport was no distance away as the crow flies, just over the mountain, and a panicked alert had called everyone in to help rescue the kids.

Every manner of boat came to assist, too, although it turned out they weren't needed. Private yachts from the Holyrood Basin, dories and fishing boats from Portugal Cove and beyond, even a couple of launches from deeper into Conception Bay. And there – yes, there was the distinctive colors of the Whale Rescue team's zodiac, that intrepid band who spent dangerous hours on the ocean in every weather freeing whales entangled in fishing lines and nets. The marine distress signal had sounded loud and clear everywhere, and all had responded. The waters of St. Jude Without had never seen such activity before, not ever.

As the stunned parents in the field came to their senses, the screaming began in earnest. Panicked mothers who, not yet realizing that no child had been hurt in this fiasco, searched through the mass of bodies, looking for their own little ones and praying that they hadn't just floated off to sea. There were shouts of 'Keisha!' and 'Justin!' and 'Brittney' and Brittany!' and over them all Carmel recognized Nancy's shrill tones demanding for Tyler and Tiffanee and Joss to show themselves. It didn't strike her that Melody's voice was absent.

And still Josh's camera clicked away amid the crowd and the dying gasps of the generator, running on fumes by now yet for no purpose. His long range lens caught the approach of the cavalry from air and sea; it caught the expressions of the individuals in the crowd, and it caught the bright festive colors of the plastic castle against the blue water.

There of course was Laney, his face red and thunderous, pushing through the throng of people as his eyes honed in on Carmel and Nate down in the field below.

'Clear the area!' he screamed. 'Move those friggin' cars and bikes, for Christ's sake!' He barked out orders to the left and to the right as he shoved the bystanders out of the way, for he was in charge and he had to be seen to be doing something.

There was no way she was going to get involved in this if she could help it. No way. This was Nate's show, and he could claim all the credit for himself. She stepped away from him, putting as much distance between them as she could among the press of the crowd.

The spot where the castle had been was now just a blank clear space, a surprisingly small area with the grass flattened and an oval of mud where the entrance had been, and nothing but tiny discarded shoes and clothing and empty popcorn bags lying around its perimeter to show the place had once held a fun house. On the far side, the generator snorted its final death as the diesel ran out.

Once the rogue wind had died down again, the ever heaving swell of the salt water quickly threw the writhing mass of plastic back onto the boulders along the shoreline as if Neptune had rejected this unexpected offering. Quick thinkers in the crowd had already run down to the rocky beach to help haul the deflated castle up past the largest rocks and onto the pebbles, and all the occupants were able to be assisted out unharmed except for a dunking in the frigid water and whatever psychological damage had been inflicted. Most of the kids, however, were thrilled to bits by the whole experience.

'Let's do that again Mommy! That was fun!' One shrill voice cried from the shore as a tot clambered over the beach and up to the meadow.

The whole incident could so easily have been deadly, thank God it wasn't, yet there would still be hell to pay. She looked again at the perimeters of the space. Had the castle had been properly affixed into the ground, or was this the result of malicious intent? She lifted her head above the crowd and looked at the island across the way now glistening innocently and brightly like an emerald against the blue of sky and water.

Either way, it simply wasn't on. If the safety of the children had been threatened because the folk of St. Jude Without had been lax, because they allowed visions of one million dollars override their common sense, well, that was simply tragic.

On the other hand, if it had been deliberate destruction, if someone had snuck over and loosened the anchors of the castle...

Carmel breathed another sigh out as she saw yet more children being helped out of the plastic castle, the helicopters hovering as near as they dared in case anyone needed to be rushed to emergency. But the ambulances were now crowding the breakwater in Portugal Cove, lights flashing and sirens sounding, waiting for to take them all to the Janeway Hospital to treat them for possible hypothermia.

It was going to end well, she realized, with all those water and air and land vehicles summoned so quickly to be at hand. Carmel swung her head to look back at the crowd, and from the corner of her eye saw Nancy acting strangely. The woman stood over by the generator with her hands framing a face that was twisted in a scream. And then Nancy let out a primordial scream to match, a scream that came from deep within her depths.

What the hell now? Carmel was heartily sick of the drama of her guests and their family, of the madness which had overtaken her home and community, and the woman's shriek was piercing her ears.

She forced herself to go to Nancy's side with her hands covering her ears for protection from the caterwauling.

'Nancy!' She shouted at the woman standing up. 'What's going on? What's wrong now?'

She rushed over to stop the noise, but her feet stopped before she reached Nancy, for her eyes were caught by the same sight that had set Nancy off.

'Oh, Jesus,' Carmel breathed as she recognized the green jeans and the neon yellow polyester blouse lying on the ground at the other woman's feet. What now? What sort of nonsense and melodrama was Melody getting on with now?

Melody lay at their feet, there was no mistaking that it was her, but then she realized that this was not more family dramatics playing out, for even she could see that Melody was dead. The back of her permed frizz was matted bright red with blood, blood that had seeped and spread all through the grass around them.

This day was not ending well after all.

S he tried to draw the dead woman's sister away but Nancy wasn't moving, and still the screams continued.

'What the hell is happening now?' Laney burst into the flattened square of grass, one eye on the rescue of the children at the beach, and the other trying to figure out the reason behind the piercing wails. He looked like he was nursing a hangover, even this late in the day, or maybe that was just his norm.

And then he saw Melody's body and he acted instinctively.

'Nobody move!' Carmel looked up to see the RNC issued revolver was aimed right at her and Nancy. She blinked to clear her eyes. This was Newfoundland, where it was common knowledge that almost every household had a rifle or three which may or may not be legally registered, but those weapons were used for hunting and for living off the land. And everyone also knew the police in the province were armed these days, but the force rarely had the bad taste to actually take the weapons out of their holsters and aim them at people. Yet here was Inspector Laney, brazenly and openly threatening to fire on her. There must be some misunderstanding. She shook her head and opened her mouth to reason with him.

'You, McAlistair – get down on the ground! And your friend too!'

Not a misunderstanding on her part, then. Carmel looked down at her feet. But there was no way she was going to lie herself down next to the very dead-looking Melody, nor could she allow Nancy to be forced to that either. 'Nu, uh,' she mumbled, but she did raise her hands up in the universal symbol of surrender.

'Down on the ground, I said!' Laney repeated himself.

She carefully pointed with one finger to the body. 'Don't want to mess with the scene,' she said uncertainly. If it was a crime. Perhaps

Melody had merely tripped and smashed her head against the metal generator?

Sure, just like Lars did, right? A small voice whispered in her head. No, she had to face the fact. Yet again, there must be a murderer running around St. Jude Without.

She looked up from where Melody's body lay to meet Nate staring at her from across the flattened meadow. His face was haggard and despite Tina's best efforts, he was again become dilapidated around the seams – his hair clumped and matted again under the battered hat, the neatly pressed shirt stained and strained against his large chest, the ends now flapping to the breeze, and his eyes were tortured, burning, like two piss holes in the snow.

Her mind was already racing in that direction. What did Nate have against Melody, except that she had singlehandedly attempted to tear down the efforts of the community to win, to finally win at something, anything.

And that was the moment when she realized that the contest, all of this, was more than just a million dollars at stake for this cove full of life's losers, Nate and all his followers. This was perhaps the last kick at success for these almost middle-aged mother's boys who had never loosened the apron strings, never held jobs, never had a reason to strive.

But murder? This was not the way to go about it. And Nate had been by her side the whole time, hadn't he? She searched the crowd wildly, looking for Phonse, but he had long since melted away.

Laney glanced down to the beach where the children were now all rescued with no serious injuries and quickly decided his priorities. He looked over at the garishly dressed body lying in the spreading pool of red in the green grass.

'Christ on a stick,' he muttered, then he pulled himself together. 'McAlistair, move over to your right ten paces! Then get down on the ground! Take your friend with you.'

She lowered her arms to encircle Nancy and forced her to move over to the side with her. The screams had faded now, but the other woman's face was still a paroxysm of pain.

'This is her sister, Laney,' Carmel said bluntly. 'Look at her – she's in shock. She found... Have a heart.'

The gun pointed at them faltered as the face behind it scowled, weighing the triumph of finally bringing Darrow down through his girlfriend against the fallout which would certainly, indubitably, occur later on when his actions were made known. This wasn't his first rodeo by any means. He brought the revolver down.

'Guys – round up every last one of the St. Jude Without crowd,' Laney threw over his shoulder. 'I want all of them behind bars pronto till we figure out what the hell happened here today.'

Out of the corner of his eye, he must have caught Josh with his camera and long lens, and he whirled around. 'You! Get out of here! No photos, this is a crime scene.'

She didn't lie down, nor did she force the recently bereaved Nancy to do so either. Laney's attention had already moved on to securing the scene of death. From where she stood, she could both watch the last of the ongoing rescue at the beach, and also the crowd being corralled up the slope. She searched through it again, looking for a familiar face amid the tramping of the police in their heavy boots. Where was Brendan? Was he with his kids? She couldn't remember if they'd been in the castle when it loosened from its moorings.

As if right on cue, Brendan reared his head as the crowd cleared and he saw the flash of green and yellow behind the hastily erected police tape guarding the area.

'Melody?' He called, his voice uncertain, looking lost with his owlish eyes behind their glasses and his body large and soft as he looked on helplessly at the busy police scene unfolding in front of him. He still wore his trench coat wrapped around him and his hands shoved in his pockets. 'Melody, get up off the ground. Where are the children? Mel?' Panic was straining his voice.

Nancy immediately raced over to him, shrieking all the way across the short expanse of field.

'She's dead, Brendan!' she said as she threw herself into his arms.

A look of distaste crossed his face at her touch and Carmel almost thought he was going to throw off his sister-in-law, but then he lifted his arms and wrapped her in a hesitant, uncomfortable hug as he continued looking over her shoulder, unable to take his eyes away from his wife's lifeless body.

Carmel walked over to the pair and put her hand on Brendan's shoulder.

'Let's get back to the house,' she said. 'We'll get a hot cup of tea in you. I don't think we should stay here. Let the police do their work.'

These kindly meant words started Nancy shrieking all over again. Brendan's eyes were round and he looked petrified to be in the line of fire of this display of emotion.

'We have to check on the kids,' Carmel said firmly. And then, relief. Good, kind Boyce was there with all three youngsters. He took his wife in his arms, relieving Brendan of that terrific burden so that he could begin to process his own loss. She led them all up the slope at the tail end of the crowd.

The police van stood at the top of the field, the back door wide open with a cluster of uniformed cops all around. Phonse sat inside, his hands cuffed, bewildered at this turn of events.

'Carmel!' he said. 'What the frig's going on? What'd I do now?'

Besides negligence, endangering the lives of uncounted children, operating a children's amusement while under several influences, and smoking substances near said flammable plastic children's amusement, she didn't really have an answer for him. He'd been angry at Melody when she threatened to sue him, ready to burst by the look on his face, but he had uncharacteristically walked away from her.

Or so she had thought at the time.

Phonse had never been one for holding back. Could he possibly have lured her behind the castle and whacked her with a rock, or thrown her against the generator?

No way, she decided immediately, for that would have required forethought and a plan, and Phonse just wasn't big on premeditation.

'Murderer!' Nancy shrieked before Carmel could answer him. Her arms were outstretched like she wanted to claw out Phonse's eyes, but her husband Boyce held her back from leaping into the van. 'You killed my sister!'

And then Laney came up behind them, with Nate cuffed and struggling and being held by two of the RNC's burliest guys.

'It wasn't my frickin' bouncy castle! I had nothing to do with it all!'

Laney stood like the avenging angel of death in the open back door of the vehicle, his hands on his hips and a smirk on his face. 'I finally got ye all,' he said.

'They didn't have anything to do with Melody's death,' Carmel said urgently. 'They couldn't have! Nate was by my side the whole time, and Phonse had already gone off and left the area.'

'Death?' Phonse's eyes bugged. In the press of the crowd, he hadn't seen the body where it had lain behind the generator. He thought he was under arrest for the castle thing. 'Who died? I thought the kids were all okay?'

Nate groaned. 'Tell me none of those kids were hurt,' he said. 'Phonse, you frickin arsehole. How the hell did that even happen?'

'The kids are all present and accounted for,' Laney said. 'No thanks to any of you. But enjoy this last bit of sunshine of your faces, because youse won't be seeing the light of day for a long time yet.'

'And all of you,' he added, whirling around to face the group of Carmel and the bereaved family. 'I don't want anyone leaving this cove till I get to the bottom of all this.'

C armel shepherded her visitors towards her home, everyone still in shock and trying to process what had happened that afternoon. They passed the cracked-off sign and she barely noted the mess of garbage and litter trapped between the boulders and in the ditches along the road. Nancy continued her weeping and wailing all the way, and the kids were uncharacteristically silent. Brendan was no help at all, merely stumbling along, lost in his own world.

It was like a funeral procession, that walk back to the cottage on the hill. The road was lined with tourists and residents alike, all aware by now of the tremendous tragedy that had struck, and everyone was silent. Only Nancy's incessant wailing accompanied them and marked the route.

She didn't stop even when they had reached the privacy of the house. Carmel tried to be charitable but the noise was really getting on her nerves. She ushered everyone into the living room – Brendan, Nancy and Boyce and the three children, then thankfully excused herself to make tea and sandwiches.

She lifted the kettle of boiling water from the stove, wincing as Nancy's voice rose up again in a sharp squeal like a pig being slaughtered. Boyce's soft murmurings of comfort seemed to be egging on the hysterics rather than quieting the woman.

'It's not as though she even liked her sister,' Carmel muttered as she poured the water into the mugs, for it really seemed over the top.

The children were starting to come to life too, she could hear, wheening and whining and demanding their share of attention from the adults, but it wasn't forthcoming, Carmel could see as she brought the loaded tray into the living room.

'I want Mommy!' Tiffanee screeched, the decibels pitched to be heard over her aunt. Tyler was plucking at his father and demanding they get their mommy while the toddler was sitting on the floor screaming its own wordless angst. Carmel looked at the other three adults expectantly but they were totally ignoring the children, Boyce more concerned with soothing his wife while Brendan sat like a solid lump of jelly in her favorite armchair, staring out the window and keeping himself apart from the scene.

'Hey, here's some tea and milk and cookies and stuff,' she tried to say brightly, but it wasn't coming out that way. She used the tray to clear the coffee table before setting it down as no one moved to help. 'Tiff, come here and help me serve.'

'My names not Tiff!' The little banshee screamed at her. 'I want Mommy! Where's my Mommy?'

How the hell had she been landed with this? Carmel bit her lip to stop herself from yelling back at the bereaved child. Nancy was still taking over most of the sofa and all of Boyce's attention with her sobbing. Carmel kicked her ankle. Hard, and with purpose.

'Ow!' Nancy straightened up from the huddle she'd been melting into and stared at Carmel accusingly, rubbing her ankle as she did.

'Oh, so sorry,' Carmel said. 'But I could really use a hand with the kids here.'

'My darlings!' Finally Nancy turned her attention on to Melody's family. 'Oh my darlings, I'm so sorry for you.'

She squatted on the floor and drew all three of the squalling brats into an embrace. 'Mommy's... gone. Mommy won't be coming back. She died. Someone killed her while we were playing in the castle.'

Carmel almost dropped the tray, not believing her ears. She didn't have kids and didn't have a maternal bone in her body, but even she knew that this wasn't how it should be done.

Then Nancy looked up spitefully at Melody's husband, still sitting lost, looking through the window. 'And Daddy didn't do his job,' she said. 'Daddy wasn't protecting Mommy at all. He let the bad people hurt Mommy.'

Carmel had no words, could only stare at the whole family in horror. Meanwhile, Brendan's only reaction to Nancy's words was the resumption of that subtle, almost indiscernible tick under his left cheek.

• • • •

It had been a truly horrible evening and night. Brendan continued to sit in the armchair, dully picking at the food that was placed before him on the TV dinner tray, but not communicating with anyone otherwise.

'Does he have family we should contact?' Carmel asked Nancy in the kitchen. She kept her voice low. 'Surely he needs to talk to someone – his mother? Siblings?'

'Him?' Nancy said loudly, not bothering to hush for her brother-in-law's sake. 'No one in his family will talk with him. No one wants anything to do with him. They took against my poor Melody and cut him off, even when the kids came. They're heartless, all of them.'

'We could at least phone them to let them know,' Carmel said. 'Surely that's the decent thing to do.'

'He can phone them himself, if he could be bothered to get out of the chair,' Nancy replied as she briskly whipped round the kitchen. 'Look at him, like a great useless lump, won't even help with his own poor motherless children.'

'That's not really fair, I mean, damn! He's in shock. He just lost his wife, for God's sake.'

'At least I'm here to look after the children,' Nancy continued in a softer voice as if Carmel hadn't spoken. She stirred the bowl of noodles and fake cheesy substance with a new tenderness. 'Oh yes, now they can have a proper home, with the love they deserve. They'll grow up on Bell Island, where they should be, with lots of fresh air and family. Boyce can finally be a dad, and he'll be fantastic. And I will look after my dear sister Melody's children as if they were my own.' She looked over in Carmel's direction, but her glittering eyes were focused on the new perfect future she saw for herself.

Carmel took a step back to stay out of the other woman's way. She felt like she was staring into a huge murky chasm of another family's emotions left to stew untended for too long. The inner workings of families are rarely a pretty sight. And it was at that moment when she began to suspect the unbelievable, that Nancy herself had killed her twin sister.

'Come on darlings, come eat this mac'n'cheese before it gets cold!' Nancy sang into the direction of the living room.

The two older ones were uncharacteristically silent, no doubt having overheard every word that came out of Nancy's mouth. Despite her dislike of them, Carmel's heart ached with guilt. They were only kids after all, it wasn't their fault they were growing up in the midst of such dysfunction. Of course, it would be easier to feel sympathy for the little ones if they had shown any redeeming aspects.

Relief was found only when Nancy and Boyce retired early to their camper van to sleep. They took the kids with them, Nancy complaining about Brendan's apathy the whole time, despite the fact that this worked to her advantage if she indeed intended to adopt Melody's kids.

Carmel stayed in the kitchen, thinking hard, trying to make sense of these new suspicions, searching for something that didn't point to Nancy. Nothing made sense. Two deaths had happened in the past week. Two deaths, both victim bludgeoned on the temple with a rock. Both victims had ties to Bell Island. But she couldn't see how else they could be related.

What else had the two in common when they were living?

To start with, both Melody and Lars were from Bell Island, although she had moved away years ago. Were the two related by blood? Carmel shook her head.

'It's a small place, so they could be kin,' she said aloud. 'But all the Andersens have big builds, and the two twins are short women.'

But the fact remained – both of the dead people had strong ties to the cove's neighbor across the water. The reasons for the deaths could quite reasonably be stemming from that island, and perhaps they had occurred on this side of the tickle to divert attention, to make it seem that the crowd from St. Jude Without were involved.

She almost stopped breathing as a thought struck her. Could Gen have known of Lars' intentions and engineered his murder? After all, it was rumored that nobody was allowed to leave that octogenarian's employ. Roland with his solid build could easily have overpowered the soft giant on those wet rocks, perhaps had hidden while Nate and Lars drank on the boulders, then when the coast was clear attacked him.

It was very possible. But what quarrel did Gen have with Melody? Why would she have taken out a hit on that irritating, yet innocent, mother of three? Carmel searched her memory of the blur of the afternoon. She hadn't noticed Roland there, and he was pretty unmistakable with his bowed legs and burly shoulders.

Dear God. Should she be worried for her own life? If Gen could set her henchman to cold-bloodedly murder her own people, then what regard would she have for Carmel who supposedly wrote the blog which had upset the old woman? No, she couldn't let her mind go in that direction, but she would make sure both front and back doors were locked tonight.

Of course, there was no shortage of people who were angry at Melody that day. In the short time she'd been in the cove, the small woman had pissed off everybody, it seemed. Carmel harked back to the hour directly preceding the discovery of her body.

Clyde had been in the crowd, his eyes wild and menacing, searching for the bright green pants of the woman who had screamed at him and frightened his goat. Melody had taken over Nate's big speech, had drawn attention to herself by her screaming and yelling about the awful things that had happened in the cove, and Tina's face had looked murderous enough in response. The guest had publicly dissed Vee Ryan's tea room, and declaimed her standards of cleanliness, and in doing so brought rage into the older woman's eyes.

But none of these residents of the cove, so angered by Melody's actions, none of them would have had anything to do with Lars' death, and the two had to be somehow connected.

Were the deaths the culmination of years of long grudges held by the neighbors, meant to discredit the rival cove? But if that was the case, well, Laney had Phonse and Nate locked up and would be searching for evidence that one or both were involved in the deaths. She shook her head. This was far too convoluted, there had to be a simpler answer.

Her mind went back to just last week, the Sunday, only six days ago when she'd seen Nate singing, drunk, at the end of Snellen's Field. He'd been celebrating what he'd thought was a brilliant plan to bring money to the cove and to push his political aspirations.

Inspector Laney still didn't know about the meeting between Lars and Nate, but on the other hand, he'd been planning to frame Phonse by playing with the video evidence.

Unless Darrow was right, and Laney had just been saying that to mess with her head. Either of the two were possible. But Nancy...

Was there some unknown reason in their pasts that would cause Nancy to kill Lars Andersen? Or perhaps it was all a setup for her twin's death, which indicated a deep level of planning, yet there was no way Nancy could have known she'd have an opportunity to kill her sister.

Carmel heavily dropped into the chair. She had to accept the fact that Nancy was the only common denominator, and Nancy stood the most to win. Her sister's children, her perfect family at long last. But how the hell could tiny Nancy have reached high enough to whack Lars, that mountain of a man, with the necessary strength to kill him?

35

B rendan remained in his seat by the window, still not moving. He hadn't eaten much of the cheesy noodles on his plate, and the whole mess had crusted around the edges by the time Carmel removed it.

'Uh, Brendan?' Carmel put her hand on his shoulder.

He jumped at the touch.

'Oh, sorry!' she said. 'I didn't mean to startle you.'

He turned his face up to hers, the owlish eyes hidden behind the lamp's glare on his glasses. There was no sign of tears on his face or the anguish she would expect from a recently bereaved man. He looked blank. Scarily, creepily empty of emotion.

'Did you want to phone your family, or do you want me to do it? I mean, you need to contact them.' She was pretty sure he should. Not having any family herself, not since her mother had disappeared on her mission all those years ago, she really wasn't sure about the social ins and outs of these things.

When he didn't respond, she tried to speak of other things, too, like the need for him and the children to stay in the cove until the RNC concluded their investigation, and when Melody's body would be released for the funeral. She tried to assure him that she would help him in any way she could.

But still he said nothing, just stared at her as if not comprehending her words.

'Well, uh, maybe you should just head on to bed,' she pushed. She was damn tired after that horrible day and the whole rotten week and she couldn't relax on the sofa until he'd left the room. Of course, she could have reclaimed her bedroom back now the kids were in the camper truck with their aunt, but that would have involved cleaning and changing sheets and she just couldn't face the thought of all that work. She just wanted to tumble onto her chesterfield and forget the world.

Finally, he must have understood, for he lumbered up from the deep armchair and headed up the stairs, every step creaking under his slow heavy feet.

With a sigh of relief she closed the living room door. Sitting on the sofa, she was ready to sleep without even blankets. She felt her phone buzz. It was Darrow.

In transit now. It's been a week of hellishness. How's yours going?

She gave a bitter laugh to herself. A week of sitting in a classroom, no murders, no crazy people, no being launched into the midst of a very messy grieving family... Sounded like heaven to her at that moment. How could she answer him? This sort of thing wasn't easy to explain over a single text message.

Meh. I'll tell you everything tomorrow.

His reply came quickly. *The kids have me booked up solid tomorrow, I'm afraid. They're leaving for their mother's on Sunday. Can we wait till then?*

Of course, she replied back immediately. Families. She leaned back and closed her eyes, willing it all to go away, just for a night. But it wasn't going away, and she wouldn't get any rest. She pressed the button to call Darrow.

'I just needed to hear the sound of your voice,' she said softly. 'And... and there's been another death.'

He was silent as it all spilled out of her, until at last she had told him all of the happenings and all of her fears. Then she heard the tapping of keys of his laptop.

'Well, I can relieve your mind of one thing,' Darrow said sombrely. 'Lars Andersen's death has been ruled an accident.'

'What?' She started up from the sofa. 'How can that be? They were both killed in the exact same manner, and they're both from Bell Island...'

'He had enough alcohol aboard him to sink a ship,' Darrow remarked dryly. She heard the tap of more keys in the background. 'Three point five blood alcohol level. That would cause severe poisoning, if not death, in a lesser mortal. And he was climbing around those great jagged boulders in that state?'

Carmel thought for a moment. 'He could have been murdered, though, while he was incapacitated,' she said. Nancy could easily have done the deed, thrown the rock into the ocean, and jumped on the ferry at the last moment. The lashing rain would have washed away any blood.

'No,' he replied. 'The forensic investigation found a boulder that exactly matched the shape of his injury, and what's more, there were grains of the same granite imbedded into his skull. Lars Andersen's death was not murder. Unlike your guest's death.'

Darrow tried his best to give her some on the spot counselling to help her deal with the trauma of the afternoon, but she recognized his efforts for what they were and insisted she'd be alright.

'I just need a good night's sleep, honestly, and I'll be okay in the morning,' she said.

She hung up the phone. Her head was whirling with this new information. Something wasn't making sense. How could the deaths not be connected? Everything, all the terrible things this past week, the madness, the brawls – all of them began with the demise of Lars Andersen.

'A sad state of affairs.' The mournful voice came from the chair Brendan had recently vacated.

She slowly lifted her eyes to the ghost of Captain Jeremiah Ryan, sitting large as life with the plume in his hat nodding.

'You,' she said. His existence had slipped her mind with all the awful happenings of the day. She looked at him thoughtfully. Surely he could be of some assistance in the matter of Melody's murder. 'You're right, it's been horrible.'

'Now there's only one of them left here,' he said, a satisfied note in his voice. 'And you can get on with the business at hand.'

Her mind immediately leapt to the only conclusion she could draw from his words, and she grabbed the sofa arm to steady herself.

'Are you saying...?' It couldn't be. The ghost hadn't left the house for two hundred years, by his own admission. How could he have summoned the courage to go to Snellen's Field and even more, lift a heavy rock with enough force to kill Melody? She looked at the spirit with new eyes. He was almost fully materialized now. He'd been a fearsome, bloodthirsty buccaneer in his day, and Jem certainly had the motive to relieve her of the noisome presence of their unwanted guests.

Captain Jeremiah could manifest into the physical world, so did that mean he could also commit acts in the physical realm, acts like murder?

'You didn't,' she said in a whisper. 'You didn't have anything to do with her passing?'

He wrinkled up his nose. 'The loud female? She's gone, although her spirit may be lingering still on the field. I'd avoid that area if I were you.'

Captain Jem crossed his right leg over the other and looked to be settling in.

'So the business at hand,' he continued. 'My biography. You can now concentrate on your very important task.'

'But Melody...' she stuttered. 'How did you do it?'

He shook his head, his expression telling her he suspected she might be crazy. 'I know not what you're talking about,' he said. 'But I have done many things. Have you paper and quill to take notes? No time like the present.'

'How did you kill her?' she asked, then she caught herself. 'I know how you did it, but how did you manage it? You left the house.'

'Pah! Utter nonsense. Haven't left the house for centuries. I told you that. No need for me to leave. I can watch everything that happens from my window.' He crossed his arms and settled back into his chair. He gave a low chuckle as he harked back to that afternoon. 'Twas quite the sight,' he added. 'That garish toy of Phonse's, sailing off with the squalling brats inside.' He snickered, and then couldn't help a chortle and a ghostly snort.

Carmel couldn't find the humor in that afternoon's horrific situation. 'Well, at least you must have seen what happened to Melody,' she said. 'You know, the loud one you hated so much in this house.'

He continued his chortling. 'Well, I didn't need to do the deed. Looks like one of the living felt as much as I did and did the job for us all.'

Carmel was not going to get anymore help from the ghost that night. She wrapped the blanket around herself including her ears, the better to tune out the echoes of his ghostly laughter.

36

It was now Saturday in St. Jude Without. As the coffee maker coughed and spit in the corner of the kitchen, Carmel flicked on the radio more out of habit than because she wanted to know what was happening in the world outside. She had enough going on in her head, and little room for anything else.

The big news was that with the murder of Melody and the bouncy castle endangering the lives of twenty-five little children, and the biting goat and the feral ponies, St. Jude Without was faltering in FaceBook likes, their narrow margin over Bell Island quickly slipping away.

The brawl at the barbeque? That had only increased the cove's popularity. The damning photos posted and shared? Newfoundlanders, it seemed, appreciated a good show of drunken fisticuffs. But the sensationalism of the grisly murder and the evidence of total incompetence in the erection of the children's play center and the photo of Clyde apparently beating his toothsome goat, well that got everyone's attention in a nasty way, and St. Jude Without was not heading into victory or the million dollars

St. Jude Without was a victim of its own greed and misguided aspirations. Whatever. She was heartily sick of it all and would play no part in any of it.

Brendan was taking a very long hot shower, she could tell from the steam upstairs. She might suggest that he go out for a walk, perhaps a long hike up to the barrens, anything to get that morose presence out of her home and away from Nancy's constant sniping.

Or maybe she would take her own advice and go on that hike. A little ashamed of herself, she realized she could not take the strain of dealing with his terrific grief, not right at that moment. If only he would speak, or cry, or something, anything to let it out of him. The man was in shock and needed a mental health professional.

'Right,' she muttered to herself as she quickly tied her sneakers and headed out the front door. 'Nancy can deal with him.'

But his sister-in-law must have had the same thought, for there was the camper truck heading down the road to Portugal Cove, probably going for breakfast. Even though it was just the next cove over, they were pushing the limits of Laney's orders, but Carmel found she really didn't care.

Now that their vehicle was no longer blocking the road outside, Carmel could see the cove again from the living room window. It was a bright, innocent looking day, with big puffy white clouds in the sky and nary a ripple on the water, the kind of day that was a photographer's dream to take snapshots of an idyllic little cove with the blue water and bright green meadows for a calendar, or for a tourism website meant to lure the unsuspecting visitor all the way across the ocean to visit.

She cut through the graveyard and headed up the hill on the path she'd taken with Brigid on their blueberry hunt last fall, when she'd first moved into the cove. The last of the orange tape, now greatly faded, still fluttered on a bush, placed there by the team of surveyors right before the Premier's brother had his throat cut down by the bridge. She shivered. So much death.

But at least the mountain was still free of McMansions and remained undeveloped. Carmel took deep gulps of the fresh, almost warm air, the salt from the water still evident even up here. Her feet followed the rabbit trail till she came to the outcrop of rock over the village, and there she sat in the morning sun to think.

She hugged her arms around her knees and gazed down to the cove below. People were beginning to stir along the road and the lanes.

Vee must have given up on her tearoom, for she was out in the yard pegging up laundry on the line, the white t-shirts and underwear, talking with her neighbor. She must be devastated with

Phonse in jail, her precious mother's boy. He was a lot of things, and the good Newfoundland word 'skeet' certainly came to mind, but he wasn't a murderer, not Phonse. Yet he'd had the opportunity to bash Melody over the head, and he'd certainly had the motive, for the woman had been ragging on him and Phonse never did take well to criticism. He'd disappeared after walking away from the bouncy castle, his pockets full of money – had he doubled back and lured her behind the attraction and knocked her down?

Perhaps, but it didn't seem likely.

Nate, though. She'd always sensed Nate had it in him to be a killer – his ambition and sense of entitlement had gotten him through a PhD in a competitive field. That, combined with his natural sense of lawlessness which came of being a descendant of Jem, well, he was almost a shoo-in to be cast as a murderer.

Her gaze wandered back to Vee Ryan, and her eyes narrowed. Melody had insulted Vee's baking, and if she'd also heard Melody threatening Phonse, then it was all too conceivable that Vee in a fit of pride and outrage could have bashed the woman's head in.

And Clyde Farrell, there he was, his dog by his side, shaking his cane at any visitors who looked interested in coming in to see the farm. With Nate no longer in the cove, he didn't have to open the 'petting zoo', and he was free to chase people off the property.

Carmel couldn't help the small smile which rose on her face when she remembered Melody indignantly showing everyone where the goat had ripped her pants. Perhaps it hadn't been biting her, as she swore to everyone, maybe the animal had probably thought the delectable bright green of her jeans was some new form of spring leafing.

But Clyde dearly loved his animals, far more so than any people in his life. And yes, he too had been in the crowd at the field when the castle blew off. Carmel sobered up, the smile dropping off her face. Melody had made a lot of enemies in the short time she'd been in the cove. There were any number of folks who would have been glad to see the end of her.

Even her sister had hated her, it would seem, or at least she hadn't liked her much. Melody had complained she wouldn't return to her homeland because she'd been bullied too much as a child growing up, and from what Carmel had seen, she was willing to bet that Nancy had been the source of much of her pain.

'Families. Who would have them?' she muttered with a shiver up her spine. But of course Nancy hadn't murdered her sister. No way.

Maybe? But she'd been by the castle the whole time, helping the little ones back in as soon as Phonse had turfed them out. Hadn't she?

'No,' Carmel said aloud. She hadn't. There was a brief span of time when Nancy wasn't there at the entrance. Where had she gone? She couldn't remember, there had been too much happening, with the crowd and the yelling and Ian's crazy music filling the cove.

Her mind went back over every jab, every twist of the knife, every unkind word Nancy had said about her sister. Nancy, who had first floored Carmel with her helpfulness and goodness, especially when compared with her sister's attitudes and complaining, until she'd realized that everything Nancy had done, every action performed, had only been to show up Melody, to highlight the difference between the two, not to actually be helpful.

But... why? Not just why did the two sisters have such awfulness between them, but why would Nancy have taken the life of her own sister? She furiously put her mind back to everything the woman had said, to see if she could find a hint.

On the surface, Nancy had appeared to be helpful, kind-hearted, thoughtful, even, and very loving towards her sister's kids. Nancy wasn't blessed with children, as Melody had so nastily pointed out, and it had been at that point that the older twin's spite had begun to seep out of her, marring the image that Carmel held of the woman.

The children. Was Nancy so jealous of her sibling's ability to have children that she would kill her own twin? Carmel remembered the show put on by Nancy over Melody's body. At the time, she'd felt it was a bit of overkill, like the woman was protesting too much. Perhaps she'd been pretending. And Nancy had even then already begun to take over the kids, pointing out that Brendan in his grief was not a fit father.

Carmel watched as the camper truck began making its way slowly back along the road far below her, her mind filling with horror at the path it had taken. Yes, perhaps Nancy was responsible for her sister's death.

But how could Carmel prove this?

37

The small cove was really coming to life now. Not on Snellen's Field, of course, that was practically empty now that the police had cleared up everything they needed from it. The flattened square of grass was beginning to spring back up, and soon only the presence of the generator left to rust would show where Melody's life had ended. Yet still some visitors, the really ghoulish ones, lurked at the edges of the field, wanting to see if there was still evidence of Melody's blood among the tall grass.

Sid and his bikers had come back, of course, yesterday, in time to watch the whole fiasco of the undoing of St. Jude Without. He'd put his buddies to work today, she could see the black leather jacketed forms along the sides of the road with big black garbage bags in their blue-gloved hands, picking up the windblown litter that occurs with crowds of people. They were attempting, in their own way, to bring normality back to the cove.

Yes, there were more tourists than ever wandering around the cove, but they didn't seem to be staying long, for aside from Ian and his haunted tours, there were very little attractions remaining for them. Clyde had finally closed the gates of his farm altogether, no one was trying to corral the ponies, and even Nate's stage had been dismantled sometime over the night.

And Josh, of course, the reporter, there he was still clicking away with his camera, trying to find crumbs of news that he could sell for his freelancing. She didn't know why he was bothering, for he would have gotten the juiciest pictures yesterday at the height of the wind and the mob's frenzy for she was sure he hadn't stopped photographing every single second of the fiasco.

Josh and his photos. Documenting the events.

'Of course!' Carmel jumped up and began a hurried descent, hopping from rock to rock down the mountain side. Josh's camera hadn't stopped clicking the whole time. If anyone had evidence of who killed Melody, it would be him.

She would have to convince him to show her the photos so she could see for herself who had disappeared behind the tent and when. The more she thought about it, the more she felt sure that Nancy hadn't been in her sights the whole time, not like Nate who'd stuck by her side, breathing heavily as he had watched his world and his dreams tumble down all around him.

Carmel raced down the slope, through the bushes, and at the graveyard, took a sharp left to run through the grasses, thereby avoiding her home where Nancy was probably unloading the kids at that moment. She cut by the back of the church, bursting out onto the parking lot where the bikers were now conferring amongst themselves, comparing the levels of garbage in their bags. They looked up at her as she jumped from the bushes, breathing heavily.

'Hey, welcome back you guys,' she paused to say as she caught her breath. 'We've missed you here.'

'What a state the place is in,' said Bill. He shook his head, and so did the others.

'Josh was just here,' she said. 'Did you see where he went? The reporter guy with the camera.'

The short biker straightened up with a scowl on his face. 'He was taking pictures of us, and we told him to get the f...'

'Went down that away last we saw him,' Bill interrupted, flicking his thumb down towards Phonse's house.

'Thanks,' she said, her eyes already scanning the meadows below them. There he was, she saw his red jacket as he leaned on the large boulder that marked the end of the land and the beginning of the beach. She set off at a more leisurely pace down the gravelled lane.

Phonse, of course, wasn't at his boat this morning, being still in the police lockup. She couldn't help the shiver that ran up her spine, remembering just a few months ago when she'd been there herself, that cold ancient cell in the old Courthouse on Water Street in the city. It had smelled of centuries of disinfectant and piss and vomit and worse – no matter how much they hosed the place down, they'd never be able to remove the stink ingrained into the stone floors and walls.

It wasn't Phonse's or Nate's first times as guests of Her Majesty, of course. It was a rite of passage for the young males of St. Jude Without to be tossed in the lockup at least once before they exited their teenage years. Getting involved in drunken brawls on George Street was the preferred method of causing their stint of incarceration, even better if you could manage to get your buddies in with you to continue the party in jail. All harmless fun, of course.

But now they were in there on charges of murder. She could feel Vee Ryan glaring at her through the lace at the kitchen window so she picked up her step.

'Ben.' She called for his attention as she approached. He appeared to be using his telephoto lens to capture shots of the gulls and other seabirds on the cliffs of Bell Island.

He turned around warily and watched as she picked her way through the grasses and rocks. The acne stood out red on his pale face, and his eyes were tired. He'd been putting a lot of time into his work over the past day or so. She sat on the boulder next to the one he'd claimed.

'Nice day for it,' she said, nodding at his camera.

'Yeah.'

'You've been shooting a lot over the past couple of days,' she remarked, throwing him a friendly grin as she did so.

'Mm-hmm.'

'I guess there's been lots to photograph, what with the crowds and all.'

'And the murder. And the total disregard for public safety.'

She inclined her head in agreement. 'Yeah,' she said. 'About that. Has Inspector Laney asked to see the shots you took yesterday?'

He sniffed. 'No,' he said. 'And I don't want him to. I'm making a photo documentary of the undoing of St. Jude Without, and if he takes these as evidence, I won't be able to use them for months, maybe years. I'm going to expose every single one of you in this, and in a timely manner.'

'Ah, right,' she replied. He had his own reasons for disliking the residents of St. Jude Without. There was another moment of silence between them before she spoke again.

'I was just wondering if I could have a look through all the ones you took yesterday, the ones down by the bouncy castle.'

He turned and opened his mouth, and she continued quickly.

'I don't want to use them or take them, just look at them,' she insisted. She leaned closer to him. 'I think I know who killed Melody, and I think, I hope, your photos will show that.'

He set his jaw stubbornly. 'Right,' he said in a bored voice. 'You'll use my work to prove something to the cops, and you'll get all the glory, and what will I get? A mention in a police report, that's all. My photographs will be tied up in the court case and I won't be able to use my own work. Forget it. You'll have to make me a better offer than that.'

'But... but this is for a good cause! I promise I'll try not to get your work involved,' Carmel said. 'Look, if I can just look at them, figure out who wasn't there at the right time, then I'll try and find some other evidence. I have a pretty good idea who killed that woman, and I just need some kind of back-up proof.'

He said nothing.

Carmel sighed. 'I don't know what I can offer you, I don't have any money,' she said. 'Is there anything I can do in exchange for this huge favor?'

Josh shoved his hands in his pockets, his camera loosely lying around his neck and remained silent for another long moment as he watched the birds circling so far off across the waters of the Tickle. Just when Carmel was about to give up and head back up the hill, he spoke.

'There is something, yes,' he said slowly.

'Great!' She leaned over to him in anticipation. 'Name it, and it's yours.'

'I overheard you talking with Nate the other day,' he continued. 'About the ghost of Captain Jeremiah Ryan.'

'Oh, no,' she said, backtracking. He must have been lurking in the bushes outside the open church windows. This was not good. 'That's not real, it's just a legend here in the cove...'

He turned to her sharply. 'Didn't sound like it. You told them he showed himself to you.' He was watching her like a hawk now, his eyes narrowed and pinning her in place as she floundered, wondering how she could get out of this one.

Carmel just shook her head. Then shook it again.

'Too bad,' he said before shifting his gaze back to Bell Island. 'I would love an interview with a ghost. That's probably the one thing, the only thing, that would get me to show you my photographs. Too bad he doesn't really exist, eh?'

He had her caught between a rock and a hard place. She needed those shots, and he knew it. The only problem was, the ghost would never agree to an interview.

'I don't think he can be photographed,' she said slowly, hedging. 'The, you know, the ectoplasm doesn't capture on film.'

'Does he speak?'

'Well, yes, but...'

'I can probably record him then,' he said. 'If he exists.'

Josh stood up and stretched. 'Well then,' he said as he reached into his wallet. 'Here's my card. You can contact me when you get it all set up, and I'll bring the key with the pictures.'

She took the flimsy piece of cardstock.

'The ball's in your court, Carmel McAlistair. Let me know what you decide,' he said. 'You might want to get a rush on, before Laney realizes the evidence my camera holds and takes them for himself.'

38

She remained sitting on the boulder for some minutes after Josh had taken himself off. How could she convince Cap'n Jem to carry through with an interview?

He was a shy ghost, a timid spirit, despite his blustering and demanding ways. Look how scared he'd been of Tyler, a mere child.

And time was of the essence, Carmel knew. Inspector Laney, or at least some bright spark on his team would remember the reporter hanging around that day, and would definitely be on to him sooner rather than later and Josh was right when he said that once his photos were part of police evidence, he wouldn't be able to use them for a long time. The police would probably even take his camera and his laptop to make sure the images didn't get out.

And she would be seeing Darrow tomorrow, after he put his kids on the plane to the mainland. There would be no space in her life then for arranging an interview with a ghost. It had to be done, and it had to be done now. She reluctantly got off the damp boulder and headed back up to her cottage.

• • • •

The family had come and gone again, she saw, for the camper truck was not in front of the house. Brendan's rented minivan and her own ancient blue Toyota were the only vehicles in the driveway, but further down the road she saw Brendan glumly sitting in a police car, having a conversation with two cops. Laney was nowhere to be seen, and neither was Josh. She put her head down and hurried past the squad car.

'And this, the final leg of our haunted cove tour, this is the very home of the original founder of St. Jude Without.' Ian's lovely Irish accent flowed over his small crowd of visitors as he thralled and enchanted them. 'And now, ah! Yes, there she is, the lady who cohabits with the ghost of this fearsome pirate! Perhaps we can convince her to show us around inside. For an extra fee, of course, and you might see the pirate for yourselves!'

'Give it up, Ian,' she muttered as she strode past the group. 'You're not getting inside. Take them all away.'

Jem would never show himself with all those folk around, in fact he was probably quivering inside a closet even now at the crowd and noise outside.

'And stop peering through my windows!' she yelled back at him as an afterthought. She ignored the loud comments he made behind her back, and pretended not to hear the crowd laugh.

'Jem?' she called out after she had firmly shut the front door behind her and made sure the house was empty of humans. 'Jem? Get out here where I can see you. We really need to talk.'

A faint stirring of the air in the living room showed his outline. She went to the window and drew the curtains shut to the murmur of disappointment from Ian's gathering.

'I need a favor,' she said, sitting herself on the sofa opposite the ghost. 'A big one.'

'You got rid of the Horribles.' He was becoming more visible. 'Except the fat one.' He looked towards the window and shivered. 'But there's a mob outside?'

'I'm afraid the 'Horribles' are only gone temporarily, and Brendan will probably be coming back in soon. We need to speak.'

'That awful young lad,' Jem said, shaking his head.

'The thing is,' Carmel began, and plunged in. 'Remember the one you said was evil? The woman, Nancy?'

He shook his head, tut-tutting.

'I think she killed her sister, the loud one,' Carmel said, keeping her voice low even though they were alone. 'And I believe someone has proof.'

He shuddered. 'Just as long as I never have to see her again,' he said. 'String her up on the yard arm, anything, just rid the cove of her presence. A nasty piece of work, with all her cleaning and bossiness.'

'But in order to get the proof I need for her to be taken away,' Carmel continued. 'I need you to speak with that person.'

'Speak?' he asked, then he sighed. 'You want me to scare them, I suppose. Scare the Bejesus out of them.' He shook his head.

'No, just have an interview with a reporter.'

He looked at her blankly.

'He wants to hear your story,' she urged. 'He wants to write about you.'

'But I have chosen you to write my biography,' Jem replied, looking disconcerted.

'We have to let him do it,' Carmel urged. 'In order to get rid of the 'Horribles' from our home.'

Jem thought a moment. 'And will it also rid us of...' He shook his hand at the window. 'They terrify me too, the mobs. It brings back dreadful memories.'

'Mmn,' Carmel replied, crossing her fingers for the lie. 'In time, they'll go.' She nodded quickly.

'And this reporter,' he said. 'One who reports, I don't like the sound of that. But is this reporter sympathetic to my plight?'

'Oh yes,' Carmel said. 'And – this interview will be great promo for your biography.'

'I mean,' she said as he began to question what this new-to-him word meant. 'This will let people know you exist, so when I write your biography, we'll already have an audience.'

He didn't look convinced.

'And,' she hissed as she continued. 'If you don't do this then I won't find the proof that Nancy killed her sister, and Laney will pin it on Phonse, your descendant. How do you feel about that?'

The ghost shook his head slowly. 'I don't like this, don't like it at all,' he said. 'I doubt if I can show myself to anyone who isn't my kin.'

Exasperated, she could have shaken him if the ectoplasm had allowed her a hold. 'You're showing yourself to me! I'm not your kin, and neither is Tyler, the little boy who saw you.'

He continued to shake his head in doubt, and his form was wavering. 'Nay, I don't like this plan,' he said.

'What's not to love about it?' She was almost screaming at this point.

He looked a little sheepish as he ducked his head. 'People,' he said, his voice whiney, then he peeked back up at her. 'People scare me.'

The sound of a truck door slamming outside caused her to look out the window. 'The family are back,' she said, her voice low and urgent. 'Josh can't hurt you, you're a ghost for God's sake. I need you to agree to do this thing.'

But she was talking to dead air. The ghost was no longer in the chair opposite her.

• • • •

'Well,' Nancy said brightly as she let herself in through the door. 'That was really something!'

Carmel looked up at the woman who had (possibly) murdered her own sister. There were no tells on her face, no furtiveness in her look. Nancy seemed as open and as happy and as false as she had ever been.

'We've all been down to the RNC station in town,' Nancy continued, ushering the children in behind her, ensuring they placed their shoes in a tidy line. 'We spoke with that lovely Inspector Laney, and it's all good news.'

'Take your shoes off Brendan!' She spoke sharply to her bother-in-law. 'I just washed these floors the other day. I don't need you mucking them up.'

'Laney, huh?' Carmel rose from her chair and leaned against the doorjamb. 'Any word on Phonse and Nate?'

'Yes,' Nancy turned her super watt smile on again and aimed it at her. 'Not supposed to say, but they have it all sewn up. They're charging the blond man with Melody's... with her... Anyway, yes, they've decided he did it, so we can all leave and go back to Bell Island.'

'No!' This burst out of her before she thought about what she was saying, and who she was saying it to. 'Phonse didn't do it!'

Nancy's eyes narrowed a little, and her voice took on an edge of brittleness. 'What makes you say that?'

Carmel forced herself to look straight at Nancy. 'Because I know who did it.' She spoke firmly and slowly.

Something clattered to the floor and smashed and they all jumped.

'Brendan, you big klutz!' Nancy scolded, bending over to survey the damage. She started to pick up the pieces. 'You broke Carmel's lovely vase! You are so stupid, I don't know why my sister ever married you.'

Carmel glanced up at him, shocked anew at Nancy's treatment of the recently bereaved man, and almost gasped when she saw the look of pain in his eyes. He quickly looked away but she could have sworn she saw the beginning of tears there. He had to be grieving deeply, but he still held it all inside. The muscle under his left eye was twitching again.

'Come on, Brendan,' she said forcing kindness into her voice as she took him by the arm and led him into the kitchen. 'Never mind that ugly old thing, it came with the house. You did me a favor, I've never liked it anyway.'

Nancy had already made herself quite at home in Carmel's kitchen, putting on the kettle and setting out the makings for tea. 'So,' she said, and there was a tightness in her voice. Her back was to Carmel as she placed teabags into the mugs. 'You don't think it was the local guy, huh? That drunken skeet who was ripping off the kids? Seems like a pretty good suspect to me.'

Was that a threat in the other woman's voice? Carmel paused, her hand still on Brendan's shoulder.

She had to tread carefully. She couldn't tell Nancy that she suspected her of killing her own sister, that would never do, not until she had proof in her hands, because she didn't trust the woman one bit. She was harboring a murderer in her own home, and there was nothing she could do about it right there and then, not till she got on the phone with Darrow.

Carmel took a deep breath. 'Oh, no, who knows?' she said, forcing a lightness into her voice that she didn't feel. 'They're the cops, they know best, I'm sure.'

She felt the mass of flesh beneath her hand relax, ever so slightly. Did Brendan also suspect his sister-in-law? She gave a tiny squeeze to his shoulder. *Hang in there Brendan,* she said in her mind. *I may not like you, but I'll get to the bottom of this yet.*

'Yes, I think the police are better at figuring out crime than you,' Nancy said, the sweetness like treacle back in her voice. 'And as I'm free to go back to the Island now, I'll just get the kid's stuff packed and in the truck. Boyce has already hitched a ride back, and he's getting the bedrooms ready.'

She handed out the mugs of tea to the three of them in the room. 'I think it best that the youngsters come back with me, wouldn't you agree?'

'Brendan?' Carmel asked. 'How do you feel about that?'

'Oh, he's not fit to look after them, not that he ever was,' Nancy continued as if he wasn't present. 'Poor Melody did all the work in that department.'

Sweet Jesus, Carmel thought. Not only had the woman killed her sister, now she was hell bent on taking the children with her. Was this what it had all been about? Nancy couldn't have kids of her own, so she was so desperate to take her sister's kids?

'Brendan, you might want to go say good-bye to the kids,' Nancy finally addressed him. She stared at him over her mug of tea as if gauging his reaction. 'It's for the best,' she repeated, her voice so firm it might be menacing.

Brendan moved slightly in his chair, whether in protest or not Carmel couldn't see, but he said not a word. Nancy hadn't even invited him to Bell Island to stay, or asked his opinion on what should happen with his children.

Carmel felt a moment of panic, but she forced herself to remain calm. She needed to talk with Darrow, and fast. She couldn't risk talking to him while she was anywhere near Nancy.

'Well, I have to go out, next door, see how things are,' she babbled as she stood up. 'See you in a bit.'

With that she took off out the back door, phone in hand and her cup of tea not even touched.

39

S he entered the old church through the smoker's door. Sid was back behind his bar, the Christmas lights twinkling all around as he polished the thin stone to perfection. It hadn't received any care since he'd been gone and the granite was in danger of staining permanently from the rings left by the coffee mugs. The old curtains and quilts remained up though, cutting off the main portion of the room.

'Thank God you're back,' she said fervently. 'The place has been a mad house.'

He nodded silently.

But she needed privacy for this conversation with Darrow, so she continued on past the curtaining. It was still being used as a tearoom for the remaining visitors, she saw, Vee's business being taken over by the bikers. But instead of tea and rock hard buns and yesterday's baloney sandwiches, they were re-selling coffee and donuts from the big franchise up by the airport. It was popular.

But this too would never do for the discussion she needed to have. She pushed on past through the old church's front door. The parking lot was surprisingly empty, so she dialed Darrow.

'Hello!' he said. She could hear a buzz behind him, like canned music and a crowd.

'Hey,' she said simply. It was such a relief to hear his voice again, and know he was near. 'I need to talk with you.'

'Wait a second, I'll find a quieter space,' he said. Then he came back. 'Sorry about that. We're at the mall, getting last minute needs. Although I told her she can get all that up at her mother's, she insisted on a mall trip.'

'Teenage girls, eh?'

'You know it. But what's up? You said you needed to speak with me?'

In a rush, she told him all that had transpired in the past twenty-four hours. Well, almost all. Again, she kept out mention of the ghost, just that she was going to look through Josh's images to see if her prediction was right.

'I wish you wouldn't get involved,' he sighed.

'But he's going to pin it on Phonse!' she cried. 'I know he didn't do it.'

'Laney is an arse, I agree,' Darrow said. 'But I told you, there's no way he would skew evidence on a murder investigation. So who do you think murdered Melody, then?'

'It was her sister,' she whispered into the phone after glancing all around to make sure she was alone in the lot with no eavesdroppers around. 'She's the evillest creature. She did it because, oh, because she can't have kids, and she's always bullied her, and oh, she's just awful.'

'Being a horrible person doesn't make her a murderer,' he told her, her voice dry. 'But I can tell you're pretty freaked out over this whole thing.'

'I think she knows that I suspect.'

He sighed into the phone. 'When are you going to see this reporter?'

'He's coming by in a bit,' she told him.

'Right,' he said decisively. 'I need to drop the kids off at their respective friends, and then I'll be out your way.'

'Oh, thank you,' she said gratefully. 'I'll see you then.'

'Who knows you suspect what?' And there was Josh. He'd come around the corner of the church unexpectedly. How long had he been lurking?

'None of your business,' she snapped as she stuck the phone into her back pocket.

'I think it is,' he observed. 'Especially as you need to see my photos.' He took out a small object from his shirt pocket and tossed it a ways into the air. It glittered metallically before he caught it again, blue and silver. Josh saw her eyes land on the flash drive in his palm and he looked over at her with a smug smile on his face.

Liking this effect, he kept his gaze on her as he gave it another toss but this time, as he wasn't watching it carefully, his aim was a little off and when he went to grab it from the air it wasn't there. Instead, he was forced to scrabble about as it bounced first off his pants, then off his right shoe, and then onto the gravelled lot before his fingers found it again. Slightly red faced, he glared at her, but she hadn't really been paying attention this time. He shoved it into his pants pocket out of sight.

'About the interview,' she began. Captain Jeremiah had outright refused to talk to the reporter, but she wasn't going to let Josh know this.

'Yeah, the interview with your so-called ghost...' Josh attempted to cover his desire with scepticism, but he wasn't carrying it off well. They both knew what such an interview would bring him – not just fame and fortune and expansion of his world, but also recognition from his peers in the local journalism industry. He would be all too happy to rub their scoffing faces in the dirt beneath his shoe.

Besides all the personal gains for Josh, though, a real interview with a real ghost would be ground breaking in so many ways. He was a millennial child, raised by his nerd parents on re-runs of Dr. Who and The X-Files and he was also born an Aquarian. In short, Josh was a Believer, and he yearned for nothing more than fulfillment of his dream's vision on earth. He wanted this so bad he could taste it.

'Come on then,' she said, reluctantly. She had to at least get him into the house. Perhaps Darrow would be able to use his authority to persuade the reporter to let him look at the photos. She led him back to her home's front door, ignoring Nancy and Brendan and the squabbling kids as they packed the camper truck round the side of the house in her driveway.

She told him to have a seat on the sofa, wondering how she could stall for time till Darrow reached the cove. The city was twenty minutes' drive away, and he first had to drop his two children off at their respective friends, who could live anywhere within its radius. Could she keep Josh here for up to a half hour without any sign of Captain Jem?

'Want a cup of tea? I'll go put the kettle on, it's still hot, won't take a minute.' Carmel remained hovering at the doorway.

'No,' he replied firmly, taking his phone out of his jeans pocket and setting it to video record, all ready for when the ghost appeared. He looked up at where she was hovering by the door, the phone trained on her. 'You promised me an interview with a ghost. I want to talk with the ghost.'

'Yes,' she said slowly. 'There's just the slightest problem there.'

'Really?' He sat back and stared at her. 'And this is where you tell me that there's no ghost after all, right?'

'Well, sort of, but there is one, it's just...' She desperately looked out the front door window, searching the road for Darrow's car. 'It's just, oh, it's not as easy as that.'

Josh huffed. 'You led me here under false pretences. You're no better than any of the crowd in this pitiful excuse for an outport. You're all liars and thieves and hooligans, not an honest one in the bunch!' He was almost in tears as he stood up, phone in hand.

He was going to leave with the evidence she needed in his tiny flash drive.

'Wait, no! Don't go anywhere,' she said desperately as she blocked the living room doorway. 'There really is the ghost of the pirate, but I can't just make him appear when I want. He's...'

Josh faced her square on. They were the same height and looked each other eye to eye. 'You're a liar! Just like the rest of the crowd in this cove. Well, you're not getting my photos. Phonse can rot in jail for all I care – he deserves it! They can tar and feather him, and hang him from Gibbet Hill like Captain Jeremiah!'

They were at an impasse. Josh had no sympathy for Phonse's plight, and he wasn't going to hand over the images until he got what he came for, and Carmel wasn't going to let him out the door without the memory stick. They could have stayed like that for a while in this faceoff, except for the smell of sulphur that began to drift in the air, just a hint at first which might be excused as the result of old plumbing in a house of this age, but then it grew stronger and more pungent until it was an unmistakably solid presence.

Josh sniffed the air around him tentatively, then screwed up his face in distaste. 'What's that smell? Did you...'

Carmel removed her eyes momentarily from the young man's, bracing the doorjambs with her arms to prevent his escape, and she glanced over his shoulder. 'No, wasn't me. It's... him.' And finally she could relax her stance, and she pointed into the room behind him.

And the ghost of Captain Jeremiah Ryan was there, sitting in his armchair as large as life, the red velvet of the chair only showing a little through his ectoplasmatic body. And he wasn't a happy spirit.

Josh gasped and ran back to the sofa, holding up his phone to catch this spectral appearance. 'Oh my God, it's a ghost! Are you Captain Jem?' he asked.

'Who do you think I am?' Jeremiah roared. 'A snivelling Clerkwell townie?' His eyes were glowing red with rage. Carmel had never seen him like this, never so solid, never so scary. He appeared to have lost his stage fright.

The young reporter gave a hesitant little smile and held his phone in front of him like a shield. 'So, so – questions for the ghost. Um, how long have you been here?'

'Since I've been dead, ye fool! Since they strung me up and tarred and feathered me up on Gibbet Hill as you would have them do to my Phonse!'

He stood up, unable to contain his anger and outrage. 'But you'll not be getting another Ryan in your clutches! Ye took me by surprise the last time, but I'll be damned if I'll let you do it again! No one will be lynching my kin, ye dastardly snivelling bastards!'

Jeremiah took another step towards the reporter who was now quivering in fear. 'Stand up and fight like a man,' the ghost said, brandishing a long curved sword which had appeared in his hand. The spectral steel flashed in the late afternoon sunlight now streaming in through the window. 'Ha! Got you quivering now, eh? Empty your purse!'

'Purse?' Josh looked all around him. He hadn't taken his briefcase with him. 'I... I...'

'Your pockets then,' the ghost said impatiently, beckoning with his free hand. 'Give me all your gold and silver!'

'Don't hurt me!' Josh squeaked as he scrabbled through his jeans pockets, unloosing all the coins and contents and throwing them in front of him. He reached round and flipped out his wallet. 'I haven't got any cash, just credit cards and my Tim's points...'

'I've got no desire for your useless paper cards! Ye scurvy wretch, have you no wealth? What kind of a man are you? Off with your head, then!'

But Josh was no longer present to be addressed in this manner, he'd seen an opening between Carmel and the door and had dashed through it, leaving Captain Jem slicing his sword through the empty air and Carmel flattened herself against the wall, taking up as little space as she possibly could.

'That's done it, then,' Jem said, satisfied. His cheeks were red with the effort and his face suffused with a glow. He peered out the window. 'Yes, he's gone, look at him tootling down the road in his carriage. Got rid of him for ye.' He proudly sat himself back into his armchair, one hand stroking his ratty beard.

'You did,' Carmel replied, dazed at the display she'd just witnessed. She threw herself into the other chair. 'You sure did. You scared him out of the house.'

The realization hit her, and her voice grew stronger. 'You also ruined any chance that I could get evidence that Nancy murdered her sister,' she accused him, then she sat up and pointed her finger at him. 'By giving this display of pirate macho, you've just sentenced Phonse to the modern day equivalence of being lynched by Laney! How could you do this? Now Josh has the evidence of your existence on his phone, and we're back at square one.'

With a scowl on his face, Captain Jem opened his mouth to give her a harsh retort, but the sound of the screen door smoothly opening on its recently oiled hinges caused him to start, and he disappeared just as quickly.

Carmel slowly dragged her head around, dread filling her gut. What would she have to deal with now? Was it Brendan with his inconsolable grief, or Nancy, the narcissistic sister with her false and manipulative ways? She would have to summon the strength to hide her true feelings and her certainty of the sister's murderous ways. She forced herself to look up, ready to paste a smile on her face.

40

'There you are,' Darrow said to her as he stood on the threshold of the living room, bringing the glorious freshness of the soft June day with him, the sun framing him from behind. 'I drove here as fast as I could.'

Darrow. It had been only a week or so, but with all that had happened it felt like a month since she'd last laid eyes on him. She drank in the sight of him, her body relaxing with relief at his presence. He was tall, but not too tall, and dark, and some might call him unhandsome with the crook in his nose that had been broken once too often in the line of duty. His eyes, though, the way they crinkled up at the edges when he looked upon her, and the smile he tried to contain but which crept out anyway. Darrow was here.

His attention was diverted momentarily as he tentatively sniffed the air. 'You really need to get those drains looked at,' he suggested. 'And – was that the young reporter I just saw tearing out of here? What's up with him? He looked like he wet himself.'

Darrow looked at her and cocked his head, those beautiful brown eyes narrowed. 'What *have* you been up to?'

Her brain finally connected with her body and she shot out of the chair and into his arms. 'Thank God, thank God you're here.' It was all she could say and she wanted nothing more than to stay in that embrace for ever and never think about the cove or the goings on or the murders ever again.

'Come on, then' he said after a moment. 'Let's sit down and you can tell me all about it. It can't be that bad, surely?'

He moved them both towards the sofa. His foot kicked something small as he did so.

'What the devil?' He looked down. 'You've been flinging your money around?' He bent to scoop up the coins on the floor.

While he did so, Carmel had found her voice again and in a hushed voice began to tell him her suspicions. 'And,' she said in a lower voice. 'That's why I think it was Nancy who killed Melody.'

'Her own sister?' Darrow jingled the coins in his hand as he thought, then shook his head. He looked up again, his eyes telling her he knew that wasn't all the story. 'Perhaps. But that doesn't tell me why Josh was here, or why he left in such a terrified flight.'

There was a spark of gold flashing in those warm eyes now. 'Did you tell him all this that you've told me?'

'No, God, no.' She shook her head vehemently, searching for a plausible explanation for Josh's terror that Darrow had witnessed, something that didn't involve a two hundred year old ghost of a pirate scaring the bejesus out of the young man. Darrow was a man of the world, yes, and had undoubtedly seen many things in his professional life, but Carmel had no intention of sharing this slice of life in St. Jude Without. She didn't want those eyes looking at her gently and soothingly with the belief that she'd finally lost her hold on her sanity. So intent was she on this goal that she babbled. 'Josh was... he was here to give me his flash drive with all the photos on it that he took yesterday so that I could see for myself if Nancy had disappeared from the crowd and I don't know what got him so agitated, he just took off and I didn't get the drive and now I don't know what to do because that might be the only evidence to save Phonse and put Nancy away...'

She only stopped because Darrow was nodding his head as if he wasn't really paying attention, and examining the coins he'd picked up.

'Do you mean this flash drive?' He held out his hand. The blue plastic and silver lay there, glinting in the sunrays streaming through the window

She drew in a quick breath. 'That's it.'

'Well, let's get this down to the station,' he said. 'No time to waste.'

She barely noticed the sound of raised voices outside as she reached out and snatched the key right out of his hand, nor did she notice the sight of the three children snivelling on the road outside. 'Yes!' she cried.

'And please, let me look at it first?' she requested as an afterthought.

'That's official evidence,' he began to say as he reached back to reclaim the key.

'Oh give me a break,' she said, holding it out of his reach. 'It's not official until it's logged, right? And we wouldn't have it except for me.'

The camper doors slammed shut, and she cringed as she heard Tiffanee's voice raised in a wail. 'Let's do it now,' she hissed. 'And then you can grab Nancy on your way back to your office and save Laney a trip.'

'Kids, go into the house.' They heard Brendan's gruff voice set out an unexpected command.

'Don't want to go in that spooky old house! Want ice cream! Want to go to Aunt Nancy's!' This cry set off the other two in their unhappy screams.

'Here, sweeties, take this ten dollars and go and get donuts from next door.' Nancy's saccharine voice directly contravened their father's order.

'I really wish you wouldn't do that!' The quarrelling voices of Nancy and the grieving widower were getting closer to the house. 'And they're my children. They're not going with you.'

Well, glory be. Brendan was finally standing up for himself and claiming his rights. But that meant he would probably be coming back inside soon.

'Quickly,' she said. And Darrow shrugged his shoulders in acquiescence. She grabbed her laptop and fired it up.

'C'mon, c'mon,' she urged it, tapping the side as if that would make the connections work faster. At last it was booted up and she plugged the key into its side.

Her guests did not enter the house, instead, she heard their quarrelling voices go back around the camper van, giving her and Darrow a few moments of respite. Josh's images from the day before flashed onto the screen, and her heart sank. There were hundreds of them, possibly thousands. It would take ages. She felt the sofa cushions sag as Darrow sat next to her.

'We're looking for the afternoon portion, just before the bouncy castle slid off to the beach,' she told him, her finger quickly sliding through the many images.

The castle shots were easy to find, for the bright yellow and red shone even in the tiny thumbnails. She paused the slide show and reversed just a little.

'Okay, we're looking for the moment when she steps out of view with Melody,' she told him. 'And they go round to the back of the castle.'

But they searched and searched and back tracked, but Nancy showed up in every single shot. Sometimes just her hand and the sleeve of her blue sweater, sometimes just the back of her short bobbed blonde head, but she stubbornly remained in every single image, even after Melody had disappeared from view, and long past the moment when the castle set off sailing through the meadow.

'This is all wrong.' Carmel sat back. 'I don't understand. How could she have done it? Perhaps she did this before...'

She scrolled back up, but saw that it was impossible. Nancy hadn't moved out of the vicinity after Melody disappeared from view. The sequence didn't lie. There was Phonse, storming off. And then there was Melody, gone from the camera's sights.

'Shit,' she said, ready to cry. 'Maybe Laney was right. Maybe Phonse finally broke and...'

The quarrel outside had escalated, muffled as it was through the old glass windows, but it no longer concerned her. She'd just proven that Nancy – perfect, detestable, manipulative, bitchy Nancy – was not guilty of sororicide. She was not her sister's murderer.

'Wait a second there,' Darrow murmured as he bent over the laptop, flicking through the images.

'There is someone else that's missing from the shots.' He stopped the flow and pointed.

'Look, there's this man,' he said. 'And then, he's disappeared from view. Yet...'

He flicked furiously through fifteen or so photos. 'There he is again in the same spot he'd been, almost as if he'd never moved. But he did. Do you know him?' He pointed to the person in question.

Did she, indeed? Did she recognize those rimless glasses glinting in the sunlight? It was her guest, Brendan, his shoulders up to his ears he was so tense, as usual, his hands shoved into his pockets. But in the last shot, when he'd reappeared, he looked like a weight had been taken off his shoulders and a smile was on his face.

Who would have thought he had it in him?

The screams outside alerted them to the escalation of the argument between Brendan (a murderer?) and his sister-in-law.

'Jesus,' Carmel breathed as her head whipped round. 'Sounds like he might be killing Nancy, too.'

Darrow leaped to his feet, and Carmel was a mere split-second after him as they raced out the front door and down the steps. She slid on the gravel at the bottom but he didn't pause to help her, so intent was he to reach the scene of the screaming and yelling before one of the voices was permanently silenced.

And so by the time she came upon the small clearing behind the camper truck, it was like she'd stumbled onto an old-fashioned tableau, a still life framed by the bright green of spring leaves and the tan camper casting shadows in the background. Darrow stood tall, his feet planted square on the ground while Brendan looked up at his own arm above his head, a ten pound rock clutched in his hand and Nancy, his wife's own sister and the aunt to his children, lay sprawled on the ground.

The only movement in the scene came from the blood slowly pooling in the gravel by her head, a dark puddle growing in the shadow cast by her camper truck.

41

'I'm arresting you for attempted murder,' Darrow said grimly as, lacking a gun to subdue the man, he firmly twisted Brendan's arm up behind his back. Yet even this small show of force proved unnecessary. The rock fell to the grass as Melody's widower listlessly relaxed his hand, hung his head and submitted to his arrest.

'Call for back up and an ambulance,' Darrow shot over his shoulder to Carmel. 'They won't be long, I saw them all parked at the Tim Horton's on Portugal Cove Road when I was coming over here.'

Her shaking hands almost dropped her phone as she punched in the 9-1-1. She quickly told the operator the address and very soon, yet again, the single road of St. Jude Without was blocked with official vehicles and their flashing lights and sirens. And the laneway was soon also filled with locals and looky-loos with their phones held up, all anxious to be a part of the continuing story of this luckless coastal village.

Nancy, unconscious but fortunately still alive, was quickly loaded up and the ambulance made its way through the crowd with much horn blowing and whooping of its siren, and she was taken to the emergency room in the closest St. John's hospital, while Brendan did not resist being placed in the back of the squad car. He sat there, head down, not paying attention to anything outside the safe confines of the vehicle.

And only then did Laney's own car come screeching to a halt and spraying gravel amid the confusion. His face red and thunderous, he quickly took in the scene with Darrow in command as he slammed his car door behind him.

'What the frig is going on here, Darrow?' Laney blustered. 'Got back from your arse-crawling on the mainland already? I'm in charge of the investigations here, got it? You can't come in half way through and be the big man.'

Darrow held up his hand in peace. 'Don't even start, Herb,' he said, his voice tired. 'This is all your file. I was just in the right place at the right time. I'm not even on the bloody clock right now.'

He drew the other man off to confer in private away from listening ears, and Darrow brought Laney up to speed to the best of his ability so that the other could, as he insisted, take over the paperwork from here. The scene of crime officers were yet again busy in the area, demarking the small clearing between the truck and the trees.

Carmel could see that her presence wasn't neither required nor welcome, she melted off around the back of the camper truck, past the yellow tape and to the sanctity of her house.

But there, lined off along her front steps, were Melody's children. Newly orphaned, or at least parentless for the moment. Mother dead, father in jail for who knew how many years, and the only other person who wanted them was in Intensive Care, possibly fighting for her life. These urchins with their clothes torn and the knowledge of their predicament written on their dirty faces, the three could have stepped straight out of a Charles Dickens' novel. And they were so silent, it almost broke Carmel's heart.

'Hey, kids,' she said, mustering up the courage and fortitude to get her through the hours to come and as she did so, her heart gave a wrench. Within the strained relationship of Brendan and Melody, the kids had acted out their stress. It wasn't their fault they'd come across as rotten brats. What words were there to say to them? It wasn't in her to fake jollity, for even as young as they were, they were well aware that their world had imploded. 'Pretty crappy day, eh?'

The three remained quiet, staring up at her with their huge eyes.

'I'm hungry,' Tiffanee whispered, her matted blonde curls coming out of the braids Nancy had fixed that morning.

'Yeah?' Carmel wracked her memory for what she could offer them to eat, but she was almost certain the fridge was empty. 'Let's go get those doughnuts and milk?'

Her heart jumped up in her throat to see the hope spring anew in three pairs of eyes. She could have cried, but instead she mustered her emotions and lifted little Joss onto her back and took the other two by hand.

'It's not much,' Carmel said. 'But it'll tide you over till we get some fish and chips delivered.'

She herded them over to the church, where the news had preceded them. The sight of the orphans touched a paternal streak lurking close to the surface in Bill the head biker. He opened his wide arms and managed to sit all three on his knees at once, and within this warm cocoon he entertained them with stories of growing up in a faraway bay, where ponies danced and seals morphed into people and fairies lured unsuspecting innocents under the light of the full moon.

Carmel leaned against the doorjamb, watching them as she waited for the food to arrive.

'I came as soon as I could,' a voice interrupted her. And there was Boyce by her side, his cap in hand and face twisted with emotion. She gave him a small hug.

'How's Nancy?' she asked quietly.

He shook his head. 'They're keeping her in hospital overnight because of the concussion,' he replied. 'But the doctor says she has a hard skull and she'll get out tomorrow. I guess...'

He looked at the three youngsters still held in thrall by Bill's stories.

She followed his gaze. 'You alright to take the kids?'

'Oh yes,' he said, his voice brooking no dissent. 'They're coming home with me. To Bell Island, where they belong. We wouldn't have it any other way. They need family, and we're all the family they have now that Brendan…'

He broke off, shaking his head and still trying to digest the revelation about his brother-in-law.

Carmel nodded, thankful with the knowledge that with Boyce at the helm, the kids were going to have a solid family experience for the rest of their growing years, despite the horrors of their parents' dysfunctional relationship. There was good in the world, and Boyce was a part of that good.

And she hoped to God that this goodness would temper any of Nancy's manipulative and narcissistic tendencies. But she mentally shrugged at this thought, for it was all out of her hands from this point on.

'Nancy had just about everything packed up before… um, you know,' she said as she straightened up and turned toward the door. 'I suppose they'll let you take the camper truck back. It's not really part of the crime scene.'

'All taken care of,' he said. 'I spoke with Laney. And it looks like we're getting fed now.' Boyce nodded toward the front entrance where the other two bikers had arrived, their arms filled with paper bags emitting the delicious smell of fried hot grease.

There was nothing like a good feed, Carmel decided later as she looked down the long table in the light of the late afternoon sun, now littered with the remnants of the feast. Nothing a good feed of hot fish and chips to smooth over the hurts and wounds and begin healing the pain, to bring the world to rights again.

42

T he FaceBook contest drew to its inevitable end the next day, and it was a short quick death for the cove. After the bouncy castle incident and the latest murder and all the rest of the bad press, St. Jude Without didn't stand a chance for winning.

'As if no one saw that happening,' Carmel murmured to herself as she looked over Tina's shoulder, watching the numbers crash.

Yet Tina, being the steadfast kind of gal that she was, remained at the helm the whole time, even after all the other residents had jumped the ship of dreams. Even Nate, when he returned from the lockup and saw which way the wind was blowing with public opinion, even this self-proclaimed mayor of the cove quickly deserted the cause and distanced himself as much as he could. Tina alone remained to steer the ship through the storm, right to the final end when all hope was gone.

'Where is Nate, anyway?' Carmel asked as she moved to sit at the table.

Tina looked up from her laptop. Despite it all, despite her disappointment and stress, her hair remained unfrizzed in its sleek bob and her makeup was perfect. Her blouse was freshly pressed and the pleats of her skirt crisp. She pasted a smile on her face, determined to remain positive.

'He needs some time to recuperate, to regroup,' she said earnestly. 'He and Phonse went off in the boat to relax and discuss where we're going next.'

'Next?' Carmel looked out the window of the old church onto the Tickle. Sure enough, there was Phonse's boat, the weathered turquoise hull in sore need of a paintjob. It didn't seem to be going anywhere, just drifting with the currents, and she knew if she had a pair of binoculars, she would see the two men hove off in the back amidst a growing pile of empty beer bottles, enjoying the warm summer breeze and with not a thought of the future between them.

Tina nodded firmly. 'This was just a practice run,' she replied. 'Nate still has his dreams and I'm going to be behind him all the way.'

She narrowed her eyes. '*All the way*,' she repeated. 'Right to the top. We're going to do it, together. We need to position him as Mayor of St. Jude Without as a starting point. He'll be Premier one day, you mark my words.'

The thought of Nate leading the province was not something Carmel wanted to contemplate. Mismanagement, nepotism, siphoning of funds... These were but the obvious pitfalls promised by a government led by Nate, and she shuddered to think what else he might dream up if he ever actually attained Tina's dream.

'Still,' she said aloud, mostly to comfort herself. 'I guess we've had worse in that office. How much harm could he really do?'

The laptop suddenly sprang to life as the winner of the Facebook contest was officially announced. Bell Island had easily walked off with the victory, of course, as everyone had predicted. Gen appeared on the screen, every wrinkle on her face creased into a victorious smile as she spoke to the reporter. She was dressed in the same fashion as when she'd visited St. Jude Without, minus the puffy coat, with her trademark bright red fleece and baseball cap low over her sunglasses. They were standing at the lighthouse on the end of the small island, the perfect spot on this perfect sunny day to showcase the pastoral setting of the emerald green meadows against the blues of sky and sea.

'We won, because we are the best,' she said in her gravelly voice. 'No one beats Bell Island.'

Gen turned slightly, and the camera followed her, zooming in on her face. In her huge wraparound sunglasses, Carmel could clearly pick out the reflection of the mountain over St. Jude Without. The octogenarian stared menacingly over the water between the two communities.

'No one,' she repeated herself. 'Ever.'

• • • •

'I've never seen your home so sparkling. Do you think you could stop the incessant cleaning for a moment and get ready to go out?'

Darrow stood by the window overlooking the cove, his arms crossed in what might be interpreted as annoyance in any other man. Both his kids were packed off for a month at their mother's home and except for the short time spent with her the previous afternoon, he hadn't been able to come back to the cove. But he was here now. 'I thought we were finally going to have our date night.'

Carmel paused at the doorway to the living room and slowly peeled off the bright blue rubber gloves.

'I know. It's been a whole day since they left, but I can still feel their essences here. I have to get rid of every speck of him and the whole family,' she said through gritted teeth. 'I want them totally gone from my house.'

Yes, she had momentarily felt sorry for the young children of Brendan and Melody. After all, she was only human and their plight had touched her heart. But now that they were all sorted and safely ensconced in Boyce and Nancy's home across the water, the horrors of the past week had come back full strength, and the only way she knew to cope was to clear the house of every last vestige of the unwelcome guests. All the bed linens had already been washed twice in the hottest setting and set out on the line, yet she still swore she could smell Melody's perfume clinging to the sheets.

'And I thought you said Nancy had cleaned the place pretty thoroughly,' he remarked.

She shivered. 'Yes, but I needed to get rid of any reminders of her, too. Do you realize I had to change my brand of cleaner? Just the whiff of lemons now makes me shudder because it reminds me of her.'

Carmel looked at the pail of hot water by her feet and realized how ridiculous her excessive scrubbing must seem to Darrow. 'Alright,' she relented.' Just give me a moment to change.'

Up in her room, she breathed deeply of the new lavender cleaning scented cleaning fluid and the polished surfaces from which every mote of Brendan and Melody's dust had been removed. The windows were wide open, ensuring that every particle breathed out by the family was gone from her house.

She rejoined Darrow wearing a sweet little mini dress, the red one with white polka dots and the flirty skirt, the kind of summer dress that, once bought, remained hanging in the closet for ten months and lasted for years because of it got so little wear in the short Newfoundland summer.

'Lovely,' he said, his brown eyes warm when they met her blue.

'Where we going?' she asked, fixing the buckles on her high red strappy sandals. 'I just want to get out of this cove.'

'I thought we'd go to Atlantica, not too far down the road so we can have a proper drink or two without driving,' he said. Then he looked down at her heels. 'If you can walk that far, that is.'

She laughed. 'I'll manage, if we go slow.'

They paused at the top of her front steps. It was a perfect evening, the clouds all red and peach around the sun which hovered over the hills of far-off Carbonear to the west. There was not a breath of wind in the sky, the air unseasonably warm for June, so she carried her light sweater.

'You know I have to ask,' she began. She'd been waiting for him to offer the information, but he had been his usual closed-mouthed self about police matters.

'Mmmn?' he replied, encircling her with his arms from the back and nuzzling at her ear.

'Don't try to distract me,' she continued. 'But if Brendan killed his wife...'

'He did,' he murmured into her hair. 'No question, full confession once he began to talk. He must have gotten the idea from Lars' death, although that was an accident.'

'Oh.' She gave a guilty start, remembering when Brendan had met her on the breakwater and she had explained in exact detail about the so-called 'sweet spot', the most vulnerable point of the skull, and how a well-aimed thump with a hard object, say a rock, could cause instant death. Dear God, what had she done? Had she set in motion his path to becoming a murderer?

'Was it... was that pre-meditated, do you suppose?' She almost didn't want to hear the answer, for it would mean that she was almost as guilty as Brendan. She turned to Darrow, biting her lip.

Darrow shook his head, and caught her by the hand. 'No, it sounds as if it was spur of the moment. That's what he's claiming, anyway. Said he couldn't take it anymore, the abuse between them and the anger. He said he saw her slip away behind the tent, she was going to turn off the generator, he thinks, and he saw a handy rock and...'

He led her down the steps.

It was a small relief. 'And Nancy?'

'Again, momentary madness, or so he claims,' Darrow replied. 'But once he'd done it and gotten away with it, the second time came easier. He won't be able to convince the judge the same thing about the attempt on the other twin.'

They paused just outside the church for Carmel to readjust her right sandal. The cove was quiet that night, with just the muted sounds of the seventies rock bands coming from the open windows of the old church. Above the sound of the music, she could hear

Tina's voice chiming into the conversation as if she'd always been a part of the cove. She'd moved into the farm with Nate and had no plans on moving out again, at least not until Nate's ship came in and he realized his dreams. Tina would be steering that ship with an iron fist, Carmel had no doubt.

All the visitors had departed from the cove, leaving St. Jude Without to the inhabitants. Phonse and Nate and the pool players were outside now, having a smoke or a toke, and she could hear their voices carry down the side of the church through the lilac bushes now in full bloom.

'Do you know how much it costs to replace that stupid piece of plastic?' Phonse drew in a deep breath of his combustible. 'Do you know, if I pay it, I'll actually be out of pocket? All that money I made, gone.'

'That's nuts.' This was Mike or Pat or Len. 'They're not seriously expecting you to cover the cost of it?'

'They can expect all they want, but they're not getting a penny of it,' Phonse vowed. 'Besides, they can't come after me anyway. I used Mom's Visa card, they can't trace it back to me. I'd like to see them take on her about it, good luck to that!'

Carmel and Darrow looked at each other, and he shook his head. She knew what he was thinking, and she merely shrugged in response.

She stood for a moment leaning against Darrow's arm. The water in the Tickle was smooth that night, not a ripple on the stretch between St. Jude Without and Bell Island.

'Who won the contest, after?' Darrow wasn't one to keep up on local affairs.

She laughed. 'Bell Island, of course,' she replied. 'They always do.'

He nodded. 'Gen wouldn't have it any other way.'

Darrow had on his best suit, Carmel could see, and his old school tie from that ancient Scottish university. His jacket was slung around his shoulders and his shirtsleeves crisply rolled up because of the warmth of the evening. She fingered the silk tie lightly.

'So... Atlantica. Must be a special occasion, then?' Carmel slid her eyes up to Darrow's.

He smiled and nodded and gave a slight squeeze. 'Perhaps,' he said. 'Or maybe I figure we deserve it. Me for having been forced to sit in a classroom all that week, and you for... well, all that's happened. And of course, the launch of your short stories.'

'I'll go with that,' she said.

'I thought perhaps we could have a long overdue conversation about getting you out of this cove,' he said softly in her ear. 'It's dangerous here, in case you haven't noticed. You're too close to the criminal elements.'

'Oh, God,' she said aloud. She'd totally forgotten about the biker bar, and how Laney had threatened to tell Darrow that she was hanging out with that creepy guy behind the bar. She turned to him, ready to offer him the full explanation. 'This is about the Hell's Angels bar, right? Laney followed me in there, and it was full of these burly hairy guys who had me surrounded...'

Her story faltered when she saw Darrow's reaction.

'Hell's Angels? You mean the Sports Bar on Boncloddy Street? What in God's name were you doing in that den of iniquity?'

'Looking for Sid... Laney didn't tell you?'

'He didn't mention it, no,' Darrow replied. His eyes narrowed, but a smile played on his lips and he gave her a hug. 'And I doubt it was you brought him there, he probably had his own business there, and the less I know about that, the better.'

He sighed, then took her in his arms again. 'As I was saying, you're getting involved with the criminal elements, living here. Perhaps it's time you moved into town. There's plenty of room in my house, you know. Or if that's too soon, there are plenty of apartments available in the center of the city.'

'Leave St. Jude Without?' She thought deeply about what he was asking. Her life could be a whole lot easier, and a lot less lonely too. She breathed deeply, taking in the smell of the starch in his shirt and the spiced soap he used, Yes, there could be definite benefits to living in the city with Darrow.

She looked around her at the cove. The ponies grazing on the point, happy and feral again and unmolested now; Phonse's boat and his rickety wharf when Gen had stood and threatened her. It was peaceful here now in St. Jude Without, the setting sun bathing the unpainted wood of the fences in soft golden light, the warm breeze coming from the water and bringing with it the vital smell of the salt air and the sounds of the seagulls settling to roost.

The parking lot of the church was now cleaned of all the litter and the detritus of Nate's dreams. Melody had stood right there on this spot, complaining of all the terrible things she'd seen in the cove and lashing out with her anger. Such an unhappy soul she'd been, seeing her whole life through a lens bleak and dark, believing she had got the rotten end of the stick when it came to life's gifts. And yet, her sister, her perfect twin, the one whose life was so full of nature's bounties, Nancy had been jealous of the one thing that Melody knew she had achieved in her life, her children. Funny how some people could only see the lack in their lives, the darkness of a painting, and not see the light that created those same shadows.

Like St. Jude Without. Yes, to the outside observer they might appear to be no more than a bunch of crooks, scofflaws and skeets. Yet she had scratched the surface, looked beyond the shadows to witness the light, and didn't have to go too far to see the real truth of her neighbors. Each and every one of them was real, true to themselves whatever that truth might be. They weren't pretending to be anything they weren't, what you saw was what you got – the dark, the light, the whole damn package.

In this modern world of illusion and mirrors and photo-shopping, this honesty of self that she'd found in her neighbors was refreshing. And she was accepted here. After years of travelling the world, she had finally found a home, and she embraced it all.

Even that bloody ghost, and she knew she hadn't seen the last of him yet.

She listened to the bits of conversation coming from the church as she thought. The conversation had turned away from Phonse's woes, and turned toward the possibilities of Nate being elected Premier and how their lives would change on that fateful day.

Carmel smiled, and brushed her cheek against Darrow's chest. He was all she had ever wanted, could ever have dreamed of in a man. And yet.

'Perhaps a little too soon,' she said. 'I think they still need me here.'

The end.

Did you enjoy this book? Please leave a review on your favorite site. For more news and latest releases, visit my webpage LizGraham.ca or sign up to join Liz (E M) Graham's Newsletter.

PS I've just opened my own online shop, so you can purchase direct from me, the author. Feel free to browse and use the loyalty coupons for discounts on your next purchase from me.

Follow Liz Graham on FaceBook and Book Bub.

Other books by Liz (EM) Graham:

The Carmel McAlistair Mysteries:
The Cut Throat
The Garrote
The Iron Dog
St. Jude Undone
The Unlikely Heroine:
An Imperfect Death
Unlikely Shorts:
The Auction (Short Story)
As E M Graham:
The Witch Kin Chronicles:
An Ignorant Witch
An Arrogant Witch
An Errant Witch
An Obstinate Witch
An Enigmatic Witch (Coming Sept. 29, 2022)
Audio versions on the way!

Watch out for *Potential Magic* – a midlife paranormal suspense! (So many stories to tell, so little time.)

Manufactured by Amazon.ca
Bolton, ON